LEGEND OF THE WHITE SNAKE

LEGEND OF THE WHITE SNAKE

SHER LEE

Quill Tree Books
An Imprint of HarperCollinsPublishers

Quill Tree Books is an imprint of HarperCollins Publishers.

Legend of the White Snake

Copyright © 2024 by Sher Lee

All rights reserved. Printed in the United States of America.
No part of this book may be used or reproduced in any manner
whatsoever without written permission except in the case of brief
quotations embodied in critical articles and reviews. For information,
address HarperCollins Children's Books, a division of HarperCollins
Publishers, 195 Broadway, New York, NY 10007.

www.epicreads.com

Library of Congress Control Number: 2023948482

ISBN 978-0-06-332719-1

Typography by Joel Tippie

24 25 26 27 28 LBC 5 4 3 2 1

First Edition

To Fred, my soulmate

致高源，我的知己

Prologue

Seven years earlier

The hemp sack over Prince Xian's head smelled of animal feed. His hands were bound in front of him, his toes raw from being bitten by hungry rats in the windowless cell where his captors had imprisoned him for two days and two nights.

He hadn't cried, though. At least not when they were around.

Growing up in the palace as the ten-year-old son of a consort among rival half brothers had taught him a lesson: Pride wasn't just his armor. It was everything he had.

They were on the move. The wheels coasted over a pothole, and his head bounced against the side of the wagon. A mushy, grassy scent tickled his nose, and his skin prickled as he recognized the smell. His mother used to bring him out of the palace to play by the lake, and he'd thought the clouds of green and blue drifting in the water were pretty, but she'd told him some algae blooms were dangerous, even deadly.

He was close to home again. So close he could imagine standing on the shore of the West Lake. The three islands, floating on the water. The Broken Bridge—it wasn't really broken, just looked that way when the snow melted on one side. Leifeng Pagoda in the distance, a sentinel on the southern shore.

The wagon slowed to a halt. Xian's heartbeat quickened. Horses neighed as boots pounded back and forth on the summer-baked dirt. They manhandled him out of the wagon and yanked the sack off his head.

He squinted at the sudden brightness of the forest's clearing. He was surrounded by armed mercenaries—but at the other end of the glade stood General Jian, his father's most trusted official.

"Prince!" General Jian's forehead was creased with worry. "Are you hurt?"

Relief rushed through Xian. He forced a brave face. "I'm—"

"You've seen the boy." The mercenary leader pushed Xian behind him. His long hair was matted and straggly, his leather brigandine covered in bloodstains. "All fingers and toes intact . . . for the time being. Now—the pearl."

Xian's eyes widened. His father had told him that spirit pearls from the highest peaks of the sacred Kunlun Mountains could cure any illness . . . and even reverse death. Countless men had died in search of them, plunging into treacherous crevasses hidden by eternal snow.

General Jian's expression was grim as he strode forward and handed over a wooden box. A murmur rose from the mercenaries.

Their leader lifted a small spherical object to the sunlight—it was the size of a marble and glinted with an unnatural glow.

A spirit pearl can cure a bite from a white snake, his father had said. *It will make your mother well again . . .*

"No!" Xian burst out. "She needs it! Don't give it to—"

A blast rocked the wagon behind Xian. The force flung him forward, and his hands, still bound, couldn't break his fall. He landed on his face. The scent of burned gunpowder stung his nostrils—he couldn't breathe, like the time his eldest half brother, Wang, had knocked him down and sat on his chest.

Xian raised his head as palace guards swarmed out from their ambush. The mercenaries shouted, their horses rearing in panic. General Jian, sword drawn, pushed through the chaos toward Xian—

Rough hands grabbed Xian from behind, and General Jian disappeared from view. Xian struggled as he was hauled toward another wagon and shoved into the back.

A second explosion hit. The rear wheel shattered, and Xian's head struck the floor as the wagon lurched sharply. A man screamed as if he were being dragged to hell.

Pain reverberated through Xian's skull, black and gray dots teeming like ants across his vision. But he forced himself upright. For the first time, he was unguarded. He had clenched his hands when they tied his wrists like his best friend, Feng, had taught him to, which made wriggling out of his bonds easier.

As he crawled out of the wagon, a horrible groan made him turn. A mercenary lay by the shattered wheel, his face contorted in agony as he clutched his mangled left thigh. The rest of his leg had been blown off.

A palace guard came up to him and drove a sword into his chest.

Xian recoiled.

The mercenary gurgled and went still. The guard pulled out the blade. Blood spurted from the wound.

As weapons clashed, no one seemed to notice Xian lying exposed on the ground. He flattened his body, trying to make himself as inconspicuous as possible. One of the mercenaries' horses, unaccustomed to battle, charged toward him. Xian dived out of the panicked creature's way a moment before its hooves landed on the spot where his head had just been.

He rolled over, panting hard. He had to find cover. As he crawled on elbows and knees toward a nearby thicket of bushes, his fingers dug into the soil. They closed around something small, hard, round . . .

Xian halted, unfurling his fingers. Nestled in his hand was an iridescent sphere, frosted with specks of dirt and dried grass.

The pearl. The tiny orb seemed to pulse in his palm like it had a heartbeat of its own. It felt strangely heavy, as if it contained the density of universes—it stared back at him, an otherworldly eye, and Xian couldn't tear his gaze away—

A pair of boots slammed down in front of Xian. He blinked up at a mercenary's roughened face. The man's eyes locked on the pearl and widened in recognition.

"Give it to me," he growled.

Xian leaped to his feet and ran.

His short, feverish strides instinctively led him toward the lake. Toward the mushy scent of poisonous algae, less deadly than the thundering footfalls gaining ground behind him. He propelled his legs faster, even though each step on his bare, torn soles was like running on burning coals.

Up ahead lay the Broken Bridge. He reached the middle and hoisted himself onto the parapet wall. His heart hammered, his breaths breaking in harsh stabs. The lake gleamed an unnatural green, forcing him to confront the one thing he was ashamed of: He couldn't swim.

The man approached. "Hand it over, boy."

"Don't come any closer!" Xian shouted. "Or I'll jump into the lake!"

"I'll let you go, promise." The man held out a calloused hand. "You can run home to your mother—"

He lunged at Xian's leg.

Xian dodged, but his foot slipped and his head tilted sharply backward—

Hitting the water was like being swallowed whole. In the green, opaque world under the surface, everything abruptly slowed and his limbs seemed twice as heavy. The algae blooms loomed like hulking monsters, their formless fingers stretching toward him.

He thrashed, kicking his legs frantically, his hand still curled in a fist. He couldn't drown. He couldn't lose the pearl that would cure his mother.

Something slithered along his arm. He froze. A flash of reptilian scales, so white they were luminous—then a long, limbless body was encircling him, graceful and terrifying, tightening around his sides like a giant tentacle.

Horror gripped Xian's chest. He opened his mouth to scream—but only a trail of bubbles emerged, rising like a prayer to the pale, faraway light.

Then the bubbles ran out, and his world went black.

Chapter 1
XIAN

"Copperhead." Xian's sturdy leather soles trod almost sound-lessly over the leaves littered across the forest floor. "Also known as the hundred-pacer. They say after you've been bitten, you can take only a hundred steps before collapsing."

"Sounds delightful." Feng hung back, his hand poised on his sword hilt. "Nothing like fresh air, sunshine, and deadly venom to start our day."

They'd agreed that Feng would cut off the snakes' heads only if they unexpectedly attacked. Otherwise, Xian wanted them alive.

Summer had arrived, which meant snakes would venture far-ther from their dens for mating season. Early morning was the best time to catch them, after the rising sun had warmed the jagged, rocky outcroppings but before the scorching heat sent them back into their burrows.

"Haven't you captured one of these before?" Feng eyed the reptile. "You've been working doubly hard since the Year of the Snake began."

Xian pointed. "See that stripe down its back? Copperheads don't usually have white markings."

If not for the white pattern on its dorsal scales, the reddish-brown copperhead would have been almost indistinguishable from the fallen log under which it coiled.

Feng leaned closer for a better look. "You think it could be distantly related to the white snake that bit your mother?"

"I'll ask Fahai when he gets back." Xian stepped forward, tongs in one gloved hand, long hook in the other. His gaiters were made of alligator skin, thick enough to withstand the long fangs of pit vipers.

He grabbed the copperhead with the wide mouth of the tongs. Startled, the snake hissed and reared its triangular head. Xian snagged it with the hook, holding it at arm's length—but the copperhead attacked, its fangs snapping within inches of Xian's forearm.

Feng raised his sword. "Watch out!"

Xian struck the back of the snake's head with the tongs in his other hand, knocking it out. It sagged, dangling limply from the hook.

Feng exhaled. "That was a little too close."

"I had everything under control. Your protective streak is really appealing, though."

"It's not a protective streak. I'm your bodyguard."

Xian put the unconscious snake into a double-stitched sack and tied it shut. He rubbed the back of his hand over his eyes and stifled a yawn.

Feng raised a brow. "Who was the boy last night?"

Xian gave his best friend an innocent look. "I have no idea what you're talking about."

"Nice try. I know you slipped out through the Pavilion of Benevolence again."

"Oh, right. You wouldn't be a good bodyguard if you didn't."

When they were younger, Xian and Feng—General Jian's eldest son—had found one of the secret escape routes that led out of the palace. The entrance was hidden behind the altar in the Pavilion of Benevolence, and the tunnel emerged in an abandoned grain silo on the other side of the outer wall. Xian had been putting the passageway to good use.

Xian grinned. "We arranged to meet in a hut near his father's farm. He still thinks I'm the son of a merchant who procures tea for the king."

Feng sighed. "I wish you'd try harder to be discreet."

"Don't worry, no one saw us." Xian lifted his chin. "And even if people found out, why should anyone make a fuss? Emperor Ai took male lovers, as did all nine emperors of the Han dynasty before him." One story of Emperor Ai was well known: When the emperor's favorite lover fell asleep on his robe, Ai chose to cut off the sleeve of his imperial garment rather than wake the young man.

"Well, you can do whatever you want when you're the king,"

Feng replied. "But right now, you know that Wang is just waiting for you to slip up. Since his guān lǐ, he's been trying extra hard to discredit you and gain your father's approval."

At the age of twenty, every noble male had his long hair—combed into a bun, as usual—crowned with a special headpiece. Two weeks ago, everyone had gathered outside the Ancestral Temple, huddled under umbrellas in the late spring rain, to witness his eldest half brother's crowning ceremony. Xian was three years away from his own guān lǐ, so his topknot was secured with just a hairpin.

The gong in the palace's wooden astronomical clock tower tolled in the distance, announcing the stroke of ten. The sun had ascended higher in the cloudless sky, and a trickle of sweat ran down Xian's brow.

"Fahai should've returned from his hometown visit by now. I'll bring this copperhead to him and see what he thinks." As Xian picked up the tied sack containing the snake, he noticed Feng's hesitant expression. "What?"

"I overheard my father talking this morning," Feng replied. "Fahai wasn't visiting his family. Your father sent him west to Mount Emei to see the oracle."

Mount Emei was the tallest of the four sacred mountains. The monastery where the reclusive oracle lived could be reached only by a narrow stairway of a thousand steps cut into the steep cliff face. Monks would carve a pilgrim's request on an ox's shoulder bone or a turtle's plastron in the oracle's ancient script. The bone or shell would be heated in a furnace, and if the oracle chose to respond, he would interpret the pattern of cracks.

Xian frowned. "What did my father want to ask the oracle? Whether he should choose Wang as the crown prince? Is that why Fahai didn't tell me where he was really going?"

Feng attempted a nonchalant shrug. "He could be on official court business . . ."

Xian narrowed his eyes. "Feng, I have a deadly snake in this bag, and I'm not afraid to use it."

"You knocked the thing out."

"A snake's fangs can still inject venom an hour after its head has been chopped off."

Feng sighed. "I didn't want to say anything . . . but I have a strong feeling Fahai's mission to see the oracle has something to do with your mother."

Xian's heart pounded as he raced across the inner court of the palace.

Everything suddenly made sense. Why his mother had been sleeping more than usual. Why the palace physicians had begun prescribing opium-poppy medicines. They were meant to make her as comfortable as possible. Why hadn't his father told him? Did his mother know her condition was getting worse? How— how much time did she have left?

His strides echoed on the wide marble steps leading to the king's hall. Its yellow gabled roof and double eaves stood grandly above the rest of the palace buildings in Xifu, capital of Wuyue and home to the West Lake.

After the fall of the Tang dynasty, the land had fragmented into ten different kingdoms, and Wuyue carved out its territory in the east. None of the kings were strong enough to take up the mantle as Tang's successor, and for a rare moment in history, there was no emperor, and each king—including Xian's father—reigned independently.

Nine was an imperial number, and his father's hall was the only building in the palace that could have nine jiān—the space between two columns—and five arches. None except the king could enter through the center arch, so Xian darted through the one on the left.

His father's guards outside the throne chamber made a feeble attempt to stop him, but he shook them off and pushed the double doors open.

The throne stood on a raised platform facing south so anyone coming into the king's presence would have to bow toward the north—a sign of respect. Tendrils of sweet smoke wafted from ornate red copper incense burners, and two huge bronze mirrors, one on either side of the throne, gleamed to ward off malevolent spirits.

Xian raised his eyes to the wooden plaque above the throne, where 一正壓百邪 was engraved in gold from right to left. *One justice can overpower a hundred evils.*

The sign wasn't just decorative. Formerly, tradition dictated that the eldest son of the empress or queen would automatically be the crown prince, but Xian's great-great-grandfather had eschewed the custom by declaring that any of his sons could be his heir. Infighting among his many sons from wives and concubines led the king to institute the practice of keeping the name of the chosen crown prince in a box behind the plaque that would be opened only upon his death. The box containing the decree was considered sacred, and anyone caught tampering with it would be put to death.

"Xian?"

Xian's attention snapped back to the imposing man seated on the throne, who had deep frown lines etched between his brows. He was decked out in a bright yellow lóng páo, a regal robe that was embroidered with nine five-clawed dragons—five on the front, three on the back, and the ninth hidden inside the front panel. On his right thumb was a signet ring made of láng gān, a blue-green gemstone even rarer and more valuable than jade.

In front of the throne stood Fahai. In his early thirties, he was younger than the rest of the court advisers. He wore a red robe with wide sleeves, and his bǔ zi—the square insignia woven on the front of his robe—was emblazoned with a crane, a symbol of longevity and of the highest rank among scholars. His yú dài—the "fish pouch" around his waist—was another mark of his senior status in the king's court.

Xian's father glowered at him. "Have I not taught you proper manners, my son? What devil emboldened you to barge into my chamber when you have not been summoned?"

Anyone who came into the king's presence without being called, even his wife or consorts, could be severely reprimanded.

And Xian should've been attired in his round-collared golden-yellow court robe—the color of princes.

"Father, I beg your forgiveness." Xian, still dressed in his hunting clothes, knelt and bowed. "I am willing to accept any punishment. But first, please tell me—what did the oracle say about my mother? Is she going to die? Is there any way to save her?"

Out of the corner of his eye, Xian could see the bases of the red columns surrounding the throne. His father used to tell him stories about the poets who wrote the verses painted on each pillar. The intertwined tenets of love and filial piety in his father's favorite poems had inspired him to marry the noblewoman his parents had chosen—but he later took Xian's mother, a commoner and his childhood sweetheart, as his first and most beloved consort.

Xian ventured an upward glance and caught his father's expression softening.

"Fahai was about to reveal the oracle's answer when you interrupted," he told Xian. He extended his palm, signaling for Xian to rise, before giving Fahai a nod.

Fahai came forward and presented a scapula-shaped bone wrapped in silk. Xian's father held the cracked bone to the sunlight to see the slanted, hieroglyphic characters, the oldest ancestor of their written language, which few alive could read.

"What is the oracle's interpretation?" the king asked.

"'The cure you seek is in Changle of Min,'" Fahai replied.

Xian couldn't believe his ears. The cure? Was there a way to not just save his mother's life but completely heal her of the terrible paralyzing pain she had suffered for almost a decade since that fateful snakebite?

"Send me to Changle," Xian blurted out.

His father shook his head. "The capital of Min is a ten-day journey from Xifu. You have never traveled so far from home on your own. General Jian will go."

"Father—"

"No, Xian," his father repeated more firmly. "Seven years ago, I took it upon myself to obtain a spirit pearl to heal your mother. As a result, I nearly lost you. *Both* of you—in your mother's fragile state, grief would've overwhelmed her. I will not let that happen again."

The king had refused to seek out another pearl, seeing the first one as a bad omen that had led to his son's kidnapping. Unlike Xian, his father was deeply superstitious—probably why he had not offered a fake pearl in exchange for his son's life, fearing that deceit would bring even more disaster.

Xian kowtowed so low that his forehead struck the floor with a loud thud. He knew which tiles had inverted mud jars placed beneath them—people believed that the more resonant the sound, the better the chances of winning the king's favor.

"Father, you once told me that crows have the virtue of caring for their parents," Xian said. "Now I implore you to allow me to do the same. I am my mother's only son. Please let me go to Changle. I must be the one to find the cure. Otherwise, I shall live with this regret for the rest of my life."

A long silence ensued. Filial piety was the foremost of all Confucian virtues, the reason both males and females kept their hair long—as a sign of reverence for their parents and ancestors. Xian invoking his filial duty would make it harder for his father to deny his request.

Xian waited. Finally, his father picked up a brush and wrote on a scroll. He took the royal seal, which had a pair of entwined dragons on the knob, dipped the square base in red ink, and pressed the insignia to the parchment.

"Prepare a delegation. You will leave for Changle at sunrise." Xian's father held out the scroll. "Fahai shall escort you on my behalf. Heed his advice as if it were mine. If this undertaking is the will of the gods, they will bless your journey and make the right path known when you arrive."

"Thank you, Father." Xian bowed as he received the royal edict with both hands. "I will not return until I have the cure."

Chapter 2
XIAN

Philosophers taught that heaven was round and the earth was square. As an homage, Leifeng Pagoda had a square base anchored to the ground and octagonal sides that appeared round when viewed from above. Whenever the evening sky was clear, people would gather on the Broken Bridge on the opposite shore to admire the sunset glowing behind the tower's vermilion brick walls. Its overhanging roof, five stories high, was covered with terra-cotta tiles glazed black, which was supposed to inspire the gods to descend to the earth. Bronze chimes hung from its wide eaves, tinkling in the wind; seen from the ground, its steeple appeared to pierce the clouds. People believed that a lightning strike to the iron spire could destroy demons.

Xian reined in his horse, dismounted close to the steps leading to the pagoda entrance, and dropped the wriggling snake in its bag to the ground. He had spent the entire afternoon preparing the delegation to Changle and requisitioning gold, jade, precious metals, and silk from the treasury. Royals often lavished gifts upon vassal states to emphasize their status as benefactors. Min was the newest vassal state of the kingdom of Wuyue; threatened by Southern Tang, the Min court had capitulated to its stronger ally in the north in exchange for protection.

Xian halted on the edge of the West Lake. Orioles warbled from the willows along the shore, and in the middle of the lake, three islands glimmered in the setting sun.

The smallest, Ruangong Islet, was where General Jian had found ten-year-old Xian, soaked and shivering after the battle with the mercenaries. Xian had clammed up whenever anyone tried to find out how he'd ended up there. People quickly stopped asking, afraid that talking about the ordeal would traumatize the young prince further.

Miè zú—execution of a criminal's family to nine levels of kinship—was reserved for the worst crimes. Kidnapping a prince was one of them. The severed heads of the two court officials who had been forced by the mercenaries to smuggle Xian out of the palace to pay off their gambling debts were hung from the outer wall. But Xian's mother had pleaded on behalf of the condemned men's relatives, and his father spared their lives. He built an altar on Ruangong Islet to thank the gods for bringing his son safely out of the belly of the lake.

Only Xian knew the truth—what had saved him was no god. No one knew he had fallen into the lake with the pearl in his hand, not even Feng. No one knew he had awakened on the islet, too frozen to react as the cure for his mother's illness was swallowed right before his eyes by a large white snake.

The snake must've been attracted to the power of the pearl. It might even have been the same cursed creature that had bitten his mother in the first place. It dragged Xian out of the lake, not to save his life but to steal from him something almost as precious. Why it hadn't strangled him after taking the pearl, he didn't know.

But that was a decision the snake would live to regret.

Xian's horse nudged his shoulder, asking for a treat. Ferghanas, slender and imposing, were the most prized horses in the land. Some believed they descended from the line of tiān mǎ—mythical steeds that carried their riders into the land of the immortals.

"Hungry, Zhaoye?" Xian stroked his horse's lustrous black mane and coat. Zhaoye—meaning "shining night"—was a fitting name for him. "Want some fruit?" Zhaoye's ears pricked up. Perhaps horses from the bloodline of celestial steeds could understand language. "All right. Let me see if I can get some for you."

Xian found an apricot tree amid the blooming peonies, and a ripe fruit hanging from an outer branch came off with a slight twist. He took a dagger from his ankle sheath, cut the apricot in half, and dug out the kernel in the center before giving the slices to Zhaoye.

An approaching beat of hooves made him turn.

"Truly a sight to behold." Fahai rode up on his bay horse, a smile playing on his mouth as he dismounted. "A prince serving fruit to his horse."

Xian glared at the court adviser. "Don't try to pretend nothing happened. After all this time we've been searching for a cure, don't you think I deserve to know that my mother's condition is deteriorating?"

Fahai sobered. "Your father made me swear not to tell you. I could not disobey his command . . . not even for you, Prince Xian. I'm sorry."

Xian forced down the lump in his throat. "How much time does my mother have?"

"Her physicians said three months, maybe a little longer."

Three months? The words cleaved Xian's chest like his dagger had sliced open the apricot earlier. Would she be able to enjoy mooncakes under the harvest moon at this year's Mid-Autumn Festival, her favorite celebration?

Fahai put a hand on his shoulder as if sensing his anguish. "Don't give up hope, Prince Xian."

Xian pulled himself together. "I captured a copperhead with unusual white markings."

Fahai nodded. "Let's speak inside."

The base of Leifeng Pagoda was built on a double-layered stone pedestal, which hinted that as much of the structure existed belowground as it did above. Xian picked up the snake bag, and he and Fahai walked around the base platform to a nondescript iron door at the back of the pagoda.

Fahai took a key from his fish pouch and inserted it in the lock. The lock clicked and the door swung open, exhaling a breath of musty air. Fahai gestured for Xian to go first.

Xian descended the smooth stone steps into a familiar underground basement. Behind him, Fahai lit the lamps on the wall sconces, illuminating the space. A wooden worktable laden with cylindrical brass vessels of different sizes stood in the center. On a bench was a jumble of scrolls filled with formulas and calculations in Fahai's handwriting. Several bookcases lined the far wall, their shelves sagging with thick alchemical texts. A sack of coal and a pair of wooden bellows lay next to a fireplace connected to a chimney.

This was the secret underground laboratory where Fahai had been working tirelessly for the past three years to carry out the king's order: find a cure for his beloved consort.

At the opposite end of the room, two dozen cages of wood and bamboo were stacked on top of one another halfway to the ceiling. Their occupants coiled and uncoiled, glossy scales gleaming in the lamplight.

Fahai had asked Xian to bring him different types of snakes so he could study their venom. Some of Fahai's tonics and poultices had given Xian's mother a measure of relief from the symptoms, but so far, they had been unable to heal her. And now she was . . .

Xian turned to Fahai. "The cure is in Changle. What do you think we'll find when we arrive? A magical spring deep in the forests of Min? A rare healing plant that only grows there? Or maybe a sage or shaman with the power to cure my mother?"

Fahai's eyes glinted. "I think the oracle is leading us to Changle to find the final piece we've been searching for all this time."

"What do you mean?"

"After three years of experimentation, I believe I've finally determined the precise alchemy for an antidote," Fahai replied. "But we're still missing one crucial ingredient for your mother's cure."

A prickle rose across Xian's skin. "The white snake?"

Sand boas, pit vipers, coral snakes, pythons, copperheads, even cobras—Xian had hunted them all. But in the past seven years, he had never found another white snake. It wasn't inconceivable that the white snake had left the West Lake after it took the pearl from him. Maybe it had escaped into the nearby Zhe Jiang, the longest river on the southeastern coast, which meant it could be anywhere by now.

Fahai didn't know any of this, of course—no one did. Xian had never told a soul about the white snake or the pearl. And each time they tried and failed to heal his mother, no one knew the guilt that gnawed at him like a parasite sucking his marrow dry.

"I am still unsure exactly what part of the white snake will complete the antidote, whether it's its venom, organs, or perhaps even its beating heart," Fahai replied. "So we will not only have to find the snake, but also bring it back to this laboratory alive."

Anticipation twisted in Xian's stomach. The oracle had told them where to find the cure—the white snake itself. The balance of fate had decreed that the snake's life would be the key to saving his mother. Xian would finally have the chance to face the creature once more—and this time, he would capture it and bring it back to Wuyue.

A large open receptacle on a low stool in the corner, apart from the cages, caught Xian's attention. He didn't remember seeing it the last time he was there. He walked over; inside the ceramic vessel was a tortoise with golden star-shaped patterns on its domed carapace.

"What's this?" Xian asked. "You got a pet without telling me?"

Fahai smiled. "I found it a few days ago while I was taking an evening stroll around the lake. It had gotten into an unfortunate scuffle with a heron and its hind leg was bleeding. I brought it back here to recuperate."

Fahai came over to Xian's side. He took some leafy vegetables from his pocket and offered them to the tortoise, which raised its wrinkled head and eagerly munched the fresh greens from his hand.

"Are those from the palace kitchen?" Xian couldn't suppress his amusement. "A court adviser handpicking vegetables for a tortoise that's lucky to have escaped being a delicacy itself?"

Fahai chuckled. "I must admit I spoil it terribly. How barbaric to butcher such gentle creatures for their meat and beautiful shells. Dr. Ping from the infirmary keeps freshwater turtles as a hobby, and he has volunteered to take care of it while we're away."

Xian's eyes cut to the cages of wood and bamboo. "What

about these? Will they last until we return?"

"Snakes can survive up to a year without food," Fahai replied.

Xian turned to him. "Thank you for working so hard to find a cure for my mother. My father doesn't trust people unless he has known them for many years, but I can see why he made you his adviser after knowing you for only a relatively short while."

"With time and patience, the mulberry leaf becomes a silk gown," Fahai said solemnly. "The years have been long, but we have not stopped trying. I hope, in this Year of the Snake, we will find what we've been seeking."

Chapter 3
XIAN

Xian walked toward his mother's bedchamber. The circular openings along the corridor and the latticed windows of her quarters did more than let in light and air—whenever she had to spend days or even weeks restricted to bed, they were her only portals to the world. Her windows overlooked gardens that were among the most beautiful on the palace grounds, landscaped with osmanthus trees, karst rock formations, and a koi pond.

His mother's handmaids bowed as Xian approached her bedchamber. He acknowledged them with a nod before sliding open the wooden doors.

Inside, candles threw flickering shadows across the painted phoenixes on the joined panels of the píng fēng, a folding screen that shielded his mother's bed from view. The windows were closed at this late hour to keep out night drafts, and the still air was suffused with the scent of sandalwood from the incense burners.

Xian shut the doors soundlessly behind him. He crossed to the dresser and opened a velvet box. Inside was a slender bamboo flute. He brought the mouthpiece to his lips and held the flute horizontally, his fingers moving smoothly over the holes along its hollow length. He continued to play as he walked to the folding screen and peeked around its outermost panel.

His mother sat in bed, leaning against the headboard, a luxurious embroidered quilt pulled up to her chest. Though she was not yet forty, strands of silver wove through her dark hair. Her sunken cheeks made the pallor of her skin starker, but her eyes still sparkled with warmth.

"Xian'er." She held out her hand. "I used to play 'The Song of the Crow' when you were a baby to lull you to sleep. Now my ears prick up whenever I hear the tune, because it means my dear boy has come to see me."

"Niang Qin." Xian lowered the flute as he sat on the edge of her bed. "Sorry I'm later than usual tonight."

His mother hid a smile. "I'm sure you had to make many preparations for your journey to Changle tomorrow."

"Father told you?"

"Your first official diplomatic mission at the age of seventeen." She beamed. "Your father has a great deal of faith in you to send you to the capital of Min. And I could not be more proud of my son."

Xian's father had instructed him to keep the oracle's words

and his real purpose in Changle a secret; they didn't want to raise his mother's hopes until they had the cure.

Xian took his mother's hand in both of his own. Her knuckles were bony, and her skin felt as thin as rice paper. "My only regret is that I won't be here to help you make zòng zi for the Duanwu Festival."

The Duanwu Festival was celebrated on the fifth day of the fifth lunar month, coinciding with the summer solstice. People would watch dragon boat races and eat zòng zi—triangular sticky rice dumplings filled with sweet or savory ingredients such as chestnuts, jujubes, red beans, and minced pork meat. Other consorts in the palace delegated the laborious task of making the dumplings to their servants, but Xian's mother's zòng zi were his father's favorite, and she took great pride in making them herself. Even after the snakebite had paralyzed her with pain and stiffness, she never missed a year. She taught Xian how to wrap the rice with two reed leaves, but he always squeezed too hard while tying the dumpling with colored string. His father remarked that he could tell which zòng zi Xian had made by the dents in them.

Last year, on the evening of the Duanwu Festival, his mother was well enough to leave her bedroom. Her attendants carried her out of the palace in a palanquin—a furnished wooden booth lifted with two long horizontal poles. She asked to be taken to the Broken Bridge, away from the crowds gathered on the eastern shore. Xian sat beside her on a cushioned stool, and they watched the dragon boats race as the sun set over the West Lake.

Now his mother winked. "Next year, I'll hide the fattest zòng zi from your father and save them for you."

Three months, maybe a little longer. Xian had to force himself not to react. Did she not know she was dying? Or was she trying to shield him from the truth?

His mother stifled a yawn, and Xian remembered the medicine with opium poppies that the physicians had prescribed for her.

"It's getting late." He adjusted her quilt. "I'll wish you good night now."

"Wait." She caught his hand. "I want to give you something before you leave on your journey tomorrow." She reached behind her pillow and withdrew a jade amulet on a silver chain. "Before I left my hometown, my mother brought this amulet to the temple to be blessed by the priest. Then she gave it to me for protection. Light-colored jade is more valuable, but dark-colored jade gives strength to overcome adversity."

Xian took the amulet. Instead of translucent emerald green, the weathered jade had a dusky shade, with dull veins and mottled specks.

"When I came to live in the palace, the jade worn by other women was so brilliant and lustrous," his mother continued. "I was afraid people would laugh at my cheap amulet, so I kept it hidden. A prince should not be seen wearing jade of such low quality, but you can carry it in your pocket. Jade is a living stone that grows stronger the longer it is worn—this amulet will protect you and ward off any evil that tries to harm you."

Xian looped the chain around his neck and slipped the amulet inside his shirt. The jade's cool weight rested against his chest.

"I'll wear it close to my heart," he told her. "I'll be home before you start to miss me."

"That's impossible. You'll have to turn and come back the moment you walk out of my chamber." His mother let out a watery laugh. "Oh, I'm just being silly. I promise to keep in good health and welcome you when you return. Bring home a souvenir from Changle if you can."

Renewed resolve coalesced in Xian's chest. He was closer than ever to finding the white snake. He could feel it in his bones, like a prophecy. Like a vow.

"I will, Niang Qin," he replied.

Chapter 4

ZHEN

Zhen raised his gaze to the full moon. Strolling through the empty main street, devoid of its daytime clamor, he felt almost as if he were back in the forest. Insects buzzed incessantly, and trout lapped in one of the tributaries of the Min Jiang that flowed through the town square. Crickets chirped in the rice fields, where crops that had been sown in the spring were growing straight and tall. He sniffed the air; he could detect the faintest scent of crushed leaves from the harvest of spring tea.

"This itches," Qing grumbled, scratching the back of her neck.

She wore an oversize rú qún—a roughly woven cotton blouse, a plain green skirt that reached to her knees, and a pair of trousers underneath. Zhen wore a coarse hemp tunic, and unlike the extravagantly wide sleeves on robes worn by noblemen, Zhen's sleeves narrowed around his wrists—practical for commoners who spent their days working on farms. These were the cheapest garments and sandals they could afford with the coins they'd gotten from selling snake skin sheds to the herbalist in the small town they were in, which lay southwest of Changle.

"Just bear with the discomfort for now," Zhen replied. The top half of his long hair was twisted in a knot secured with a bamboo stick; the rest hung down past his shoulders. Qing's dark locks were tied back in two braids. "When we have more money, I'll get you new clothes that fit better, all right?"

A red banner fluttered past, liberated by a stiff gust. On it was a pair of badly drawn snakes with huge eyes and forked tongues—a discarded decoration from the spring festival a couple of months ago that had marked the beginning of the Year of the Snake. He and Qing had perched on a high tree branch outside Changle watching people light water lanterns and release them on the Min Jiang, where they floated like flickering stars in an ever-changing constellation.

"Are you sure you know the way?" Qing puffed a stray strand of hair away from her face. "I don't want to get lost. My legs are killing me."

"I know where we're going," Zhen replied a little defensively. "Traveling through towns is trickier than navigating through forests, that's all. The landmarks are different."

"And we can't read the signposts," Qing said. "You know, we really should ask someone for directions or get a map or something."

A woman's singing accompanied by music from stringed

instruments drifted through an open doorway, mingled with men's voices talking and laughing. A yellow lantern illuminated a flag painted with the character 酒; it flapped in the crisp night wind.

Qing grabbed his arm. "Hey, I've never been inside a tavern. Let's check it out."

Zhen frowned. He had tasted wine before, but Qing had not. "No. We don't have enough money for wine."

"I never said anything about drinking," Qing replied. "I just want to see what's going on. Every time I pass by a tavern, the people inside sound like they're having a great time."

"Qing, we're not supposed to draw attention to ourselves—"

"We'll stay at the back! No one will even notice us." Qing rolled her eyes. "If you're going to be such a spoilsport, you can wait here—"

"There's no way I'm letting you out of my sight." Zhen sighed. "Fine. Just for a few minutes. We'll keep close to the door. The moment there's any sign of trouble, we get out. Agreed?"

Qing smirked and dragged him through the entrance.

Inside the dimly lit establishment, the jaundiced glow from torches in sconces threw gnarled shadows across the uneven stone walls. Bones of chicken and fish littered the floor, which was tacky with spit and spilled wine. Barmaids served overflowing goblets to men who sat at haphazardly arranged tables with half-logs for benches. Some were in rowdy groups; others sat sullenly on their own.

The tables near the entrance were occupied, so Zhen and

Qing had no choice but to sidle to a vacant table in the far corner with two barrels for stools. The female singer finished her song, and as she and the musicians stepped off the cramped stage at the front, a drunk man jumped up and started spewing rude poetry. Other patrons guffawed and threw groundnut shells at him.

Zhen glanced toward the door. The sooner they could get out of there, the better. Next to him, Qing looked around with wonder instead of wariness. She didn't seem to notice men jerking their chins in their direction.

An unpleasant prickle went up Zhen's spine. He put a hand on Qing's arm. "I think we should go."

"What? We just got here!" Qing shook his hand away. "Let's see if the singer comes back after a break. I want to listen to one song before we head off."

A muscled, bullnecked man detached himself from his table of friends and walked toward them.

Zhen tensed.

"Welcome to our humble tavern, young lady." Bull Neck eyed Qing with interest as he offered a mock-gentlemanly bow. "Haven't seen you here before."

"Oh, we're just passing through," Qing replied. "By the way, do you happen to know which way out of town is better if we're headed to Mount Emei?"

"Mount Emei? That's over a thousand miles away." Bull Neck cocked his head. "Why don't you stay awhile? My friends and I would love to show you around."

"Actually, we're leaving." Zhen stood, pulling Qing to her feet. "Have a good evening, sir."

"It's rude to reject a kind offer of hospitality, young man." Bull Neck's eyes glinted as he blocked Zhen's path. He turned to his friends and whistled. "Brothers, we have newcomers. Let's give them our signature hearty welcome!"

Dread curdled in Zhen's stomach as two of Bull Neck's friends maneuvered toward them from opposite directions. Bull Neck leered, reaching out to touch Qing's cheek—

Zhen's palm flew up, stopping the man's hand even though it was nearly as big as a bear's paw. Qing looked startled, and surprise crossed Bull Neck's face at Zhen's unexpected strength.

"We don't want any trouble." Although Zhen's heart was pounding, he kept his tone steely. "But I must warn you to keep your hands off my sister."

"Ah, she's your sister, is she?" Bull Neck let out a bark of laughter. He beckoned to his friends, who drew closer, backing Zhen and Qing into the corner. "Seems like trouble has a way of finding you two."

The tavern around them had gone quiet. The other patrons stopped what they were doing and turned to watch. The barmaids hung back nervously.

Qing glowered at Bull Neck. "You're such a brute. Only cowards pick on strangers. Now, get out of our way before my brother kicks your—"

Zhen grabbed Qing and pushed her behind him. Bull Neck's eyes narrowed dangerously.

He swung at Zhen's jaw. Zhen dodged with lightning reflexes. Bull Neck lunged again, but Zhen evaded his strike with serpentine grace and Bull Neck collided with the wall behind them.

A scatter of laughter rose from onlookers.

Bull Neck growled as he heaved a large porcelain wine jar at Zhen, who dived out of the way. The wine jar hit one of Bull Neck's friends instead, bowling him over before shattering on the floor and sending wine everywhere. Some patrons scrambled out of harm's way while those at a safer distance roared with mirth and clapped.

"Zhen, look out!" Qing shouted.

Bull Neck barreled toward Zhen, a dagger in his hand. Zhen twisted away, narrowly avoiding the blade as it sliced past his ear. Bull Neck attacked again, aiming for Zhen's ribs—Zhen swiveled out of reach just in time, and the dagger slashed across one of the sacks in a pile stacked nearby.

Raw soybeans burst out of the gash and spilled and bounced across the floor. One of Bull Neck's friends slipped on the beans and fell, arms and legs flailing; he landed on his ass with a dramatic groan.

A pair of hands grabbed Zhen's head from behind. Before he could turn away, someone threw pepper in his face. Zhen flinched, his eyes burning. A solid fist connected with his stomach, knocking the wind out of him, and he doubled over as blows rained down—

Qing screamed—but it wasn't in fear.

Zhen focused his stinging eyes in time to see Qing leaping

forward with reptilian agility, her face white with rage. Her forked tongue and fanged teeth flashed before her jaws clamped onto Bull Neck's left forearm.

Bull Neck's eyes went wide. The dagger in his raised right hand, poised to descend on Zhen, fell from his grip and landed with a loud clatter.

Qing let go.

Bull Neck staggered backward. He opened his mouth, but no sound emerged—instead, blood spurted out. His friends gasped and jumped away. Bull Neck's eyes rolled back in his head as he keeled over. His arms were splayed out, revealing two stark puncture wounds on his left forearm.

Dead silence echoed before the tavern erupted in chaos.

Stools toppled over, and goblets and plates of food crashed to the floor as everyone yelled in wild panic, colliding with one another in a desperate scramble for the exit. Zhen jumped to his feet, rubbing the blinding grit out of his eyes, and pulled Qing toward the door—

The edge of a sword against his neck made him skid to a halt. Next to him, Qing did the same. Grim constables surrounded them on all sides, their swords drawn.

"Kneel!" one of the constables shouted. "Don't move, snake devils!"

Chapter 5
ZHEN

As Zhen walked toward a bridge, he glanced up at the evening sky, which was streaked with brushstrokes of vermilion and violet. The sunset was the same as other days, and yet it felt different. Standing on two legs gave him a new perspective on everything.

He passed an old man near the riverbank, but when he caught sight of what the man was holding, he stopped in his tracks.

In the man's hand was a bright green snake—it wasn't struggling, only twitching spasmodically. A full-bodied jolt of horror went through Zhen as he realized why.

The man had sliced the snake's belly wide open.

"What are you doing to that snake?" Zhen called out.

The old man looked up and flashed a rotted-toothed grin.

"Have you ever seen a snake's gallbladder?" Between his thumb and forefinger, he held a bloody sac about the size of a grape. "I'm going to make snake-bile wine. It helps my arthritic knees and hemorrhoids. I'll sell the snake skin to one of the merchants in the morning." He thrust the half-dead snake in Zhen's face. "Such an unusual shade of green, isn't it? Almost like jade. It'll fetch a nice coin."

The snake's beady eyes met Zhen's. A sour taste rose in Zhen's throat.

"Stop! I'll pay you for this snake." He knelt and pretended to dig into his boot as he surreptitiously plucked a blade of grass. When he straightened and extended his palm, in place of the blade of grass was a silver coin. "This should be enough."

The old man seemed suspicious. "Why do you want a snake, young fellow?"

Zhen recalled what a vendor selling musical instruments had told him. "I play the èr hú, which is made with snakeskin. That snake you have is young, and the elastic skin will help me achieve the perfect resonance."

"Ah, a musician!" The old man took the coin and handed over the limp snake. "Very well. My catch will have a noble purpose. May your èr hú sing to the wind!"

Zhen's heart pounded as he waited for the old man to disappear. Then he hurriedly brought the dying snake to an obscured spot under the bridge and laid her on the ground. Blood seeped under his fingernails as he tried to pull together the serrated cut down the length of her belly, although he knew his efforts were futile. Even if he'd had a needle and thread to stitch her up, she was too badly injured to survive.

The green snake's eyes were like dying embers, but she still fought to keep them open. Her tongue flicked out. "Thank you."

"No," Zhen said fiercely. "I need you to hold on. I won't let you die."

He placed his hands on the snake's eviscerated body. Then he squeezed his eyes shut and concentrated. The spirit pearl's energy stirred within him. He had never used its power in this way or pushed it to such limits—but he just had to try.

He reached into himself, straining hard until he felt something deep within his core cracking wide open. Suddenly every part of him was ablaze, and his skin felt like it was burning off his flesh, his flesh off his bones. His ears exploded with his own anguished screams. Blood spewed from his mouth as he stumbled backward and collapsed.

He had no idea how long he lay there, convulsing with agony. Tears and sweat mingled, briny and metallic on his lips. He felt as if his own organs had been ripped out.

Through the blistering haze, he felt a lesser pain twist through him—he was transforming back into a snake. The sun had set, and the sky was dark. The silver coin he'd given the old man could hold its transmuted form for only a couple of hours; it would've already turned back into a blade of grass.

The green snake lay a distance away. She wasn't moving. With excruciating effort, he slithered to her side, his scaly white body undulating over the uneven ground.

"Are you all right?" He prodded the other snake with his snout. Her open eyes were glassy, unseeing—but all that remained of the horrific gouge on her belly was a raw scar. "Can you hear me?"

Her tail twitched. She feebly raised her head and turned it from side to side. "Where am I? Who—who are you?"

His body uncoiled in relief. He flicked his tongue in greeting. "My name is Zhen. What's yours?"

The green snake's tongue darted out. "My mother used to call me Qing."

The iron manacles bit into Zhen's wrists and ankles, tethering him to the stone wall. The hard floor of the jail cell was covered with a scattering of hay.

Zhen turned to Qing, who was shackled next to him.

"You shouldn't have used your spirit powers on that man at the tavern," he told her.

"He came at you with a dagger! What was I supposed to do?" Qing shot him a mutinous look. "You're the one who didn't want to ask for directions."

"I should've noticed that your tongue hadn't fully changed." Zhen reached out his cuffed wrist, took Qing's chin in his hand, and pulled her jaw open. "Your fangs must've still been folded in their sheaths."

Qing was a pit viper, a breed known to be short-tempered and combative. In contrast, pythons like Zhen would curl up in a ball rather than lash out when they felt threatened.

She swatted his hand away. "Just our luck that a bunch of constables were in the private room of the tavern. How convenient that they didn't intervene when that brute first attacked you."

Zhen sighed. "I know you were trying to protect me, but you mustn't lose control like that again, Qing. You already don't have your gallbladder. You can't afford to put unnecessary strain on your body before we reach Mount Emei."

Qing made a frustrated sound as she tugged at her restraints.

"Can't we find our way to Mount Emei as snakes? You said traveling on the roads as humans would be faster and less dangerous, but . . ." She gestured around the cell. "Look where we are now."

The first snake spirits had cultivated their powers on Mount Emei. When they gained immortality after a thousand years and ascended to heaven, the bodies they left behind made a special kind of milfoil bloom on the mountain slopes every summer that could give healing to other snakes. That was where he and Qing were headed.

"Hopefully we'll be far from here by the time they discover we're gone." Zhen estimated that about an hour had passed since they had been thrown into the cell in the basement of the constables' station. "I'll go upstairs first to make sure it's safe to leave."

Zhen shut his eyes and focused. A familiar tug on his spine, a sudden twinge, a cross between a shudder and a spasm—his body lengthened, and his limbs retracted like a turtle drawing its flippers back into its shell. His tunic and pants pooled in a heap, and the iron cuffs hit the floor with a dull clang.

Zhen turned to Qing, flicking his tongue. His words, in the language of snakes, emerged in a hiss. "Wait here. Don't follow until I give the signal."

His dorsal scales gleamed with pearly translucence as he slid between the bars, then glided across the basement floor and up a narrow flight of stairs to the constables' station. The front door was locked from the outside, but the back door was bolted from the inside. That would be their way out.

Zhen raised his head and listened intently. As a snake, he didn't have ears, but he was far from deaf. Bones and membranes inside his head could pick up sounds and vibrations that the human ear couldn't: The faint scurry of rats prowling through a rubbish mound in the back alley. The flutter of a moth's wings as it settled on the rafters above. The distant howl of foxes.

No sign of human movement. This was their chance to escape.

He made his way back to the top of the stairs. "Pssst. You can come up now."

Silence.

"Qing?" he called. "Can you hear me?"

Her choked cry pierced the air.

Zhen slithered down the steps faster than he'd ever moved in his life. He reared up, poised to attack whoever or whatever was stealthy enough to have evaded his senses—

Qing was alone in the cell. Her face was flushed, her hands clenched into fists as she let out another strangled scream.

"I can't transform!" she wailed. She hurled herself at the bars, but the chains around her wrists and ankles restrained her. She clawed at her face, raking angry red lines down her cheeks. "What's wrong with me? Why can't I turn back? I'm scared, Zhen—don't go without me!"

Using her spirit powers on that man at the tavern must've weakened her more than she'd expected, even affecting her ability to transform.

Zhen slipped through the bars. Within a few heartbeats, his scales had morphed into skin. He quickly put on his pants before wrapping his arms around Qing. She clung to him, sobbing against his chest. A patch of scales on her arm flared crystal green, like an angry chameleon at midday.

"Don't be silly." Zhen stroked a comforting hand over the back of her head. "You know me better than this. I would never leave you behind."

"We're stuck here because of me, and I'm the one who can't get out." Qing's voice was choked. "I don't want you to stay, but I don't want you to go without me."

Zhen pulled back. "There's always another way."

Qing sniffled, wiping the back of her cuffed hand over her tear-streaked cheeks. "What do you mean?"

Zhen's fingers found a rusted nail buried in the hay, and he showed it to Qing.

She frowned. "We can't pry open the lock with this. It's too small and blunt."

Zhen's hand closed around the nail, and when his fingers unfurled, a plain iron key lay in its place.

Qing's eyes went wide. "How did you—"

"It's a skeleton key." Zhen inserted it in the keyhole in Qing's cuff and turned it; there was a click and the cuffs loosened. "It'll open any locks."

Qing stared at her liberated wrist. She shoved Zhen's shoulder. "I can't believe you didn't do this earlier instead of making me have a breakdown!"

Zhen shook his head. "Remember what I told you about using your powers? The stronger the emotion, the stronger your powers, but using them will drain you to almost the same degree. You know what dài jià means, don't you?"

"What something costs?"

"It's the cost *of* something," Zhen replied. "We have to pay a price each time we use our powers. That's how everything stays in balance."

Qing's gaze slid down to a smooth, silvery weal on the left side of Zhen's torso, just above his waistband. "I never noticed your scar. It was hidden by your scales before. What happened?"

"I got careless around a snake trap. A lesson I'll never forget." Zhen put on his tunic, covering the scar. A faint noise caught his attention, and he stiffened. "Did you hear that?"

"Um, that was me." Qing's hand went to her stomach, which let out another rumble. "I'm starving. This must be another side effect of our transformation."

"You're hungry all the time, whether snake or human," Zhen said. "Let's get out of here."

He unlocked the cell, and together they crept upstairs. Zhen pushed open the back door leading out of the constables' station; the stench of rotting garbage had never smelled more like freedom.

They slunk along the shadows of back alleys and small lanes, staying off the main streets. Zhen hadn't been in this part of town before, but he let the sounds of nature guide him toward the forest.

He breathed easier once they ducked under the canopy of trees. As a human, he did not hear the soft hoot of an owl as a warning to take cover; the rustle of rodents in the brush wasn't a hint that supper was close by. Still, he was driven by urgency to keep moving. Not until Qing stumbled, her face pale with exhaustion, did Zhen stop by a stream to rest.

While Qing cupped her palms and gulped the water thirstily, Zhen foraged nearby. He returned with his hands full of small, rounded fruits with a rough pinkish-red exterior.

"Lychees." He gave Qing some, and they sat side by side against a rock and ate the sweet and tangy fruit, peeling off the coarse skin and spitting out the seed in the center.

Qing frowned and turned to him. "You said using our powers will drain us to almost the same degree." Realization dawned in her eyes. "Saving my life was what weakened you, wasn't it? That's why you need to go to Mount Emei for healing as well."

At first, Zhen had wanted only to stop the old man from stripping Qing's skin and selling it. He'd just hoped to let her die with dignity. But when he gazed into her dying eyes and saw the fire in them, he knew he had to give her something better than a merciful death. She deserved more. So much more.

Zhen had summoned the pearl's powers to revive her, turning her into a snake spirit, the same thing that had happened to him when he swallowed the pearl all those years ago. But the immense toll of healing her hadn't just weakened him. It had taken a part of him, altered him forever. Still, he didn't want Qing to bear the burden of knowing that. She shouldn't have to feel guilty about the price he'd paid to save her. The choice had been his. It was his dài jià.

"Why?" Qing's voice was thick with emotion. "Why did you do it?"

"Because I couldn't let you go," Zhen replied. "And I would do it all over again if I had to. Don't worry. Once we get to Mount Emei, the milfoil will replenish my strength and cure the deficiency caused by your missing gallbladder."

Qing sighed. "My mother used to say I was more mischievous than all my siblings combined. She would've been so mad if she knew how much trouble I got us into tonight. Probably given me a dozen lashes with her tail."

She sounded as if she would gladly accept the punishment if only her mother were around to mete it out. Among snakes, pit vipers were the only breed that cared for their young. Mothers would fiercely guard their babies until their first shed. The only thing talkative Qing had been taciturn about was her family, and Zhen hadn't pressed her for details. He stayed quiet now, and silence settled between them until Qing finally spoke.

"We lived in a bamboo forest, and I loved to explore the groves and streams around our burrow. One day, my mother warned us that a thunderstorm was coming and told us to stay home. But I refused to listen and went out to play." Qing's voice frayed a little. "The storm hit before I could get back. I hid up in a tree as the rain poured for days and the forest flooded. When the waters receded, I made my way home. Our burrow was destroyed. My mother and siblings weren't inside, so they must've escaped in time."

Now Zhen understood why Qing had broken down in the cell.

She'd thought Zhen had no choice but to leave her behind, like her mother had, and once more, she had only herself to blame.

Zhen took her hand and gave it a comforting squeeze. "I believe your mother stayed for as long as she could. She waited for you to come home until she had to take your brothers and sisters to safety."

Qing's eyes glimmered in the darkness. "I was the one who wanted to go inside that tavern. You tried to stop me, but I wouldn't listen. Everything that happened was my fault."

"Hey," Zhen said. "If your mother had seen the fearless little snake you were tonight—how loyal and brave her daughter had grown up to be—she would've been so proud."

Qing blinked. Tears ran down her cheeks. She let out an embarrassed sound. "Crying still feels so weird."

As snakes, they couldn't blink or shed tears. Zhen put his palms on the sides of Qing's face and brushed away the wetness with his thumbs.

"Another reason why humans have these," he said, wiggling his fingers.

Qing gave a teary chuckle. Above their heads, the moon had passed its zenith. There wasn't much time before the first light of dawn.

"We have to keep moving." Zhen got to his feet. "They'll be even more convinced we're devils when they discover we broke out of jail."

Qing brushed off the dirt and grass that clung to her green skirt. "Where will we go?"

"They know we were planning to travel west to Mount Emei, so they'll probably search in that direction first," Zhen said. "We'll head north instead. We don't have enough money for the rest of the journey, so we need to stop for a while and find some work to feed ourselves. Our best chance of doing that will be in the capital, Changle."

Chapter 6
XIAN

According to ancient books of rites, an emperor or king rode in a carriage drawn by six horses, while a prince rode with four. But Xian refused the carriage and insisted on riding Zhaoye. He didn't care about tradition. His goal was to reach Changle as soon as possible.

Xian set out at daybreak, accompanied by Fahai, Feng, and the rest of his delegation. He hadn't set foot in the capital of Min since the smaller kingdom declared allegiance to Wuyue. Last year, Xian's father spent two weeks visiting the palace in Changle; he had brought his royal entourage, including his wife, consorts, princes, and princesses. But Xian had chosen to stay behind. He wouldn't leave his mother alone just to have a good time.

In the middle of their journey, they arrived at a way station and were told by scouts who had gone ahead that fallen trees were blocking the main road. The horses could pass but not the wagons laden with gold, jade, and silk. Workers would take a day or two to remove the debris.

"We'll split the delegation," Xian said. "Fahai and I will go ahead. Feng and the guards will stay behind with the wagons until the road is cleared."

Fahai nodded. He understood the urgency of their true errand. Feng, who also knew the real reason they were going to Changle, was unable to hide his misgivings.

"I'm supposed to be your bodyguard," Feng said early the next morning as he helped Xian put on his armor in his room. "No offense to Fahai, but he's trained in court affairs, not martial arts."

"I'm sure Fahai can punch any attackers with his scholarly fists and whack them in the face with his fish pouch," Xian replied, taking his helmet from Feng. It was made of lamellar metal trimmed with leather and had yellow plumage to distinguish him from the other cavalry.

Feng shot him a withering look as he secured Xian's overlapping breastplates to his torso with toughened laces. "I'm not joking. How can he defend you if anything happens?"

General Jian had begun teaching his firstborn son martial arts when he was a child; by the time Feng was ten, he was so skilled that he was sent to Shaolin Monastery for three years to learn from the world-renowned masters there.

"You and Fahai are the two I trust most." Xian adjusted the

metal greaves that extended from his belt to his knees. "I need one of you to stay behind with the valuables and make sure nothing goes missing. You know the guards your father picked for this journey better than I do. They'll obey your command."

Outside, Zhaoye neighed and stomped his feet.

"Rong got food poisoning last night and will have to stay behind," Feng said. Rong was Zhaoye's keeper. "Your horse won't let anyone but you and Rong put on his armor, so you'll have to do it yourself."

Zhaoye still wasn't happy when Xian fastened the plate armor to his head and face. Xian leaned forward and rubbed his neck. "Yeah, you and me both."

Xian and Fahai set off at first light with a small entourage of two scouts, five guards, and a packhorse carrying the supplies they needed. Traveling without wagons allowed them to cover more ground. Ferghana horses excelled at endurance riding and had to drink water only once a day even in the sweltering heat of summer. Zhaoye rode like fire scorching a narrow canyon, spurring the other horses to increase their pace to keep up.

The rest of the journey passed without incident, and Xian sent the scouts ahead to announce he would be arriving at Changle a day earlier than anticipated.

The capital was decorated ostentatiously for his royal visit. The streets were lined with lanterns and banners painted with blessings for the prince of Wuyue, and people thronged the road to the palace, playing flutes and cheering. But as Xian rode through the city, he noticed the sparse trees had brittle bark and low-slung branches that bore small fruit or none. The kingdom of Min had been faltering at the end of a drawn-out conflict with Southern Tang—which was what had prompted its capitulation to Wuyue—and the austerity was visible beneath the gold banners and red-lettered glamour.

As at the palace back in Xifu, the sprawling outer court was where official ceremonies were held. Festive celebrations and victory parades took place there, as well as public punishments. As was the custom, no trees were planted nearby, as they would overshadow the majesty of the king's presence—and provide a hidden vantage point for an assassin.

Guards saluted as Xian and Fahai dismounted, and stable hands quickly took their horses. An impeccably attired man approached, bowed deeply, and introduced himself as Governor Gao.

"The rest of my delegation has been delayed by the impassable road, but my adviser and I rode ahead, so we are here a day earlier than expected," Xian said. "The welcome banquet can proceed tomorrow as planned. The gifts we have brought will have arrived by then."

Gao bowed again. "The Min court appreciates the prince of Wuyue's kind consideration, but for an auspicious start to the visit, we as hosts must hold the welcoming festivities on the day of Your Highness's arrival. We request that you and your counselor grace us with your presence at the banquet this evening. The royal manor has been prepared for you and your entourage."

All palaces were constructed along the same south–north

axis; the buildings on either side of the central line were built with painstaking precision to ensure each half was symmetrical, and the left was always given more honor than the right. A vast gate with five archways separated the inner and outer courts. Two stone lions flanked the center archway, which could be used only by the king. Gao respectfully gestured Xian toward the archway on the left, which was reserved for the royal family. The other officials, including Gao and Fahai, entered through the archway on the right.

The royal manor stood in a guarded compound with high walls on all four sides. The main building, with its yellow-glazed roof crowned with carved dragons and double eaves that curved outward and upward, was at the north; the vermilion entrance gate faced south.

The bedroom arranged for Xian was second only to the king's chamber—it was traditionally occupied by the crown prince. Xian couldn't suppress a smirk as he imagined Wang's chagrin. The room was so spacious that he and Feng could probably have had a sparring session if they shifted a few pieces of furniture aside. The platform bed was as wide as it was long, elegantly framed with gauze curtains and pennants. On the elaborately carved wooden dresser stood an incense clock, minutes and hours calibrated by incense sticks. To the left, a set of doors connected to an adjoining room, which was where his bodyguard would sleep.

In the corner of the chamber was something Xian didn't have in his room back home: a gold lacquered bathtub. Bathing was ritualistic, meant to cleanse body and soul; priests and even the king himself had to bathe before offering sacrifices or performing rites. This gilded bathtub, however, was clearly made for pleasure rather than piousness.

But nothing was quite as blatant as the small ceramic bottle placed by the side of the bed. Xian didn't need to remove the stopper to know what the contents were meant for.

A good-looking boy around his age had quietly followed Xian into his chamber. He stepped forward and bowed low. "Will Your Highness allow his humble servant the honor of assisting him in removing his armor?"

Feng was usually the one in charge of this task, but he wasn't there. Xian extended his arms, and the boy skillfully unknotted the ties holding the pieces of armor together and hung them all on a wooden rack. Then he filled a copper basin with clean water for Xian to wash his face and hands.

"What's your name?" Xian asked.

"My name is Deng, Your Highness. I am the most senior among the courtesans under the age of eighteen."

A courtesan. It explained why he was faultless not just in his duties but in his expressions. On any other occasion, Xian would've let himself indulge. This was the first time he had been away from home on his own—he didn't even have to sneak out for a roll in bed with an attractive boy.

But the reason he was here was too important. He couldn't allow himself to be distracted.

"I can take it from here, Deng," Xian said. "You may leave."

Deng couldn't hide his surprise at the abrupt dismissal. He retreated and closed the doors behind him, leaving Xian alone in the vast room.

Xian washed his face with water from the copper basin, rinsing away the grime and sweat from a long day of riding. He opened his luggage and took out his golden-yellow lóng páo for the banquet. Its dark blue satin collar and cuffs were hemmed with gold thread; embroidered on the front of the garment were five-clawed dragons, embellished with thousands of tiny freshwater seed pearls, as well as motifs of cloud scrolls, medallions, and crashing waves.

Xian released his long hair from its bun, combed the locks, and twisted them in a loose knot. He would tie his hair properly before the banquet. He shrugged on a comfortable white robe with green trim and a matching sash. As he adjusted the cross collar, his fingers brushed the jade amulet hidden beneath his inner shirt.

A wistful smile curled on Xian's mouth. When his mother was finally cured and well enough to travel, he would ask permission from his father to take her to the small palace in the eastern court of Yuezhou to recuperate. The character 東—east—was made up of 日, the sun, and 木, a tree. Both elements represented spring—a time for growth, for new beginnings to take root. Being back east, close to her hometown, would be good for his mother's recovery.

A large bowl of fresh fruit sat on the table. The apricots were exceptionally fragrant, and Xian slipped two into his pocket before heading out of the chamber.

The guards outside saluted as he passed. If they were bemused at his informal outfit, they had been trained not to show any reaction. Beyond the walls of the royal manor, no one cast a second glance at Xian. The prince of Wuyue, as far as everyone was concerned, wore a plumed helmet and full ceremonial armor wherever he went, probably even the bathroom.

Instead of going to the Ancestral Temple, where royals offered sacrifices to their ancestors and bowed before their memorial tablets, Xian made his way to the Spirit Hall, where the commoners who worked in the palace worshipped. Most Daoist temples were built entirely with timber and without the use of a single nail; interlocking wooden brackets ingeniously transferred the weight of the overhanging roof to vertical columns.

The uneven stone steps leading up to the Spirit Hall had been weathered by years of pilgrims' feet. The temple had three doors. By the door on the right was a statue of a dragon, while a tiger statue stood by the one on the left. The middle doorway was for spirits, not humans.

Xian walked through the dragon doorway on the right, making sure he crossed the threshold with his left foot first. He would later exit through the tiger doorway with his right foot first. His mother always reminded him to step over, never on, the red wooden plank across the bottom of each door that blocked evil from entering the temple.

At that hour in the late afternoon, the temple was empty. The walls were covered in stelae of human figures among a menagerie of beasts and birds; images of deities were carved onto the pillars. Unlike his parents, Xian had never been religious. The rituals he performed at the Ancestral Temple each year were perfunctory, and while the priests chanted lengthy prayers, his mind would drift to how he would sneak out to meet the latest boy who had caught his eye.

Xian halted in front of a statue of Guan Yin, the goddess of mercy and his mother's most beloved deity. On the altar were an oil lamp, two candles, a porcelain incense burner, and three small cups. The cup on the right contained tea, the left one was filled with water, and the one in the middle held grains of uncooked rice. Tea represented yin, water symbolized yang, and uncooked rice was the union between the two.

Xian took three incense sticks—always offered in uneven numbers—and lit them with the flame from one of the candles. He knelt in front of the altar, shut his eyes, and inhaled deeply, letting the earthy scent of the incense fill his lungs.

"Prince of Wuyue."

Xian opened his eyes as the priest emerged from the inner shrine. He had a black satin hat with a round hard brim on his shaven head. He was dressed in a dào páo, a wide-sleeved, crossed-collar robe that Daoist priests wore to tend to their daily duties in the temple.

The priest walked toward Xian. "I'm surprised to see you here, Prince of Wuyue, instead of at the Ancestral Temple."

"Dao Zhang." Xian bowed his head as he uttered the respectful title. "My mother is a commoner, and she grew up worshipping in temples like these."

The priest nodded solemnly. "The gods look with favor on

your filial piety. Concealed danger lurks nearby, but you have been blessed with protection from your mother's amulet."

The jade amulet, hidden behind the folds of Xian's robe, suddenly felt warm against his skin. Perhaps the priest was able to sense its protective aura.

"My mother has been ill for many years." Tendrils of smoke from the incense sticks clasped between Xian's palms continued to rise, curling heavenward before vanishing. "My father, the king of Wuyue, sought the wisdom of the oracle of Emei, who directed us to Changle to find a cure. I have come here today to petition for further direction from the gods."

The priest gestured toward a wall at the far side of the room. "Since you have offered incense, we shall now ask for guidance."

Qiú qiān was a common practice in temples throughout the land. The wall was made up of rows of bricks numbered from one to a hundred, each with a circular hole about an inch in diameter that contained a small rolled-up scroll. The priest handed Xian a hollow bamboo cylinder filled with flat sticks, each painted red on one end and inscribed with a number that corresponded with one of the bricks.

Xian tipped the cylinder slightly downward and shook it until one stick jumped out and landed on the floor. He leaned down, picked up the stick, and held it out to the priest with both hands. The priest looked at the number on the stick, withdrew a small scroll from one of the bricks, and gave it to Xian.

Xian's heartbeat quickened as he unfurled the parchment, revealing the words written in tiny, slanted lettering: 強龍難壓地頭蛇.

"'Qiáng lóng nán yā dì tóu shé,'" he read out in a quiet tone. *Even a powerful dragon struggles to overcome a snake in its native haunt.*

Yet another reference to the white snake. But what did it mean? Was it a warning that he, as a prince and the king's emissary—represented by the dragon—was still an outsider in Changle, while the white snake was in its natural element?

The priest must have noticed the contemplative look on Xian's face.

"The answer will reveal itself at the right time," he said. "May heavenly blessings be with you."

Xian bowed low. "Thank you, Dao Zhang."

He turned to leave, making sure he stepped over the red plank of the tiger door with his right foot.

Chapter 7
XIAN

A bronze carving of a flying horse was nailed above the stable entrance. The harried stable hands didn't pay any attention to Xian as they rushed back and forth with armfuls of bedding, sacks of feed, and buckets of water. Changle's stable was half the size of Xifu's, and several horses had been brought out to the paddock to free up space for their visitors' steeds.

Xian walked along the stalls, searching for his horse. The only two people Zhaoye allowed to groom him were his keeper, Rong, and Xian himself. Maybe Xian would be able to save some poor soul from getting kicked in the face for getting too close.

He found Zhaoye in the last stall in the row, which was larger than the rest. A stable boy around Xian's age was there, dressed in coarse cotton trousers and a shirt with narrow sleeves rolled up just below his elbows. He was talking to Zhaoye in a low, soothing tone.

Xian stopped.

The boy leaned forward and tapped Zhaoye's front leg as a signal to lift his foot. "Come on, hoof up."

Zhaoye raised his hoof. The boy bent over, a pick in hand, and meticulously dug out the mud and debris trapped in the horseshoe.

Xian was so stunned by his horse's calm demeanor that he didn't react quickly enough when the boy turned; he caught Xian watching.

"Hello." The boy let down Zhaoye's hoof and straightened, looking at Xian inquiringly. "You are?"

"That's, uh, the prince's horse," Xian said. He realized how dumb the words sounded as soon as they were out of his mouth.

"I know," the boy replied. "Our guest of honor here caused quite a ruckus earlier."

"What happened?" Xian walked toward them. "Is he all right?"

"Don't worry, he's fine." The boy patted Zhaoye's flank, and the horse made a satisfied noise. "While he was cooling down after running all day, someone noticed watery red drops trickling down his coat and yelled that the prince's horse was bleeding, which sent everyone into a panic. I told them there was nothing to worry about—he's a hàn xuè mǎ, after all. When they run, they look like they're sweating blood."

Xian hadn't expected a stable boy to know this unusual trait of Ferghana horses. Their skin was thin, almost transparent, and exertion made their blood vessels become more obvious, giving the sweat on their necks and shoulders a metallic-red hue.

"How did you know that?" Xian asked.

"Oh, I've met them before," the boy replied. "In the east, close to the Tibetan Plateau. A few Ferghana horses broke free from a noble's stable and made their home on the steppes."

Xian raised an eyebrow. "Do you come from a family of nomads?"

The boy chuckled. "You could say that." He ran a hand down Zhaoye's mane, gazing admiringly at him. Zhaoye preened, basking in the attention. "Without a doubt, he is one of the most beautiful creatures I've ever laid eyes on."

Xian could have said the same about the boy. Feng would probably scoff, but this boy was, without exaggeration, beautiful in a way Xian had not seen before. His features were delicate but defined, and his long hair, tied back in a half-knot that had loosened, framed his face with a tumble of soft, dark locks that Xian wanted to run his fingers through. A sheen of sweat gleamed on his alabaster skin; he was unusually fair for someone who spent most of his time working outdoors. But it wasn't a sickly kind of paleness . . . more like moonlight, luminous in a way that was almost otherworldly.

Xian was captivated. Not just by the boy's looks but by his unpretentious charm—he probably wasn't even aware of how appealing it made him to Xian.

"He kept tapping his left front foot as I passed by, and I figured there must be some grit irritating his hoof." The boy held out the hoof pick to Xian. "Here. I hope you don't mind that I started grooming him. I didn't mean to take over your duties."

His duties? Xian blinked—then realized that, in Rong's absence and because Xian was dressed in a plain robe, the boy had assumed *he* was the horse keeper of the Wuyue delegation.

"Have you been working here for some time?" Xian asked.

The boy shook his head. "I just arrived in Changle a week ago. Everyone has been talking about the prince of Wuyue, and the palace staff have been working around the clock to prepare for his arrival. It's the reason my sister and I managed to find temporary work so quickly."

"Your sister works in the palace too?"

"She was sent to the kitchen; I was assigned to the stable." The boy paused. "My name is Zhen. What's yours?"

Xian thought quickly. "You can call me Xu."

Zhen offered a courteous bow. "Good to meet you, Xu."

"So what have you heard about the prince of Wuyue?" Xian couldn't resist asking. "It sounds like his reputation precedes him."

"They say his father favors him even though he's not the first-born, which means he must be very capable." A furtive smile lifted the sides of Zhen's mouth. "They also say he's handsome."

"Hmm. Prince Xian—that's his name—might have a few skills, but between you and me?" Xian leaned forward until he was inches from Zhen's ear and said conspiratorially, "I'd rather deal with his horse." The other boy had an earthy musk that reminded Xian of sandalwood and grass after summer rain. "I mean, what kind of show-off arrives a day earlier than expected with no gifts, sending the poor host into a frenzy to get the banquet ready? Who does he think he is?"

Zhen arched an eyebrow. "You have a strong opinion of your lord. Have you been working in the palace in Wuyue all your life?"

Xian couldn't suppress a grin. "Yeah, you could say that."

Zhen glanced around the stable. "So which of these horses is the one you rode?"

"Uh . . ." Xian pointed at Fahai's horse. "That one."

Zhaoye neighed and scratched his hoof on the ground.

"You're lucky to have the chance to care for and spend time around such fine creatures." Zhen looked at Xian wryly. "To tell you the truth, I'm only supposed to be mucking out the stalls, not grooming the horses. I might get in trouble if they found out. I hope you won't tell on me."

"You have nothing to worry about," Xian replied. "What I just said to you about the prince is enough to get me a dozen lashes and a week in the stocks."

Zhen smiled. "I won't say anything if you won't."

"Deal." Xian took one of the apricots from his pocket, cleaned his dagger on his sash, and cut the fruit in half. He gave one piece to Zhaoye and offered the other to Zhen. "Try this. It's ripe and fragrant."

Zhen regarded the apricot with amusement. "Am I worthy of taking fruit meant for a prince's horse?"

"Let's find out." Xian showed the second half to Zhaoye. "Do you want to share this with your new friend?"

Zhaoye snatched the fruit without hesitation. Xian and Zhen

exchanged looks, and they both laughed. Xian liked the sound of Zhen's laughter, as pleasing as the tinkle of copper chimes teased by the wind.

"Good thing I came prepared." Xian took out the second apricot. He touched Zhen's shoulder and beckoned him away from Zhaoye's stall. "Let's leave the selfish horse and share this one."

They moved to a corner of the stable where the fodder was stored. Xian sliced the apricot in two and handed one piece to Zhen. "Here."

Their fingers brushed as Zhen took the fruit. "Thanks."

Xian ate his half, not taking his eyes off Zhen as the other boy bit into the yellow-orange flesh. The way Zhen's tongue flicked out to chase the drops of juice on his lips sent a thrill through Xian.

"Where did you find such a delicious apricot?" Zhen asked. "Surely you couldn't have brought it all the way from Wuyue."

Xian couldn't tell him the apricot was from a fruit bowl in his royal chamber and had likely been sent to the capital from one of Min's finest orchards. "Just a lucky pick along our journey."

Zhen leaned against a post. "I was told your delegation would be staying until after the Duanwu Festival. Do you have any days off?"

"I'm not sure the prince of Wuyue understands the concept of days off. He's a brutal taskmaster." Xian tilted his head. "If I could get away, what do you have in mind? Would you show me around Changle? You said you only arrived a week ago."

"I'm familiar with the forests outside Changle," Zhen replied.

"There are some beautiful scenic spots not many people know of. Perfect for half a day of riding . . . I mean, if you're up for that."

Xian's heart lifted. Zhen could be their guide for a snake-hunting expedition in the forests around Changle. Perhaps his visit to the temple had won the favor of the gods, and this chance meeting with Zhen was more than just serendipitous.

"Sounds perfect," Xian said. "I would love to."

Zhen looked pleased. A distant shout made them both turn.

"I'm afraid I have to get back to work before the steward of the stable gives me the sack," Zhen said.

"Of course. It would be a shame if I found myself with a day off and no one to spend it with."

Zhen's eyes glimmered with mirth. "I hope we'll see each other again soon, Xu."

Xian grinned. "I have no doubt we will."

Chapter 8
ZHEN

"I think I'm turning back into a snake," Qing said.

Zhen's head whipped in her direction. The scaly green patch on Qing's arm and the forked edge of her tongue had disappeared before they arrived in Changle. "What's wrong?"

Qing held up her reddened fingers. "I've been shredding ginger and chopping garlic until I can't feel my hands. And I've been on my feet all day—my legs feel boneless."

Zhen poked her in the ribs. "Don't scare me like that."

"Two hundred kitchen staff had to spend the entire afternoon rushing around to prepare over fifty dishes, far more than this snobbish bunch of nobles can finish." Qing rubbed her ankles ruefully. "This is the least efficient method of feeding ever."

The sky had darkened to cobalt, and Zhen and Qing were perched on the roof of the dining hall. Snakes were natural climbers, and for them, sneaking up to the roof unnoticed wasn't difficult. They were obscured by a row of ceramic figures along the ridge: a bird, a fish, a bull, and a lion. The red clay that cemented the glazed roof had weathered down and cracked, and they'd pried up a few tiles so they could peer at what was going on in the banquet hall below.

A square gold lacquered table stood at the north, facing the rest of the hall. Sitting against the high backrest of an armchair was the prince of Wuyue, dressed in a regal yellow robe. To his left was an older man in a burgundy robe and a black gauze hat.

From his high vantage, Zhen could see nothing more than the top of the prince's head. His hair was gathered in a perfectly coiffed bun—the only indication of his youth was the gold hairpin that secured his topknot. Zhen still had a lot to learn about human customs, but he knew that a man received a headpiece when he turned twenty.

"Humans are weird," Qing remarked. "So many have to toil to serve a few. That prince can't be older than a teenager. What makes him more special than the rest? Who gets to decide?"

She had a point. Humans had a puzzling way of distributing power, placing it in the hands of the less experienced just because they were born into certain families. Snakes weren't social creatures and usually hunted alone, but among the animals with herd hierarchy that Zhen had met, such as wolves and horses, the leaders were stronger than the rest of their group.

Qing nudged him. "Hey, see that pot of soup? Did you know it's not made with the meat of swallows but with their *nests*? Apparently the nests aren't just edible—they're an emperor's delicacy! I caught a couple of swallows when I was a snake, but I never once thought to eat their nests!"

"What about the other dishes?" Zhen asked.

"That's duck soup with yam. Next to it is wild herb salad with cauliflower. Cauliflower tastes disgusting, by the way. That dish over there is made of deer tail—which, again, is not the first part of a deer I would've chosen to eat. Way too close to the butthole, you know?"

Zhen cracked a smile. "Sounds like you missed out."

"I must say, humans have clever ways of preserving food," Qing said. "Madam Hua showed me the icehouses today. They're filled with blocks of ice hewn from frozen creeks during winter, so they can store vegetables and fruits inside and serve them at other times of the year. Salt keeps fish and meat from going bad, and seasoning different kinds of food with vinegar, honey, or oil can make them last longer. Imagine snakes could do that—we wouldn't need to hibernate! Napping for months is such a waste of time."

"What would we do in the winter?" Zhen asked, amused. "Catch falling snowflakes on our forked tongues? And then freeze to death because we're cold-blooded?"

"Killjoy." Qing snapped her fingers. "I've been meaning to ask—when are you going to teach me transmutation? That'll surely come in handy in the kitchen. I could transmute grains of rice into the dishes I'm supposed to prepare so I don't even have to cook! They'll keep their form for long enough to be eaten, right?"

"I only managed to learn the skill after five years of cultivation, and at the beginning, the objects I transmuted lasted for barely a couple of minutes," Zhen replied. "You need to spend time cultivating to refine your internal energy into skills. And that involves being able to sit still for more than five minutes."

Qing huffed. "I can sit still for five minutes! Watch me." She made a show of sitting perfectly still and putting on a serene expression. A short time passed before she started humming to herself. She caught Zhen hiding a grin and realized why. "Not fair, that doesn't count!"

"I think you lasted two minutes," Zhen told her. "Good start, though."

They reclined on the roof, eating steamed buns stuffed with minced pumpkin and mutton that had been rejected by the chefs because they were slightly misshapen. Madam Hua, one of the kitchen ladies who had taken Qing under her wing, had let her have them.

"Guess what?" Zhen said. "I met a handsome boy at the stable today."

"Ooh." Qing perked up. "Tell me everything. I want details."

"His name is Xu, and he's one of the horse keepers in the Wuyue delegation. I met him while I was grooming the prince's horse, which is supposed to be his job, but he didn't seem to mind. We talked, and he shared an apricot with me."

"That's all? Did he push you up against the wall and flick his tongue against yours?" Qing smirked. "Male vipers do that when they're interested in mating with another snake. First they flick their tongues, then they vibrate their bodies—"

Zhen coughed and quickly cut in. "He was surprised the prince's horse, Zhaoye, was so friendly to me. The horse was standoffish at first, but he warmed to me when he found out I could speak his language."

"You can do that?"

"You'll be able to, in time," Zhen replied. "Spirit creatures like us can communicate with different kinds of animals."

"So did the horse share any gossip about the prince?" Qing asked.

"Not really. The funny thing was, while I was talking to Xu, Zhaoye was chortling to himself. After Xu left, I asked Zhaoye what was so amusing, but he refused to tell me, like it was some kind of inside joke with his keeper." Zhen shrugged. "Anyway, I told Xu that I know the forests outside Changle pretty well, and when he gets a day off, we can go riding together. And guess what? He said 'I would love to.'"

Zhen was startled by his own desire to spend more time with the horse keeper from Wuyue. It went against not just his reserved nature but his better judgment. He had warned Qing that they shouldn't draw attention to themselves while they were working in the palace. Perhaps he had let his guard down because Xu, like him, was an outsider in Changle. There was something strikingly familiar about the boy, like a face Zhen had seen in a dream . . .

"You know how to ride a horse?" Qing asked, breaking into his thoughts.

Zhen nodded. He had left the West Lake shortly after becoming a snake spirit, and he'd spent the past seven years learning everything about human life that he could. How to ride, how to kindle a fire, how to identify healing herbs and treat injuries, how to drink and hold his liquor . . . all the skills that he needed not just to survive but to pretend he belonged.

Qing brightened. "Then you can teach me to ride, and we'll buy two horses and get to Mount Emei sooner!"

"A horse costs about fifty bolts of silk," Zhen told her. He'd discovered that the old skins snakes naturally shed had medicinal value and could be sold for money, so he saved up their skin sheds and sold them so they could feed themselves whenever they transformed into humans.

Qing puffed out her cheeks. "Seriously, things were a lot simpler back in the forest."

That was true. There were times when Zhen got homesick, when the clarion call of the forest hummed in his heart—he would revert to his natural form and return to the burrows and the dens where he had been meant to live out an ordinary snake's lifespan of ten to fifteen years. But after a while, the woods would feel small, stifling, and he would find himself longing to venture among humans again. Perhaps this was why animal spirits had to cultivate for a thousand years before gaining immortality—so they would have the chance to immerse themselves in many lifetimes on this mortal world before ascending to the celestial realm.

Qing nudged him.

"We've been here just a week and you've already met the first boy you want to flick your tongue at. Careful—soon you'll have so many trailing after you that you'll have to beat them off with your tail." She gave him a sidelong look. "When I talked about the mating rituals of male vipers, why did you seem so shy? Haven't you ever . . ."

For all that Zhen had learned about being human, there was one aspect that he had yet to experience. He had never been with a mate, not as a snake or as a human.

"When I was an ordinary snake, I was more curious about exploring the world than finding a mate," he replied. "After I became a spirit creature, I no longer went through the same cycles as other snakes. Things just felt . . . different."

Snakes didn't mate for life, but he envied creatures that did, like wolves and cranes. He didn't crave different partners. He wished for only one who could find a place in his heart—and who held a place for him in his. Even as a human, his attraction to other boys was always vague, remote. But when Xu gave him the fruit and their fingers touched . . . the unexpected rush of warmth that went through him was entirely new and exhilarating.

Lively music drifted from the banquet hall below, bringing Zhen's attention back to the festivities. Qing peered through their spyhole. "Hey, looks like some kind of performance is about to start."

Lanterns illuminated the four corners of a square stage that had been prepared for the evening's entertainment. At the table to the prince's left, Governor Gao stood and bowed to the young royal.

"We are privileged to have the prince of Wuyue as our

honored guest," Gao said. "We wish to present the prince with a personal attendant to serve him during his stay in Changle. We have selected eight of our most talented courtesans for the prince to choose from."

A murmur of interest rose from the court officials seated at other banquet tables as eight teenage courtesans—four girls and four boys—dressed in different-colored costumes streamed onto the stage. The girls wore long, flowing skirts decorated with sequins, and the boys donned embroidered capes with tassels. The courtesans took turns greeting the prince and introducing themselves—the girls with a curtsy, the boys with a bow. A boy named Deng, in a teal outfit, his hair plaited as elaborately as the girls', was especially attractive.

"The courtesans have prepared a special dance for the prince," Gao announced. "Please enjoy the performance."

The prince nodded. Zhen could still see only the back of his head.

Lamps in wall sconces were dimmed with black cloth, and musicians began playing pan flutes and reeds accompanied by an hourglass-shaped drum and a zither. The courtesans danced, their long silk sleeves flaring and billowing as they swirled across the stage.

"He's going to pick one of the boys," Qing said.

Zhen raised an eyebrow. "Don't tell me you've somehow figured out the prince likes boys from all the way up here, because I won't believe it."

"I don't know or care who he likes. But Madam Hua says if he picks a girl and she gets pregnant, he'll have to marry her, which will mess up whatever court business he's here for. So if he's smart, he'll pick a boy. He can have fun without consequences."

Zhen's mouth quirked. "What makes you think the prince intends to sleep with the one he chooses?"

Qing rolled her eyes. "Come on—a personal attendant to serve him during his stay? I'm sure the governor wasn't talking about getting up in the middle of the night and giving the prince a nice . . . cup of oolong tea."

Zhen couldn't suppress a laugh. "Where did a young snake like you learn to talk like that?"

"The girls in the kitchen caught me up on how teenage boys are," Qing replied. "Pretty sure the last thing the prince of Wuyue will be doing tonight is sleeping."

When the performance ended, everyone applauded. The courtesans stood in a row on the stage, their faces flushed with exertion and excitement.

Gao spoke. "We now invite the prince to make his selection."

The clapping faded. Anticipation rippled across the hall as the prince of Wuyue stood, stepped onto the stage, and turned around.

Zhen choked as if he'd just swallowed a whole egg. His hand caught Qing's wrist. "That's him."

"Yes, I know, that's the prince," Qing said impatiently. "I've got to say, he's way cuter than I—"

"No, I mean that's *him*! The boy I met at the stable today!"

"Wait—what?" Qing's head snapped to him. "*That's* the boy

you flirted and shared an apricot with? The *prince*? Don't pull my tail!"

Zhen couldn't tear his gaze away from Xu's face. Dressed in a glorious yellow ceremonial robe, his presence calm and commanding, his topknot secured with an ornate hairpin that probably cost more than a commoner earned in a year—he behaved nothing like the boy with the rakish grin who had walked into the stable earlier that day.

"Thank you for the exceptional performance." The prince's eyes were bright and piercing as he regarded the eight courtesans. "Changle's excellence in dance and music shall be something I will praise when I return to my father's court. As for the matter of selecting an attendant—to tell the truth, I had already made up my mind before the performance. Now I'm even more convinced I've made the right choice."

The courtesans exchanged eager glances. Deng, dressed in teal, seemed smug. Zhen guessed that the boy had interacted with the prince before the banquet, and the prince's remark hinted that he was the obvious pick.

"We are gratified that one of them has won your approval," Gao said. "Please let us know whom you have selected."

A hush fell across the hall. The courtesans stood ramrod straight.

"The one I have chosen is not here," the prince said. "His name is Zhen."

Chapter 9

ZHEN

Zhen froze.

A restive murmur rose. Everyone seemed confused. The courtesans appeared crestfallen.

Gao broke the silence. "Excuse me, Your Highness?"

"He works in the stable," the prince replied. "I don't know his family name. If there's more than one person named Zhen, bring them to me and I'll tell you which one."

Next to Zhen, Qing spoke. "Yeah, the prince definitely likes boys."

A tall man in a gray robe came forward and bowed to the prince.

"Your Highness, I am Chu, steward of the courtesans. The person you speak of is not among those I have trained. However, I shall send for him without delay." He signaled to a pair of guards, who promptly exited the hall. "We seek your patience. He will be in attendance at your chamber by the end of the evening."

Zhen's heart dropped. He had to get back to the stable. But a guard was now stationed by the column they'd climbed to get up to the roof. And the next column was too exposed.

"I'll distract him," Qing said. "When he moves away, you climb down."

Zhen caught her arm. "What about you? I can't leave you here by yourself—"

"I'm not the one they're sending for right now!" Qing batted his hand away. "What do you think will happen if those guards don't find you at the stable?"

Before Zhen could stop her, she threw a tile fragment a distance away. The guard spun around; his hand went to his sword as he moved away from the column to investigate.

"Zhen, go!" Qing hissed.

Zhen's stomach knotted. *He* was supposed to be watching out for *Qing*; she shouldn't be putting herself in danger to help him. If anything happened to her, he would never forgive himself. But if the guards couldn't find him at the stable, they would call for a wider search—and being discovered on the roof would get them both in worse trouble.

Qing shoved his arm and muttered a swear word. "Now!"

Zhen slid down the column and landed noiselessly on the ground. He didn't look back, just ducked behind a manicured shrub hedge and sprinted to the stable as fast as he could.

The permanent stable staff had their own quarters, but temporary hires did not. Most lived outside the palace in Changle and went home at the end of the day. Madam Hua allowed Qing to share her room, and Zhen slept in the barn behind the stable where hay bales, feed, and equipment were stored.

Zhen approached the rear of the barn, breathless from running. The flare of torches and voices drew closer; the guards had already checked the stable and were heading to the barn. Which meant he couldn't go through the front entrance, and the back door was locked from inside, so the only option left was an open window.

Torches bobbed as the guards entered the barn—

Zhen dived headfirst through the window and narrowly avoided snapping his neck when he landed on a bedding of hay in an awkward roll. The human body had way too many breakable bones. Snakes had bones too, more than a hundred, but they were lightweight and flexible enough to coil and constrict.

Zhen scrambled to his feet as the guards halted in front of him. He bowed, his hair falling in his face in a wild tangle. "Good evening, sirs."

The guards eyed him askance. "What's your name?"

"I'm, uh, Zhen."

"You sure he's the one we're supposed to bring?" said the second guard. "He looks like he hasn't washed his hair in weeks."

The other shrugged. "Seems our guest of honor likes his gemstones *very* unpolished."

"Come with us." The guards' hands closed around Zhen's arms. "You've been summoned by the prince of Wuyue."

Zhen had never been inside any of the halls in the palace, but the shape and color of their roofs hinted at their importance and function. The banquet hall was rectangular and had a green roof with overhanging eaves and ceramic figures lining the ridges. The grandest building in the inner court had a yellow gabled roof with wide double eaves and carved dragons that rose above the four walls that surrounded its compound.

A tingle went up Zhen's spine. That was probably where the prince was staying—and where he would be sent to serve him later that night.

The guards escorted Zhen to the Hall of Training Courtesans, a square building with a pavilion roof. The tall man in a gray robe who had introduced himself in the banquet hall as the steward of the courtesans came out to meet them.

"I'll take the boy from here," he said curtly, and the guards left.

The steward's forehead creased as he regarded Zhen, who self-consciously ran a hand through his hair, trying to shake out bits of hay and debris caught in the long strands.

"I am Steward Chu, in charge of the training and upkeep of our young courtesans. For some unfathomable reason, the prince of Wuyue has chosen you to be his attendant." Chu caught Zhen's chin and turned his head from side to side. "You have pleasing bone structure. Remarkable symmetry. But you stink of horse. You're in dire need of a bath."

Chu marched Zhen down a corridor and into a large bathroom. A pair of middle-aged women in maids' uniforms dispassionately stripped him of his clothes, ushered him into a metal tub overflowing with suds, and scoured him so vigorously that he wished he still had scales. The abrasive strokes of the pumice momentarily distracted him from the embarrassment of being naked in front of two women who, in human terms, were both old enough to be his mother.

Chu stood by, watching the relentless scrub-down with a hawk's eye.

"Don't just luxuriate, pay attention and learn," he ordered, as if Zhen's grimacing could be mistaken for the expression of someone luxuriating. "You will need to draw the prince's bath when he tells you to. The soap is made of plant ash and soap-berries from the Tibetan mountains. Rub the bar between your palms to create lather."

After the bath, the women slathered thick cream that smelled of plum and white lotus all over Zhen's stinging skin. One of them combed and braided his hair while the other tended to his fingernails with a file. He was then dressed in a flowing silk robe that reached to his ankles—"White," Chu had instructed, "it will bring out the fairness of his skin."

Zhen stared at his reflection in the large copper mirror. His white robe was exquisite, its wide sleeves surprisingly heavy. The top half of his hair had been twisted into an elegant knot fastened by a white jade hairpin. The rest flowed onto his shoulders and down his back in soft, straight locks.

He had never been so finely attired before . . . but something in him bristled. He couldn't help feeling as if the carved hairpin and elaborate braids marked him as property instead of a person, even though courtesans were treated above other palace workers, since they possessed not only beauty but also talents such as dancing, singing, and playing musical instruments.

Which made Zhen all the more bewildered that the prince had chosen *him,* of all people. He didn't have any skills, and he had no idea what the proper etiquette was to wait on nobles, much less a royal. He had been hired to muck out horse stalls—and the prince *knew* this. So why had he picked Zhen?

"We have barely made you presentable, and our time is nearly up!" Chu looked harried. "All right, quickly now—show me how you walk. From here to that cabinet and back again."

Zhen walked in a straight line. The cabinet was on a raised platform, and he lifted the hem of his robe off the floor as he climbed the steps the way he'd seen noblemen and noblewomen doing. He made his way back and looked to Chu for approval.

Chu threw his hands up toward the ceiling. "I must have wronged heaven in some way to be given this impossible task! What are you doing? We want the prince to behold the gracefulness of a crane, not the waddling of a flat-footed duck!"

Zhen winced. "I'm sorry."

Chu glowered at him. "You're sorry . . . what?"

"My lord. I'm sorry, my lord."

"Never forget to address the prince as Your Highness at all times. As his attendant, you must also kneel before him in greeting whenever he enters the room. Rise only when he tells you to. Failure to show respect will be severely punished. Do you understand?"

"Yes, my lord."

"A cot has been brought to the prince's chamber; that's where you will sleep unless he instructs otherwise," Chu continued briskly. "The hour is late, and you will likely be called upon to do only two things for the prince tonight. I will show you how to make a pot of tea."

Chu gestured at a pair of purple clay teapots and several delicate porcelain cups.

"You will find a similar set of tea ware in the prince's chamber. A high-fired teapot, like this one, is made of thin clay. It can be used with any tea but is a must for rolled leaves with a strong fragrance, such as green, white, and oolong. The other teapot is low-fired, made of clay that is thicker and more porous. It's suitable for large leaves with low fragrance, like black and pu'er."

Chu described how to fill the teapot and told him the different brewing times for each tea, and Zhen tried to absorb as much of the instructions as he could.

"You will serve dried plums and pistachios as snacks along with the tea," Chu finished. "Can you remember all of that?"

"Uh, yes, my lord." Zhen's mind was racing. "What about the second thing the prince will want?"

Chu met his gaze. "Whatever else the prince asks you for, do the best you can. Use the contents of the small bottle by the bed."

Zhen stiffened. Qing was right—the prince would have one thing in mind on his first night away from home. Animals mated out of instinct, sometimes even forcibly. Humans weren't much different.

Chu must have noticed Zhen's reaction.

"You are by no measure an ideal candidate for the prince's attendant," he said. "Deng is our finest male courtesan—I specifically sent him to welcome the prince, and I'm baffled as to why the prince did not spare him a second glance. If the prince is displeased with you tonight, Deng shall be your replacement. But if you somehow manage not to get dismissed, I'll teach you the rest of your tasks tomorrow. If you serve the prince satisfactorily during his stay, after he departs, you won't have to return to the stable. You're clearly not cut out to be a courtesan, but I'll have you assigned to other work in the palace that pays better."

Zhen bowed his head and followed Chu out of the Hall of Training Courtesans. When they arrived at the royal manor, Chu informed the guards at the gate that Zhen was the prince's new attendant and should be allowed entry at all times.

Zhen blinked when they walked inside the walled compound. The main building in the north was flanked by two smaller buildings, one on each side. In the middle was a square courtyard, divided into four equal quadrants by paved walkways. In one quadrant stood a quaint white gazebo furnished with a round table and stone seats; in another was a pond decorated with rock formations and a miniature waterfall. Two mandarin ducks floated on the surface among the lotus flowers. Zhen was reminded of the West Lake on a calm spring night. He breathed in; the scent of magnolias tickled his nose.

Chu led the way up the marble steps and through the elaborate red door of the main building that opened into a spacious dining room. Before Zhen could take in the decor, Chu hurried him down a corridor on the left and halted in front of a pair of doors.

"This is where you shall serve the prince," he told Zhen. "Quickly, now."

Zhen entered the prince's bedchamber, and Chu shut the doors behind him. As Chu's footsteps retreated, Zhen stood alone in the middle of the vast space. This was the first chance he'd had to catch his breath since sliding off the roof.

Braziers suffused the chamber with a warm glow, and the floral aroma of jasmine candles mingled with the earthy sandalwood from the incense clock. Perfumed sachets filled with dried chrysanthemum hung from pennants at the four corners of the sprawling platform bed, which was surrounded by delicate white gauze curtains that had been parted and tied back.

As Chu had described, a lacquered tray with two purple clay teapots and porcelain cups had been placed on a mahogany table. A kettle sat on a ceramic stove. Lumps of coal had been banked underneath the circular burner hole, and there were several pine sticks dipped with a dried yellowish substance to strike a flame.

Zhen recoiled. Sulfur. Snakes could not tolerate it.

In a corner, close to one of the latticed windows, was the plain wooden cot where he would sleep . . . unless the prince had other ideas.

Zhen's gaze fell on a small bottle next to the bed. That was what Chu had told him to use. He removed the stopper and peered inside. The thick liquid had a slippery, sticky texture and smelled like red seaweed. The thought of using it made him queasy.

He could escape before the prince returned. Transform back into a snake, slither through the open window, and flee the palace. He'd figure out a way to get word to Qing.

But another part of him didn't want to leave. The thought of seeing Xu again filled him with anticipation that was sharp, strangely pleasurable. But would he feel the same way when he was with the prince?

The sound of the doors sliding open made Zhen whirl around. His heartbeat quickened as a familiar figure stepped inside the chamber.

"Hello, Zhen." The prince shut the doors, a smile twitching on his lips. "Told you we'd be seeing each other soon."

Chapter 10
ZHEN

His face and voice were Xu's—but in every other way, he was the prince of Wuyue. They were the same person, and yet they weren't.

Xu, the irreverent horse keeper who had leaned in and whispered teasingly in Zhen's ear, didn't exist. In his place was the prince—imposing and impressive, wearing an air of detachment with even more effortless grace than he wore his lóng páo. He was like a leopard, its presence revealed not by any sound it made but by the silence it created. Birds would stop chirping, and the forest would hold its breath, as Zhen was doing now.

Zhen dropped to his knees, lowering his eyes. Chu would have had a fit if he'd seen him gawking at the prince. "Good evening, Your Highness."

Footsteps moved forward. "There's no need to call me that."

"Steward Chu made it clear this is how I should address you at all times, Your Highness."

The prince's expression was veiled. "And what if I ordered you not to?"

"Then I would ask you not to put me in a difficult position . . . Your Highness."

The prince's black leather boots halted in Zhen's line of sight. Zhen ventured an upward glance. By the gods, the prince was devastatingly handsome in a completely different way than Xu. His hair was pulled back in an austere knot that sharpened the angle of his jawline. His cheeks were tinged with a light flush, probably from the wine he'd been drinking. But when he gazed down at Zhen, his eyes were clear as pools reflecting moonlight.

"I wasn't lying about my name," the prince said. "I'm called Xu Xian, but I prefer to go by Xian."

Zhen understood enough about human honorifics to know it was highly unusual for a prince to reveal his given name to a commoner, much less his short name, which was reserved for his family and closest friends—certainly not for a stable hand he had just met.

Xian. Zhen liked the sound and shape of the name. Not that he imagined the prince was giving him permission to use it. *Xian.* He wondered what the name meant.

Xian held out a hand as if to pull Zhen to his feet. "After so many oily dishes at the banquet, I'm in the mood for a cup of pu'er tea."

Nothing in Chu's instructions had included how to respond

if the prince extended a hand while he was kneeling. It seemed rude not to take his offered hand—but as the prince's attendant, wasn't it disrespectful for the prince to be the one helping him stand up?

Zhen made a quick decision—his hand closed around Xian's and he was firmly tugged upward, but he let go as soon as he was on his feet.

He ducked his head and hurried to the stove to make tea. He was careful not to touch the yellow tips of the sulfur sticks as he rubbed them together, kindling fire to light the coal. A large jug of water stood nearby, and he filled the kettle. Chu had said something about bringing the water to a boil for at least a minute. Which teapot was for the pu'er tea? Which leaves were pu'er?

He surreptitiously peered into each of the four tea canisters. None were labeled; they didn't need to be, since all the courtesans could probably prepare a perfect cup of tea with their eyes closed. Three canisters contained dark-colored leaves, and the fourth had leaves that were more shriveled, herby-looking. Pu'er sounded herby, so it had to be that one.

As he scooped up the leaves with a wooden spoon curved on both sides like a canal, he felt Xian's eyes on him, which made him fumble and spill some leaves onto the tray. Chu had mentioned that the teapot with the smaller opening would keep the fragrance longer, so he put the leaves into that one and added boiling water. He let it stand before pouring the pale yellow tea into a porcelain cup.

He offered the cup to Xian with a nervous smile. "Your Highness."

Xian's expression betrayed nothing as he took the tea and sipped. Zhen held his breath. If he accomplished this task, there might be hope for him yet.

Xian lowered the cup and looked him in the eye. "You've never brewed tea in your life, have you?"

Zhen turned red. Steward Chu had predicted that he'd be dismissed by the prince in the morning, but he might fail to meet even the lowest of expectations by getting kicked out that night. He would probably lose his job in the stable too. If he had to leave the palace, what about Qing? Madam Hua treated her well, and she was safer living in the palace than outside its walls.

Zhen fell to his knees and bowed so low that his forehead touched the floor.

"Please forgive me." His dignity was worth less than being able to watch over Qing. "I beg for another chance to do better."

To his surprise, Xian chuckled. "I knew what I was getting into when I asked for a stable hand as my attendant. Get up, and I'll show you."

Zhen couldn't hide his astonishment as he climbed to his feet. "You know how to make tea?"

Xian grinned. "You forgot to add *Your Highness* at the end of that question. Keep it up." He walked to the table and picked up the teapot with the larger opening. "This teapot is for brewing pu'er." He took another canister of dark-colored tea. "And these are pu'er leaves. The ones you used were oolong."

Zhen covered his face, mortified. "I'm sorry."

"Here's how to tell them apart." Xian pointed at the leaves Zhen had used. "Oolong is somewhere between black and green tea. The leaves are wilted and bruised, while nearly all other tea leaves are needle-like and flat. Oolong is cooling, perfect for a hot summer afternoon."

He opened another canister and beckoned Zhen closer.

"Pu'er, on the other hand, is a fermented tea," he continued. "The leaves are blackish brown with a reddish tint. Unlike other types of tea, pu'er tastes better as it ages, and it's mild enough to be drunk at night."

Zhen tried to memorize everything, but standing close to Xian turned his brain into a sieve.

"First, we need to 'awaken' the leaves by blanching them." Xian scooped some pu'er leaves into the teapot, added boiling water, and drained the leaves almost immediately. "Now the tea is ready to be steeped. Pour the kettle just above the teapot to reduce exposure to air, which helps preserve the tea's flavor. And don't throw away the leaves after. They can be steeped up to ten times, and the taste evolves with every brew."

Xian tipped the teapot and filled two porcelain cups. The tea was clear but had the rich color of red wine, bright and dark at the same time.

"You're a prince," Zhen said, still amazed. "How do you know all this?"

"My mother comes from a family of tea farmers in the eastern province of Guangwu." Xian held out a cup, and Zhen automatically took it from him. "I wouldn't be a good descendant if I hadn't picked up a few tricks of the trade."

Zhen froze as it hit him: The prince of Wuyue had *just offered him tea*. And he'd *accepted it*.

Steward Chu was going to kill him.

Xian seemed oblivious to Zhen's consternation as he brought his own cup to his lips and inhaled deeply. "Spend a moment savoring the aroma before taking the first sip."

Zhen raised his cup and sniffed, but his mind was racing too much to register the scent. Did Xian realize he had just served him tea? Surely he must have. Was it a trick? A test? Should Zhen apologize? But the other boy didn't seem to mind one bit. It was almost as if he were Xu again and they were back in the stable sharing an apricot. Was the prince of Wuyue treating him less like a servant and more like . . . a friend?

Zhen sipped too quickly, scalding his tongue.

Xian noticed. "Drink slowly. Let the flavor of the tea unravel. Linger over the aftertaste."

The tea was as much a contradiction as the person who had steeped it: strong and earthy with an intriguing lightness, bitter with a returning hint of sweet.

"So, tell me." Xian lowered his cup and popped a dried plum into his mouth. Zhen had completely forgotten to offer the snacks. "The rumors you heard about the prince of Wuyue . . . do you think they're true?"

Zhen's cheeks burned. Earlier, in the stable, he'd told the prince that he was rumored to be handsome. Right to his face.

And it was certainly true. People also said that the prince was unconventional, contrary, willful. But no one had mentioned that his mother was from a humble family of tea farmers or that the prince's laugh was such a pleasing sound. Zhen would do anything just to hear it again.

Zhen met his gaze. "The rumors didn't tell the half of it."

Xian drained his cup of tea and set it down.

"I wasn't exactly truthful with you about my identity," he said. "I can see why you might be uncomfortable calling me Xian. I don't want to make things difficult, so when others are around, you can address me as Your Highness. But when we're by ourselves, I want you to call me Xu. At least something about the first time we met was real."

"I understand the reason you did it—" The words spilled out before Zhen could think them through. He broke off, afraid he had spoken out of turn.

"What reason is that?" Xian's expression was not reproving but questioning, encouraging him to continue.

Zhen bit his lip. "I imagine it's not easy to know if people are responding to you or to your position. If you hadn't pretended to be someone you weren't, I would never have dared to speak to you. And we might not be standing here right now."

A languid smile curled on the edges of Xian's mouth. "Perhaps we were meant to meet the way we did."

Zhen was acutely aware of his pulse jumping in his wrist, in a vessel in his neck. "Is there . . . anything else I can do for you?"

"Actually, there is." Xian unbuckled the pendant belt around his waist and raised his arms by his sides. "I'd like you to help me out of my lóng páo."

A warm shiver prickled over Zhen's skin, sending a fluttery feeling through his stomach. *Whatever else the prince asks you for, do the best you can—*

Zhen swallowed hard as he moved forward. His fingers were clumsier than they should have been as he removed the heavy ceremonial robe from the prince's shoulders. He brought the robe to a horizontal wooden rack nearby and carefully draped the fabric so it wouldn't be creased.

When he turned around, Xian had removed his inner shirt and was wearing only linen pants.

Zhen's breath caught in his throat. Xian's body was on the lighter side of tanned; the muscles in his shoulders and arms were lean but wiry, like taut cords beneath his skin. A jade amulet on a silver chain rested against his bare chest.

Something stirred in Zhen's lower abdomen. Did Xian disrobing mean he was supposed to as well?

Xian walked forward, still shirtless, and halted in front of Zhen. They hadn't even been this close in the stable earlier—they were as near each other as two people could be without touching.

Xian spoke. "There's one more thing I want you to do for me."

He was a couple of inches taller than Zhen, and when Zhen raised his gaze, Xian's eyes were like the tea he had steeped—bright and dark at the same time, their color clear yet heady and intoxicating. The air was alive with an inexorable connection that seemed to draw them together. Zhen was sure the prince would reach for the front of his robe, and when he pulled it open, Zhen would not stop him—

"Do you remember what you offered to do if I had a day off?" Xian asked.

Zhen blinked. "I said . . . I would bring you riding in the forests outside Changle."

"I intend to take that trip, and I chose you as my attendant because I want you to be my guide." Xian stepped back, breaking the magnetic pull. "We will set out once my bodyguard arrives with the rest of my contingent."

Zhen's heart sank. He had a feeling the prince wasn't talking about a scenic tour, which meant it would be a hunting trip. Obviously, as a snake, Zhen had hunted, but that was out of nature and necessity. He hated the thought of killing animals for sport.

Xian walked across the room and took a sleeping robe hanging on a rack. He shrugged the robe onto his shoulders, and the jade amulet around his neck disappeared behind the front folds when he fastened the robe with a sash.

He looked at Zhen. "It's windy tonight, and your cot is facing the window. Make sure you use a blanket when you sleep."

Zhen couldn't hide his surprise. Was that all Xian planned to do—sleep? Alone in his huge bed? Didn't Qing say that was the last thing he would be doing tonight?

Xian climbed onto the platform bed and rested his head on the silk pillow. He didn't remove his hairpin or release the bun.

"You can dim the lights now."

"Oh. Yes, of course." Zhen went around the chamber, snuffing out the candles and extinguishing the braziers. The embers glowed, suffusing the shadows with faint illumination.

Zhen had balked at the idea of sleeping with someone he'd just met, but now he wasn't sure if he was relieved or disappointed. Xian obviously knew that asking for pleasure was within his rights. So did his lack of overture mean Xian wasn't attracted to boys—or was he just not interested in *him?* Is that why the prince made it clear he had chosen Zhen only to be a guide on his hunting expedition?

Zhen unfolded the blanket at the foot of Xian's bed and draped it over the prince, pulling it up to chest level. Xian's eyes followed him, his expression unreadable. Zhen untied the curtains, letting the gauze canopy fall around the four-poster bed.

He hesitated before he spoke. "Good night . . . Xu."

Through the gossamer layer, he caught the prince's smile. "Good night, Zhen."

Chapter 11

XIAN

Feng and the rest of the delegation arrived the next day with all the gifts and valuables accounted for. Governor Gao had sent soldiers from Changle to help clear the debris and escort the Wuyue contingent to the capital; with the added security, they had ridden through the night and made up for the delay, arriving as originally scheduled.

Feng wiped a hand over his sweaty brow as Xian embraced him. "Careful. Don't let my grime stain your robe."

"It's true, you do stink. I have a bathtub in my chamber that will fix that."

"Your very own bathtub? They really went all out to impress you."

"That wasn't the only extravagance they offered to our prince," Fahai remarked obliquely. He gave Feng a welcoming nod. "You handled the unexpected task admirably well. General Jian will be pleased. Wash up, have something to eat after your journey. I'll take over from here."

Feng bowed. "Thank you, Counselor Fahai. I'll leave the rest to you."

"Sorry to inform you that you missed the feast," Xian told Feng as they headed to the royal manor. "But I've already told the kitchen to whip up your favorite dinner, braised pork belly with steamed buns. With a side of smoked duck and mushrooms as well as radish with osmanthus."

Feng slowed his pace and arched an eyebrow. "What did you do?"

Xian gave him an innocent look. "I can't order my best friend his favorite dishes?"

When they entered the walled compound, instead of appreciating the architecture or the landscaped gardens in the courtyard, Feng eyed their surroundings critically.

"We'll station two of our own guards outside your chamber," Feng said. "Another two will patrol the walls. I'll take the first watch tonight to observe Changle's security and their shift changes."

When they stepped into Xian's bedchamber, Zhen was smoothing out the creases of Xian's lóng páo on the wooden rack. He turned with a tentative smile, which vanished when he saw Xian wasn't alone.

Zhen swiftly knelt. "Good morning, Your Highness."

Feng frowned. "Who's this?"

"Feng, this is my new attendant, Zhen." Xian gestured for Zhen to stand. "Zhen, meet my bodyguard, Feng."

Feng narrowed his eyes at Xian, who offered a blithe smile before turning to Zhen.

"Please bring some steamed buns for my bodyguard," Xian said. "Hunger always makes him bad-tempered. Oh, and a pot of oolong tea to lower his temperature."

"Yes, Your Highness." Zhen bowed and left the chamber.

Xian gazed after him approvingly. "I must say, white really is his color."

Feng glowered at Xian. "I let you out of my sight for one day, and the first thing you do is jump into bed with a pretty boy who looks good in white?"

"I couldn't possibly reject the Min court's hospitality. I kept them on their toes, though—they offered their best courtesans, but I chose Zhen. We met in the stable when he was grooming Zhaoye. I was dressed in an ordinary robe, and he mistook me for a horse keeper—"

"If you could be a prince masquerading as a horse keeper, he could be an assassin pretending to be a stable hand." Feng's gaze swept across the chamber and fixed on the cot. "Am I supposed to sleep there?"

"No, that's Zhen's bed. Your room is through those doors." Xian pointed to the adjoining room. Feng looked incredulous. "I know, it doesn't have its own bathtub. Feel free to come over and use mine."

"That's not what I meant." Feng stared daggers at him. "For

obvious reasons, this attendant should *not* be allowed to sleep in your chamber. I can't believe Fahai didn't object. This is exactly why I—"

"He slept here last night without incident."

Feng made an exasperated sound. "If you insist on allowing him to sleep in your chamber, then I'll have to as well."

"If that's how it's going to be, you can take the cot and he'll share the bed with me." Xian waggled his brows at his best friend. "Unless you insist on joining us, in which case, things could get interesting."

Feng raised his eyes to the ceiling. "I can't believe I rode five hundred miles to continue facilitating your trysts."

"Just hear me out." Xian reached into his sleeve and took out the rolled-up parchment. "I went to the temple yesterday to inquire of the gods what I should do next. I shook the bamboo sticks and got this."

Feng read the phrase out loud. "'Even a powerful dragon struggles to overcome a snake in its native haunt.' What do you think it's supposed to mean?"

"Despite having my father's backing, we still need the help of someone local to find the snake," Xian replied. "That's the reason I chose Zhen as my attendant. He's familiar with the forests around Changle. When we go snake hunting outside the palace, he can be our guide. Not to mention he's also the only stranger I've seen come close to Zhaoye without getting kicked in the face."

"Excuse me if I don't count Zhaoye as a credible character

witness." Feng sighed. "I still don't think this is a good idea. You don't know who he is, and he's going to be sharing your bed for the rest of our time here? Or at least until you get tired of him?"

"If you really must know, I didn't sleep with him last night."

Feng scoffed. "What happened, you were too drunk?"

"Unfortunately not. Trying to go to sleep was hard in ways I didn't expect."

"I can teach you a few Shaolin meditation methods to help with that." Feng paused. "Did the priest say anything else? Did he warn that we should be on the lookout for any threats?"

Xian didn't like keeping secrets from his best friend, but Feng was already suspicious of Zhen. If Xian mentioned that the priest had said his mother's amulet would protect him from a hidden danger lurking close by, Feng would overreact and refuse to let Zhen stay in Xian's chamber.

"The answer will reveal itself at the right time," Xian replied. "That's all he said."

Feng's expression turned serious. "Listen, we aren't children anymore. I'm here as your bodyguard now. It's my sworn duty to protect you with my life."

Xian put a hand on Feng's shoulder. "There's no one I trust more to have my back. Not just as my bodyguard but as my best friend." He smirked. "Does this mean we can't go searching for secret escape tunnels in the Changle palace?"

Feng let out a half groan, half chuckle. "If your father doesn't have my head for that, mine certainly will."

Chapter 12

ZHEN

Zhen sat cross-legged on the floor. Xian sat on a straw mat on the other side of the low table between them, which held a square wooden board with grid lines that ran vertically and horizontally. Next to the board were two bowls of stones—one bowl was all black, the other all white.

Feng had left a guard in his stead before he exited the chamber to roster the other guards and show them their posts. The prince's bodyguard had been cold and curt toward Zhen since he'd arrived earlier in the day. Then again, if he wasn't distrustful, he wouldn't be very good at his job. Zhen figured the more he tried to gain Feng's approval, the more suspicious Feng would be.

Xian himself was another enigma. At the break of dawn, Zhen had lain awake in his cot, wondering if the prince would ask for . . . something to start the morning, but he did not. Zhen had spent the rest of the day learning more about his duties from Steward Chu, which included a tour of the various palace buildings—the kitchen, the scullery, the workshops, the library—so he would know where to get what the prince needed.

"Have you played wéi qí before?" Xian asked.

Zhen shook his head. "I've seen people playing this game in the marketplace. Can you teach me?"

"Wéi qí is a game of encirclement," Xian replied. "The rules are simple: Each player takes turns putting black or white stones on the intersections between the grid lines. You gain points by capturing opponent stones or expanding your territory into empty spaces on the board."

"Are there rules about where we have to put the stones?" Zhen asked. "Or can we put them anywhere we like?"

"A stone can be placed on any unoccupied point, but after that, it can't be moved unless it has been taken prisoner—that is, surrounded on four sides by the opponent."

"And the one who captures the most stones wins?"

Xian nodded. "But don't worry about winning or losing for now. Just learn how to work your way around the board. You take white and I'll take black, which starts first."

He put a black stone on one of the points in the upper right corner.

Zhen mirrored his first move, putting a white stone in the lower left corner. "You must have started playing when you were very young."

"My father used to make me play against my oldest half brother, Wang, in some kind of misguided hope that we would bond over the game," Xian replied. "We were well matched, but because I was three years younger, he was embarrassed and enraged whenever I beat him. I guess he thinks he's invincible because his name means 'king.'"

"What does your name mean?" Zhen asked.

"Well, *Xu* is the generation name shared by all my half brothers. *Xian* is the name my mother chose for me, with my father's blessing. It means 'immortal.'" Xian looked wry. "Mothers are always so optimistic."

He put another black stone on an intersection, capturing one of Zhen's white ones.

Zhen leaned forward, studying the pattern of black and white stones forming on the board with keen interest. "This game seems simple, but each move leads to countless possibilities."

"No two boards are the same at the end," Xian said. "Games played between grand masters can last so long, they have to be split across two days. Since Fahai became my father's court adviser a few years ago, he and I play a game every week. He's even better than the palace teachers."

When the game ended, the heap of white stones in Xian's prisoner pile stood in sharp contrast to the lone black stone in Zhen's. He wondered if Xian had ceded that one on purpose to give him some encouragement.

"Do you mind if I leave the board this way?" Zhen asked. "I'd like to study it more carefully."

"Of course. You did very well for a first game." Xian sat forward. "I want you to bring your sister here tomorrow."

Zhen tensed. What trouble had Qing gotten herself into now?

"Did she do something wrong?" He couldn't conceal the trepidation in his voice. "If Qing has offended you or the Changle court in any way, please don't hold it against her. I am willing to bear the punishment in her place."

"Don't look so worried." Xian reached across the table and put a hand on Zhen's wrist. "Your sister isn't in trouble. She's the only family you've mentioned, and I would like to meet her. Where are both of you from? It's hard to tell from your accent."

"Actually, I was born in Wuyue," Zhen replied. Xian looked surprised, and Zhen continued, "We moved away when I was young. My family . . . isn't used to living among people. It's just me and my sister now."

"What's her name?"

"Qing," Zhen said. "I'm certain she'll be excited to meet you."

Xian got to his feet. A tingle of anticipation went through Zhen. The prince hadn't made any advances toward him so far, but would the second night be different?

Zhen's gaze followed Xian as he walked to the clothes rack where his sleeping robe hung. He took off his shirt and then turned to Zhen. Zhen blinked, trying not to stare at Xian's bare chest, his lean torso . . .

"Get a good night's rest," Xian said, putting on his sleeping robe. "Tomorrow afternoon, if the weather is fine, we'll go riding in the countryside. Feng and Fahai will come with us, and you will be our guide. We shall head west, which will give us the longest stretch of daylight before the sun goes down—that's the time snakes come out to search for food."

An invisible noose closed around Zhen's neck. "Snakes?"

"Yes." Xian had a glint in his eye. "That's the only creature I'm interested in hunting. I'll show you."

Xian beckoned him over to a rectangular rattan case in the corner. When he unsnapped the latches and opened the cover, Zhen's blood ran colder than it ever had.

Inside was a collection of hooks, tongs, poles, nets . . . They had been cleaned, but Zhen could detect the residue of dried snake blood on them. There was a cruel metal trap identical to the one he'd been snared in when he was a young snake. His hand instinctively went to the scar on the left side of his torso.

"Why—why do you have so many tools for killing snakes?" he breathed.

"I don't kill them. I want them alive." Xian let out a mirthless sound. "Although I'd slice every one of them wide open if that would make my mother feel better for just five minutes."

It was like watching an ugly transformation, an outer skin splitting down the middle and peeling back. Xu had never existed, and from beneath his visage, the prince's true form emerged.

Zhen fought the nausea that rose in his throat. "What happened to your mother?"

"She was bitten by a white snake." Xian's voice was a blade. "For almost ten years, she has been confined to her bed, and at times the pain is so agonizing that she's paralyzed for days.

And when my father brought back a spirit pearl from the Kunlun Mountains to cure her—the white snake resurfaced."

Zhen felt as if icicles had sprung up inside his lungs.

When he'd first seen Xian in the stable, there had been something strikingly familiar about him, like a face he had seen in a dream—

"I've been hunting snakes of every breed for Fahai, my father's adviser, and he's been working on an antidote," Xian continued. "All we're missing for the cure is the white snake. An oracle predicted we would find it in Changle, and I intend to capture it and bring it back alive. We're closer than ever. I can feel it."

A metallic scent filled Zhen's nostrils. Blood gushed from his nose, spilling onto the floor and the front of his robe. Startled, he took a step back, but his knees couldn't hold his weight—

"Zhen!" Xian was at his side in an instant, steadying him. "Are you all right?"

Zhen was so lightheaded that he couldn't help leaning into Xian's arms. He opened his mouth but couldn't form any words.

"What's wrong?" Xian led him to a chair. "Are you ill? I'll take you to the infirmary."

"No," Zhen managed hoarsely. His fingers reflexively closed around Xian's wrist. "I . . . I'll be fine."

The boy who fell from the Broken Bridge. The one Zhen dragged onto the shore of the tiny islet in the middle of the lake. The last time Zhen had seen him, he was a terrified, bedraggled boy gripping a pearl. In the past seven years, Xian had matured so much that he was completely unrecognizable.

Zhen tried to tilt his head back to prevent the blood from trickling out of his nose, but Xian stopped him.

"Don't. The blood will flow into your stomach and make you sicker. Lean forward and breathe slowly through your mouth." Xian cradled Zhen's head against his chest and pushed a stray strand of hair away from his face. "Does it hurt anywhere? Tell me."

More than anything, Zhen wished he could tell him. Tell him the truth. But Xian would stare at him like he was a monster. Maybe even kill him on the spot.

"I'm sorry," he whispered. "I've made such a mess."

"Shhh." Xian lifted the cuff of his sleeve to Zhen's nose and gently dabbed the blood from his upper lip. "Try not to talk."

Zhen relented, closing his eyes. He could only hope that the other boy would never find out what he was truly apologizing for.

Chapter 13
ZHEN

When Zhen was an ordinary snake, he loved to swim along rivers and canals that meandered through towns. He would poke his head above the surface, avoiding the docked merchant boats and crab traps that fishermen hung along the waterways, and curiously watch humans hurrying across bridges, always needing to be somewhere else. They seemed oblivious to their surroundings, a luxury most creatures didn't have.

He wanted a chance to live like them. To leave his own footprints on the paths of the world. And when he saw the gleaming orb in that little boy's hand . . . he knew at once that it was a mythical spirit pearl, the kind the old tortoise had told him about. A pearl that would change everything.

Zhen had told no one how he became a snake spirit. Not even Qing. Maybe that was another reason he had been compelled to rescue her—as a way to atone for taking the pearl. If he used its stolen power to save another life, perhaps what he had done would be a little less wrong.

He left the West Lake and traveled far and wide—north beyond the Huang He, south to the Pearl River, and east to the Tibetan Plateau, which people called the "roof of the world." Still, he thought often about the little boy he'd abandoned on that islet—his scared, ruddy face, his long, dark hair plastered to the sides of his head. He'd wondered what had become of him.

Now he had the answer.

Zhen stood alone in the middle of the prince's bedchamber. Cold morning light streamed through the open window. Xian had left half an hour ago for a meeting with Governor Gao and his court officials. Zhen had scrubbed the stains on the floor from his nosebleed, but the sleeve of Xian's sleeping robe, hanging on the rack, still had traces of his blood.

Last night, the memory, the shock, the realization—it was just too overwhelming, like a monstrous wave that had sucked him out to sea. Even now, his eyes strayed to the latched rattan case in the corner of the room, and he imagined his fellow snakes captured alive, tortured, maybe even used for experiments . . . his stomach curdled, and he had to force down the urge to be sick again.

All these years, Xian had been hunting snakes, hurting them—all because of him. Zhen hadn't bitten Xian's mother, but he had taken the pearl meant to cure her. If only he had known how much suffering he would cause by taking that shiny little orb—

He had to leave. Get out of Changle. Put as much distance between himself and Xian as possible. Xian could never find out that the stable wasn't the first place they had met.

Zhen started toward the door but halted as he passed the wéi qí board. The pieces were just as he and Xian had left them the night before. He leaned down, picked up a white stone from the bowl, and turned it over in his fingers.

Some people believed cold-blooded creatures couldn't feel emotions. That wasn't true. The feelings that Xian stirred in him were painfully real. When Xian had used his own sleeve to wipe the blood from Zhen's nose, the tenderness had been almost more than he could bear.

"Goodbye, Xian," he whispered.

He dropped the single white stone into the bowl of black stones. Then he turned away and walked out of the prince's chamber for the last time.

The palace kitchen was on the eastern side of the inner court, close to the storehouses. It was divided into a main kitchen, a tea kitchen, and a bakery. Qing had told him that meticulous records were kept of which cook prepared each dish. If the food was good, the dishes could be easily reordered; if something bad happened, the culprits could be identified just as swiftly.

"Zhen!"

He looked up as a motherly woman in her forties hurried toward him. She wore a waistcoat with half-length sleeves and a button in front, indicating her position as a senior kitchen staff member.

"Hello, Madam Hua." Zhen glanced around. "Is Qing here? I need to talk to her."

Madam Hua chuckled. "Oh, your sister was fretting about you all of yesterday. I told her now that you're the prince of Wuyue's attendant, you'll have all kinds of duties to take care of, and you'll come and see her as soon as you can. But she was still so distracted, she ruined an entire batch of fried sesame balls—"

"Zhen!" Qing burst out of the kitchen and hurtled toward him as if they hadn't seen each other in years. She threw her arms around his neck and squeezed so tightly that he gasped. "I've been so worried about you!"

"Qing, go on and take a fifteen-minute break with your brother." Madam Hua gave Zhen a wink. "I'm sure you'll have some juicy gossip to share. I'll let you two catch up . . ."

Zhen forced a smile and waited until Madam Hua went back into the kitchen before he turned to Qing. "We need to get out of here. Right now."

Qing frowned. "Wait, what? Why?"

"It's not safe here any longer," Zhen replied urgently. "Please, Qing, I need you to trust me on this. Go back inside, don't appear suspicious, and pack your stuff—"

"But we don't get paid until next week! Isn't that the whole point of stopping in Changle? To earn money for the rest of our journey to Mount Emei?" Qing's eyes narrowed. "It's the prince, isn't it? What did he do?" She took Zhen's face between her palms. "Did he hurt you? Is that why you're so pale? Did he have you chained to his bed all this time?"

"No." Zhen swatted her hands away. "He did nothing of the sort. In fact, he treated me very well. I'll explain everything later, but for now, we have to—"

"Are you Zhen, the prince's attendant?" came a male voice behind them.

Zhen spun around. A teenage boy dressed in a blue robe with wide sleeves and a matching sash stood there. He was the courtesan who had been in the teal costume at the welcome banquet.

"I am." Zhen bowed. He hoped the boy hadn't overheard their conversation. "Is there something I can help you with?"

"My name is Deng." The boy returned the bow. "Steward Chu has asked me to take over your training today."

Zhen groaned inwardly. He tried to stall. "I'm actually . . . feeling unwell."

"Ah, yes." Deng gave a knowing nod. "I imagine the prince didn't let you get much sleep for the last two nights. We have the perfect remedy for that. Come with me to the Hall of Training Courtesans, and I'll get you a bottle of pills."

The timing couldn't have been any worse. Zhen exchanged a dismayed glance with Qing, but he had no other choice. "Of course. Please lead the way."

Qing went back into the kitchen as Zhen set off with Deng. As they walked across the wide marble terrace, heads swiveled and people nudged one another and pointed at Zhen. The embroidered white robe that designated him as the prince's attendant fitted him like a silk glove, but the attention it drew chafed like rough hemp. Another bitter reminder that whatever Xian saw in him was nothing more than an illusion.

He wasn't who Xian thought he was—and he could never be.

"No wonder everyone is so fascinated with you," Deng remarked. "I've never seen anyone go from mucking horse stalls to serving a royal within a day."

His tone was as pleasant as a calm lake, but his words felt like rocks beneath water. Zhen pressed his lips into a thin line and said nothing. The sooner he could get away, the better.

They reached the Hall of Training Courtesans, and Deng led him to a storeroom at the back of the building. The shelves were stacked with all kinds of items: porcelain lamps, lanterns, candles, bundles of incense sticks, even umbrellas.

"You can collect more candles, incense sticks, and tea leaves for the prince's chamber," Deng said. "You should also refill the bottle by the bed. You wouldn't want to run out of that in the middle of the night."

Zhen's face flushed. Deng had assumed the same thing everyone else had, even Qing.

He turned to Deng. "What type of incense should I bring for—"

An open palm slammed into the side of Zhen's head. Starbursts of red exploded in his eyes—then another strike connected with the front of his neck, knocking all the air out of his throat and sending him sprawling onto the floor.

"My father was good at martial arts when he wasn't a mean drunk." Deng's boot shot out and kicked Zhen in the stomach.

"He taught me one thing: how to hit where it hurts most without leaving any trace."

At any other time, Zhen would have been able to fight back like he did in the tavern, but the nosebleed last night had badly drained his qi. He hadn't felt this weak since he'd saved Qing's life.

Zhen grunted and curled in on himself, his ribs rising and falling as Deng loomed over him. Deng grabbed the front of his robe with one hand and dragged him to his feet with surprising strength, given the other boy's lithe build.

"I didn't run away from home and sleep my way to where I am just to lose my place in the prince's bed to some lowly stable hand," he hissed in Zhen's face.

Deng drew back his fist and swung, sending a stab of excruciating pain through Zhen's abdomen. Bitter copper bubbled up his throat, filling his mouth before his world went dark.

Chapter 14
ZHEN

The first time Zhen saw a dead snake was on a small islet on the West Lake. The snake had bitten a fishhook and torn his jaw trying to get free. The fisherman had taken the rest of his catch and left him behind. A blue heron descended and stabbed the mangled carcass. But it didn't eat the snake, just flew off with a blood-smeared beak.

Outrage washed over Zhen. He had been snared in a trap before—he knew the terror and desperation that the poor snake must have suffered before succumbing to a slow, painful death. He had to do something, even though the snake was already dead. Maybe he could bury him. He'd seen a girl putting a squirrel's body into a hole in the sand. He could use his tail to dig.

As Zhen slithered toward the carcass, a raspy voice spoke. "Don't."

Zhen stopped. A large tortoise, craggy and wizened, lumbered forward.

"Why not?" Zhen replied. "You rescued me when I was caught in that trap."

"You were lucky. He was not. There's nothing more you can do for him."

Zhen's tongue flicked out. "All creatures have to die, but he didn't deserve such a terrible end."

The tortoise picked up a stick in his mouth. He drew a circle on the sand, added a wavy line down the middle, and put in two dots, one in each half.

"What does this mean?" Zhen asked.

"Yin and yang—opposites in balance, connected and flowing into each other," the tortoise replied. "I've lived for hundreds of years, but you are young and mortal, Little White One. Maybe one day you will understand the unchangeable law of the universe—the equilibrium always finds itself."

Zhen opened his eyes.

His surroundings were airy and spacious, filled with a clean, medicinal scent. He raised his head. He was in the infirmary, lying in a corner bed of an empty row. Deng was nowhere to be seen. A metallic tang of blood lingered in Zhen's throat, a reminder of the blistering moments before he blacked out.

He tried to move and winced. He wasn't used to having so many body parts that hurt.

A distance away, a physician was talking to a familiar figure: the prince, accompanied by his bodyguard.

A jolt of panic went through Zhen. He didn't want Xian seeing him like this. He wasn't supposed to meet Xian again. He and Qing should've been miles from the palace by now.

Before Zhen could shut his eyes and pretend to be asleep, Feng looked in his direction and nudged Xian.

Too late.

Xian sidestepped the physician and walked swiftly to Zhen's bed.

Zhen put on a brave face and struggled to sit up. "Your Highness—"

"Don't move." Xian stopped him with a hand on his shoulder. He touched Zhen's forehead. "What happened? Does it have anything to do with your nosebleed last night?"

If Zhen breathed as shallowly as he could, the pain on his left side wasn't so bad. He could get through this. "Your Highness, I—"

Xian put a finger to Zhen's lips.

"Remember what I said? Don't call me that when we're by ourselves. Or with Feng. You can speak freely in front of him." He leaned forward, his eyes dark and intense. "I want you to tell me who did this to you."

Before Zhen could respond, Qing burst into the infirmary. She caught sight of Zhen lying in bed and rushed over to his side.

"Zhen, are you all right?" she exclaimed, her face flushed, breathless from running. "They said you were ill and that I should come immediately—"

She broke off, suddenly noticing the two people on the other side of the bed.

Xian spoke. "You're his sister?"

She blinked, as if surprised that he knew, and bowed. "Yes, Your Highness. My name is Qing."

Xian turned back to Zhen. "Tell me the truth. Are you ill or did someone hurt you?"

Zhen dropped his gaze to his hands. They were unmarked. No defensive injuries. Deng hadn't given him a chance to fight back. The other boy might not have caught him off guard if he hadn't been so distracted figuring out how to get away from the palace as quickly as possible.

"I've had this blood condition since childhood," Zhen lied. Fortunately he had learned a little bit about traditional medicine over the past seven years. "The summer heat disrupts my qi and makes my blood flow backward. I must have fainted and hit my head."

The equilibrium always finds itself.

The old tortoise was right. Deng had trained long and hard to be the perfect courtesan. Zhen had appeared out of nowhere and won a place that wasn't meant to be his—and Deng would do anything to take it back.

Xian spoke. "The physician has prescribed dāng guī bǔ xuè tāng, which will nourish your qi and help with any internal pain. I've taken the concoction on a couple of occasions when my sparring partner here"—he nodded at Feng—"decided to show me that his skills are far superior to mine."

Feng's cheeks colored as he looked at Qing—the first time Zhen had seen him blush.

"You will rest here until the physician is satisfied that your condition has improved," Xian continued. "Your sister can stay and keep you company."

He walked to the door without a backward glance. Feng gave Zhen a pointed stare before he followed. As soon as they disappeared from the infirmary, Qing leaned forward.

"Who hurt you?" she whispered, wrapping both hands around Zhen's. "No one can hear us. Was it the prince's bodyguard? Is that why you were afraid to say anything just now?"

Zhen shook his head, thoroughly miserable. "It was Deng."

"The courtesan who came looking for you when we were talking? He hurt you because he was jealous the prince chose you instead of him?"

"He wasn't just jealous. He wanted my place." Zhen's chest felt like lead. "Steward Chu said he was the obvious choice from the start. Now that I'm in the infirmary, guess who will be my replacement?"

"Why didn't you tell the prince all of this when he asked you earlier instead of saying you have a blood condition?" Qing demanded.

"And end up looking like the liar?" Zhen let out a humorless sound. "If I accuse Deng, the other courtesans will surely take his side. We're outsiders here, Qing. We don't belong. We never will."

Qing's brow creased. "Is that why you wanted to leave all of a sudden?"

"We came here to blend in but ended up drawing more attention. It's too dangerous." That wasn't the most important reason, but it would have to do for now. "I'm sorry. I know you like working in the palace kitchen, and Madam Hua treats you well—"

Qing cut him off. "When you saved my life, I swore I would always stay by your side. You may have forgotten, but I haven't."

Zhen smiled in spite of himself. "Don't be silly. I won't hold you to that promise."

"I'm not going—or staying—anywhere without you." Qing's tone was resolute. "But you need to rest and recover before we leave. Hopefully we'll have gotten our wages by then." She pursed her lips. "Hate to break it to you, but you're the worst liar I've ever met. I don't think the prince believed you for a second."

Zhen's heart sagged. Last night, the way Xian had carefully wiped the blood from his nose and comforted him . . . he wanted more than anything to feel that tenderness again. To touch Xian back, to pull him close until their lips met . . .

But he wouldn't be returning to serve the prince. Tonight, Deng would be in the cot where Zhen had slept. Or maybe the cot would be empty, and Deng would spend the night in Xian's bed.

Jealousy lanced through Zhen—startling, thorny, a barbed wire that coiled and twisted around his insides. Maybe this was how it felt to be slowly crushed. What an irony, considering he was a python.

Deng had made it clear the prince was to be his conquest. And the only thing worse than thinking about Deng's satisfaction as he enjoyed his prize was imagining Xian's pleasure as he did the same.

Chapter 15
XIAN

"Zuǒ xū bù liāo," Feng said. "Swinging up the sword in the left empty stance."

Xian stood across from Feng in the Hall of Concentration, the martial arts training gallery. He wore a black sparring robe, while Feng was dressed in his brown Shaolin robe cinched by a black belt. They both had black wraps around their bare feet and their shins to prevent splints from long hours training on hard floors. They hadn't sparred in over a week, and jiàn shù—the skill of swordsmanship—had to be kept honed.

Xian raised his training sword, which, unlike a real one, had rounded edges and blunt steel. "Haven't we practiced this move about a hundred and twenty-nine times already?"

"Hopefully you'll execute it flawlessly on the hundred and thirtieth," Feng replied. "Remember why it's called the empty stance. Your front leg must be empty of any pressure. Your body weight should be fully on the back leg to free up your front leg to kick your opponent."

Xian kept a steady grip on his sword hilt, not so loose that the weapon could be knocked out of his hand, but not so tight that he wouldn't be able to quickly rotate the handle to parry an attack from an unexpected angle. The swordless hand was a counterbalance, as important as the one that grasped the sword.

Xian attacked first, wielding his blade in a circular slashing movement as he aimed for Feng's arm. The strength behind each sword stroke didn't come from the arm but the dān tián—the internal energy center inside his core, just below the navel.

Feng deflected his downward blow and demonstrated a perfect example of swinging up the sword in the left empty stance. Show-off. Xian parried before counterattacking with short, percussive stabs. As Feng thrust the tip of his sword at Xian's shoulder, Xian dodged, exposing his left side. Feng didn't miss a beat—he followed up with a powerful backhanded stroke.

Xian couldn't move away in time as Feng had expected him to. The blow caught Xian on the side of his head—he stumbled a few steps back but managed to stay on his feet.

Feng quickly lowered his sword. "Are you all right?"

"I'm fine." Xian grimaced. "Can't say the same about my pride."

Feng came forward, took Xian's chin, and tilted his head from side to side. "Any sharp pain in the temples? Blurred or double vision?"

"Your jawline is as chiseled as ever, and the bridge of your nose still looks like the gods carved it from rock."

Whenever Feng performed martial arts routines during palace festivities, maidens would giggle and jostle for a better view. Some young men would have more than admiration in their eyes as they stared at Feng's broad shoulders and toned abdomen.

But Feng was indifferent, showing no interest in boys or girls. Perhaps the monks at Shaolin had taught him to use his martial arts training to control his impulses. Feng was definitely someone Xian could be attracted to—but he was strictly off-limits. Xian cherished their friendship much more than a fleeting grope.

Feng stepped back.

"You're too distracted." He led Xian to a bench to rest and sat next to him. "I'm guessing that has something to do with your attendant flat-out lying to your face back in the infirmary."

Xian hadn't missed Zhen's pained expression before he left. The lie, it seemed, had cut into both of them. "He must have his reasons."

"You're still making excuses for him?" Feng sounded aghast. "He lied to a prince. He should be charged with irreverence—that's punishable with eighty blows of the heavy stick. I might even ask to flog him myself."

Xian's mouth quirked. "Didn't know you were into that kind of thing."

"I'm not joking. You shouldn't tolerate such insolence. The sixth of the ten abominations includes disrespecting a member of the royal family."

"Under the nine levels of kinship, his sister would have to be punished in the same way," Xian pointed out. "Sure you can bring yourself to flog her too?"

Feng looked mutinous. He pointed at Xian's sword lying by his side. "Let's try again."

Xian's brow furrowed as he got to his feet. He couldn't shake the feeling there was something Zhen wasn't telling him—exactly what, he didn't know. He didn't blame Zhen for being cautious; he and his sister had been in the palace for only a short time, and the inherent power imbalance between him and Xian made everything more complicated.

But Xian was convinced their paths had crossed for a reason—and the more Zhen seemed to want to hide the truth, the more he wasn't going to let it go.

When Xian entered his chamber later that evening, a slender figure dressed in a teal robe was waiting for him.

"Your Highness, I am your new attendant." The boy gracefully dropped to his knees. "My name is—"

"Deng." Xian closed the doors behind him. "I know who you are."

The surprise in Deng's eyes quickly gave way to a pleased expression.

"You remembered." He rose, walked to Xian, and brushed his fingers over Xian's collar. "May I help you remove your outer robe, Your Highness?"

Xian's gaze flitted down to Deng's hand. "That won't be

necessary. I'm heading out to visit Zhen in the infirmary. I understand you were one of the courtesans who found him?"

Deng stiffened almost imperceptibly. "Yes. Poor Zhen. All of us were horrified when we saw him lying in the storeroom unconscious with blood flowing from his mouth. He must have passed out and hit his head."

"That's what he said too." Xian lifted his chin. "But I believe you might have left out a few crucial details."

Deng's lips flattened, but he kept his composure. "Your Highness, the other courtesans were also there. If you ask them, they'll tell you the same—"

"I don't have to. You just told me everything I need to know." Xian caught Deng's hand and twisted it to reveal his reddened knuckles. "You know how to hit someone without leaving marks on them, but you forgot about yourself. After the other courtesans saw what you did to Zhen, do you think they would dare to contradict your story?"

Deng's expression faltered. "Please, it's not what you think—"

"Save it. I have an older half brother who despises me, so I know exactly what it's like to be the victim of someone's fists and try to hide it." Xian's tone was deadly. "If you think I can't figure out who benefits from putting Zhen in the infirmary, then you're guilty of another crime—insulting my intelligence."

Deng's face blanched. He fell at Xian's feet.

"Your Highness, forgive me!" Unlike in the throne chamber, no mud jars had been placed underneath the floorboards, so there was only a dull thud each time Deng's forehead made contact with the wood. "I have been training all my life for this, and I so badly wanted to serve you. Please don't dismiss me, or I'll lose everything—"

"Despite what you did to him, Zhen still lied to keep your secret." Xian grabbed a fistful of Deng's robe and yanked him to his feet. "My forgiveness isn't as important as his, and you'd better pray that he is in the mood for mercy, because you sure as hell don't deserve any."

When they stepped into the infirmary, Xian looked so grim and Deng so tearful that the physicians bowed and hurried away to tend to their duties.

Xian strode to Zhen's bedside, dragging Deng behind him.

Zhen pushed himself upright, eyes wide. "Your Highness?"

Xian released his grip on Deng's arm. "He has something to say to you."

Deng collapsed to his knees in front of a bewildered Zhen. "I hurt you because I was jealous. I deserve to be punished. But this life in the palace is all I have—I'm begging you, please forgive me . . ."

As Deng sobbed, Zhen's expression changed from astonishment to empathy. A kind of empathy Xian hadn't seen—or felt—in a very long time.

Zhen spoke. "I forgive him."

Xian could tell he meant it. Deng gazed at Xian beseechingly.

The infirmary doors opened and Feng entered, accompanied by Governor Gao, Steward Chu, and a pair of guards. Deng looked horrified as they came toward them and bowed to Xian, who did not acknowledge their greeting.

"This vile person has confessed to assaulting my attendant out of spite and malice." Xian's tone was terse. "Remove him from my presence and deal with him accordingly."

Zhen sounded panicked. "But I for—"

Gao spoke. "Such treacherous behavior will not be tolerated in this palace. I assure you that he will be punished to the severest degree."

Deng's face crumpled, and he began shaking and sobbing uncontrollably as the two guards hauled him to his feet. "Please, have mercy on me!"

"Your Highness." Chu stepped forward and lowered his head. "I am deeply ashamed that you had to witness such behavior from one of my courtesans. I seek your pardon."

Xian shot him a steely glance. "May this be a lesson to the rest of your courtesans: I do not want a replacement. Zhen will be my attendant or I shall have none."

Deng's wails grew more hysterical as the guards dragged him out, his cries echoing in the quiet of the night until they faded away. Zhen looked horrified.

Gao and Chu exited the infirmary, and Feng stepped away, leaving Xian alone with Zhen.

"What's going to happen to Deng?" Zhen asked.

"That's not important." Xian fixed him with a stern stare. "Why didn't you tell me he was the one who hurt you? Why did you lie to me, Zhen?"

Zhen's lashes fanned downward. "My sister and I are strangers in this palace. Deng is the most senior courtesan and Steward Chu's favorite. I didn't imagine anyone would believe me over him."

"I would have."

Zhen blinked. "I'm sorry." He pressed his lips into a thin line. "Deng was a victim himself. His father beat him, and he ran away from home. Maybe violence was the only way he knew to survive."

Xian frowned. "That's why you hid the truth?"

Zhen was quiet for a moment.

"Someone wise once told me why each half of the yin-yang circle has a small dot of the opposite color," he said. "It means that in every choice, we have to consider the good of the other person in some small way. Only then will things turn out well."

Doing a small thing for the good of one's enemy—would that be beyond Xian when he finally captured the white snake? Could he find it in himself to show mercy to the merciless, as Zhen had done?

Xian didn't know if he could. The boy who had fallen off the bridge into the West Lake wasn't the same person who had been rescued from it. He had lost more than the pearl that day. He had lost his belief in the fundamental goodness of all creatures in the world, in the existence of fairness and justice that didn't have to be taken into one's own hands.

Xian reached out and lifted Zhen's chin so the other boy had to meet his gaze.

"Promise me one thing," Xian said, looking steadily into

Zhen's eyes. "Don't lie to me again. You sleep in my room. I don't care that Feng doesn't like it, but I need to be able to trust you. And I want you to feel that you can do the same."

A glimmer of emotion passed across Zhen's face, so fleeting that Xian couldn't decipher it.

Zhen nodded and gave a tentative smile. "I promise."

Chapter 16
XIAN

Dull red glowed behind his closed lids. His fingers curled in sandy dirt. A breeze tickled his nostrils, filling them with the odor of dead fish and rotting algae.

His lids fluttered open. Sunlight hit his eyes. A bitter fountain of bile and water bubbled up his throat. He tried to roll over to throw up, but something was wrapped around his torso, restricting his movement.

A large white snake was coiled around his body in three full loops. Its pale, gleaming scales were like a thousand tiny plates of armor. On its left side was a deep, pitted scar several inches long.

He froze. His fingers reflexively unfurled, revealing the pearl in his palm. The snake opened its mouth wide; its forked tongue flicked out, and he braced for the death bite—

But the stab of fangs didn't come. The snake began to unwind, its scaly underside sliding over his arms. He'd thought its skin would feel like a corpse's, but it was cool, dry, leathery, like the weathered cover of an old book.

The snake raised its head, meeting his gaze. Its inhuman eyes were emerald voids, holding him in a trance. He tried to move his limbs, but they were numb, as if his body was trapped in some kind of paralysis.

Finally the snake turned away and slithered into the lapping waters of the lake.

A gleam of bone white, then it was gone.

And so was the pearl.

Xian's eyes sprang open.

He sat up, his heart still beating fast. He hadn't dreamed of the white snake for some time, and its recurrence while he was in Changle had to be significant—another reminder of his purpose there.

He parted the drawn curtains in front of his platform bed. Zhen was still in the infirmary, and the cot in the corner was empty. Through the latticed window, he could see the faintest streaks of dawn lightening the sky outside. The vestiges of the dream still lingered, and the panic his ten-year-old self had felt was still all too real. No point trying to get back to sleep.

Xian shrugged on an outer robe; the guards outside his chamber saluted as he exited.

When he walked into the dining room, one of the carved wooden seats was occupied by a familiar figure. Several scrolls were spread out in front of him, and he was reading them by candlelight.

Xian cracked a smile. On the journey to Changle, in true

scholarly fashion, Fahai had spent his free time at way stations with his nose buried in a scroll instead of drinking wine with the rest of the delegation.

"You're up early." Xian slid into the seat next to the court adviser. "What are you reading?"

"Good morning, Prince," Fahai replied. "I went by the Hall of Knowledge. The Min court has a decent library, and I borrowed a few ancient texts on alchemy and taxonomy." He closed the scroll in front of him. "I hear you caused quite a stir at the infirmary yesterday evening. You seem intent on eschewing the courtesans offered by the Min court and choosing someone entirely untrained for the job."

"I like keeping them on their toes," Xian replied. "Besides, their courtesans might have been trained to eavesdrop on our private discussions. We certainly wouldn't want that."

Fahai's tone was dry. "So choosing the stable hand as your attendant was entirely . . . strategic."

"Zhen is familiar with the forests around Changle," Xian said. "I intend to arrange a hunting expedition as soon as he recovers. He shall be our guide."

He was closer than ever to finding the white snake. He could *sense* it, as if what had happened that fateful day seven years ago had forged some kind of connection between himself and the cursed creature—one that Xian would use to his advantage to capture the white snake and bring it back alive to Wuyue.

"You care about the boy," Fahai observed.

Xian met the court adviser's gaze. "I care about finding the white snake."

The diplomacy—the pretext of his visit to Changle—was frustratingly time-consuming. Instead of searching for the cure his mother urgently needed, Xian had to keep up appearances by attending the seemingly endless meetings and meals arranged by Governor Gao. He had spent the entire day touring the Changle armory and two nearby garrisons, accompanied by Feng and Fahai.

When Xian returned to his chamber late that night after an evening meal with Gao and the most senior court officials, Zhen was already there. His hair was freshly washed and combed, the top half tied back in a braided ponytail instead of a bun. His cheeks were still pale, which accented the ivory white of his silk robe. He would probably look good in other colors too, but white just seemed perfect for him.

Xian walked toward him. "The physician said you're well enough to be discharged?"

"No, I sneaked out without his permission," Zhen deadpanned.

Xian couldn't suppress a grin. A sense of humor was a good sign. "In that case, you're forbidden to do any kind of work in my chamber."

"Too late." Zhen gestured at a teapot with steam rising from the spout on a tray close by. "I thought you might enjoy a cup of pu'er tea after your evening meal."

Zhen poured some tea into a small porcelain cup and then offered it to Xian with both hands.

"Your Highness," he said.

He spoke the honorific that Xian had expressly told him not to use, but he did so with a twinkle in his eyes and a small curl playing on the edges of his mouth. It made something twinge inside Xian's chest, a sudden, sharp yearning.

Their fingers touched as he took the cup from Zhen. The tea was certainly not the best Xian had ever tasted, but that didn't matter. Far more satisfying was the expectant look on Zhen's face as he watched Xian sip the tea he had brewed.

"This is good," Xian said. "Although if you call me Your Highness again when we're alone, I'll have to send you back to the infirmary so the physician can determine if your injuries have resulted in some form of memory loss."

Zhen gave a furtive smile, which Xian relished far more than he should.

"By the way, I've spoken to Governor Gao," Xian told him. "Starting tomorrow, Qing has been assigned to serve us our meals, so you'll get to see each other more often."

Surprise lit Zhen's face. "Thank you."

"Qing isn't your real sister, is she?" Xian kept his tone even, without the slightest accusation. He wondered if the other boy would lie again, but Zhen nodded.

"Last year, I rescued her from a man who wanted to kill her," he replied. "Neither of us had anyone else, and she became like a sister to me. That's why it's my duty to take care of her the best I can."

Zhen's words struck a chord within Xian. He thought of his

mother—a commoner concubine, often derided by other noble ladies behind her back or sometimes less discreetly. His father loved her, but his loyalties were split between his kingdom, his wife and consorts, and his children. He was divided—which was why Xian could not be.

Xian removed the outer garment he'd worn to dinner—not his lóng páo, but still a formal robe. As he reached for his undershirt on the clothes rack, out of the corner of his eye, he glimpsed Zhen looking in his direction. But when he turned his head, the other boy quickly averted his gaze and busied himself with snuffing out the candles and dimming the lights.

Was that stolen glance just out of curiosity . . . or something more?

Xian put on his sleeping robe, and as he walked past the table that held the wéi qí board, the single white stone in the bowl of black stones drew his attention. He wondered how that white stone had ended up there. It reminded him of the small dot of the opposite color in each half of the yin-yang circle.

As Zhen started toward his cot in the corner of the chamber, Xian spoke.

"Wait," he said, and Zhen stopped. "I want you to sleep in my bed tonight."

A flicker crossed Zhen's face, which made Xian realize how the other boy must have interpreted his words.

"Your cot is too cramped, and sleeping in a bad position can slow the healing of your internal injuries," Xian quickly added. He put a rolled-up blanket in the middle of the platform bed, separating them like a rampart. "I'll sleep on this side. You can sleep over there."

Xian climbed onto the bed; a moment passed before Zhen went to the opposite side. He released the cords that tied back the gauze curtains, and they enveloped the bed like a cocoon. Xian lay on the silk pillow, which was long enough for them both to share. On his half of the bed, Zhen unfolded his limbs with effortless, almost sinuous grace. The silence settled on them, a shadowy blanket.

Xian shut his eyes. With Zhen lying just inches away, he was now more awake than ever. He tried to distract himself by thinking about an advanced wéi qí strategy Fahai had taught him before they left for Changle. But all he could conjure was the memory of his first game with Zhen, the way the other boy absently turned a white stone between his fingers as he mulled over his next move. Xian couldn't stop himself from imagining how Zhen's fingertips would feel against his own skin. In his mind, Zhen dropped the white stone into the bowl of black ones and leaned over the wéi qí board, his hands sliding up Xian's shoulders and linking behind his neck—then Xian swept all the stones off the table and pulled Zhen forward into an open-mouthed kiss . . .

Xian inhaled sharply as his eyes sprang open. A familiar tightness dragged through his abdomen, funneling lower.

Next to him, Zhen lay with his eyes closed. Quiet, even breaths escaped his slightly parted lips, and Xian wanted nothing more than to press his own mouth to them . . .

No. He had assured Zhen they would be doing nothing else but sharing a bed. Anything more would be a betrayal of Zhen's trust.

Xian got up, careful not to disturb him, and slipped out of the chamber and into the courtyard.

The absence of the moon was a reminder that the fifth lunar month had just begun. The Duanwu Festival was a few days away. He lifted his chin and inhaled deeply. The cool rush of night air had the same effect as a cold bath, dispelling images of Zhen that were both unwanted and wanted.

An unmoving figure sat under a fig tree at the other end of the courtyard: Feng. His back was ramrod straight, palms and feet facing upward, fingers interlaced and thumbs touching. He opened his eyes as Xian walked toward him.

"Sorry," Xian said. "Didn't mean to interrupt your meditation."

Feng unfolded his legs. "Can't sleep?"

Xian sat next to him, rested his elbows on his knees, and steepled his fingers. "Do you know how it feels when you can't stop thinking about someone but you can't do anything without messing everything up?"

Feng made a sardonic sound. "This has to be a first. The prince who can have, and has had, anyone he wants suddenly can't bring himself to make a move on a boy whose job description includes sleeping with him?"

"That's the problem. How do I know if he actually wants to sleep with me or if he's only doing it because he thinks he has to?"

"When did that ever matter to you?" Feng replied. "I'm still getting letters asking about you from that fellow student you seduced that summer you came to visit me at Shaolin."

"I did catch Zhen sneaking a glance at me when I was changing into my undershirt," Xian mused. "Do you think that means anything? You don't feel the urge to watch me when I take my clothes off, do you?"

"No, because I've seen you since you were a scrawny five-year-old with twigs for arms."

Xian absently twirled a blade of grass. "Do you think he has ever been with another boy?"

"I'm *not* having this conversation with you." Feng rolled his eyes. "I came out here to meditate because I was sure you and him would be going at it tonight like a pair of rabbits."

Xian shot him a narrow-eyed look. "He's still recovering. I'm not an animal, you know." He reclined on his elbows. "I can't figure out why Zhen is different from other boys. He just is."

The way Zhen had faltered when Xian asked him to sleep in his bed was still vivid in his mind. Like Feng said, he could have anyone he pleased—that was the good part about pretending not to be a prince with his other conquests. He never had to second-guess their motives for being with him. If only he had been able to keep his fake identity after his first meeting with Zhen in the stable. At least he'd know that whatever unfolded between them would be because Zhen wanted it to, not because he thought he had no choice.

Feng spoke. "I heard what Zhen said to you in the infirmary.

It was shrewd of him not to tell on Deng. And very decent of him to forgive him."

That was probably the closest thing to Feng's approval that Zhen could earn.

Feng folded his legs again, gracefully putting each foot facing up on the opposite thigh. Xian tried to imitate him, but the position was a lot harder than it looked. "How do you do that?"

"This is the full lotus pose. Perfectly symmetrical and grounded, with all five energy points facing the sky, which concentrates the qi in the dān tián. It takes practice, along with a lot of flexibility in the hips."

Xian smirked. "Maybe you can teach Zhen."

Feng swatted at him. "Don't disgrace the sacred Daoist traditions, you heretic."

Xian chuckled. He crossed his legs and nestled his palms close to his navel, knuckles overlapping. "I think I need to learn one or two of your Shaolin meditation methods after all."

Chapter 17
ZHEN

"And nothing happened?" Qing asked.

"We slept on opposite sides of the bed." Zhen unwrapped a glutinous rice cake that Qing had brought for him. "He put a rolled-up blanket between us."

They sat on the open terrace near the southern gate that separated the inner court from the outer. It was a favorite spot for palace workers to spend their midday rest, enjoying the crisp summer breeze or taking a nap under the shade of scholar trees. Majestic cypresses towered along the gate arches; two had interlocking branches, and the gnarled bark of another looked like a pair of dragons were coiled around its trunk.

Zhen bit into the sticky, chewy rice mixed with minced meat. "I pretended to be asleep, and he didn't try anything. After a while, he got up and left the room for about half an hour."

Qing's eyebrows shot up. "Did he go off to . . . you know, take care of himself?"

Zhen eyed her askance. "Where did you learn about that?"

She smirked. "Girls talk."

"I peered through the window. He was out in the courtyard talking to Feng. Then they meditated together."

Zhen thought he'd be ashamed that the prince only seemed interested in him physically—but as it turned out, that was the only thing Xian *hadn't* asked him for.

Qing took a large bite of a steamed bun. "If you like him, you need to get your tail out of a knot because you're the one who has to make the first move."

Zhen couldn't suppress a smile. "Are you giving me love advice?"

"Who else is going to? Boys are so clueless." She poked his side. "I saw the way he looked at you in the infirmary. If you didn't mean anything to him, he would've just slept with you and tossed you aside. The fact that he hasn't tried to pressure you into anything means he actually has feelings for you. It's kind of romantic."

After he was discharged from the infirmary, Zhen had seriously considered getting Qing and leaving the palace instead of going back to Xian's chamber. They'd be miles away by the time anyone noticed they were missing.

But something held him back. Something that went against the instincts he'd always trusted. He had left Xian behind once before, when he was a helpless little boy who had almost drowned, and the guilt still haunted him. Maybe the gods were giving him a chance to make things right. He had no idea how, but he did know that running in the opposite direction wasn't the answer.

Zhen looked at Qing soberly.

"There's something I need to tell you," he said. "I'm the one the prince wants."

Qing chuckled. "Sure took you long enough to figure that out."

"No, that's not what I mean." Zhen drew a deep breath. "His mother has been ill for many years after being bitten by a white snake. An oracle told him to come to Changle to find the cure: another white snake. That's the real reason he's here. He's going snake hunting, and he wants me to be his guide."

Qing's eyes went wide. "Is that why you wanted us to leave the palace so urgently the other day? Because the prince is here for the sole purpose of killing snakes?"

"He won't kill them. He intends to bring the white snake back alive. It's the last ingredient in the antidote that his adviser is making."

"Ingredient?" Qing looked aghast. She grabbed Zhen's arm. "Let's get out of here. Right now."

Zhen shook his head. "I've changed my mind about leaving. I don't want to be a coward." *And a thief,* he didn't say. He still couldn't bring himself to tell Qing about the pearl. "Running away isn't going to solve anything."

"Uh, nothing except taking away an imminent *threat to your life*—"

Qing was interrupted by the resounding echo of a gong being struck. They both turned toward the outer court.

"What's going on?" Qing jumped to her feet as the gong sounded again.

They joined other curious palace workers streaming through the gate. On the other side, in the middle of the vast, treeless outer court, a crowd had gathered around a raised platform with a broad wooden frame about twice the height of a regular doorway.

A familiar figure was shackled between the posts of the wooden frame. His back was facing the crowd, and his wrists were tied over his head by ropes attached to the top beam. Governor Gao and Steward Chu stood by the platform, and Zhen quickly ducked behind a tall man so they wouldn't see him.

Gao spoke. "The court of Changle has found this young man guilty of the crime of causing hurt to another person out of revenge. A second, more serious crime of declaring falsehood to the prince of Wuyue was also taken into consideration."

Deng had been stripped down to his undergarments, and as unnatural as clothes still felt to Zhen, he knew that, to humans, having this dignity forcibly removed was deeply shameful.

"He is sentenced to forty blows with the light stick," Gao continued. "He will be left hanging in the outer court overnight to reflect on his sins, after which he will resume his palace duties. The punishment shall now begin."

An official struck the gong with a hammer. The ominous knell reverberated inside Zhen's chest. He couldn't see Deng's face, but the way he hung his head and slumped his shoulders was hard enough to watch.

One of the guards stepped forward, a long bamboo stick in his hand. The nodes of the bamboo had been rasped away, which made the stick somehow more menacing.

Zhen's mouth went dry. A hush fell over the crowd. On the platform, Deng trembled.

The guard raised the bamboo stick and brought it down with brutal force. The stick whistled through the air and landed with a loud thwack on the back of Deng's thighs. Deng's body tensed and arched like he'd been struck by lightning. The ragged scream that ripped from his throat was one of the most horrible sounds Zhen had ever heard.

Zhen's hands closed into fists. Qing glanced at him.

The beating was swift and searing, carried out at one go. The lashes bled into one another, a pattern of cruel streaks criss-crossing Deng's back and thighs. Zhen hoped someone was keeping track, because he had lost count and Deng had stopped crying out as each blow landed.

When the guard finally lowered the bloodstained stick, a collective exhalation rose from the onlookers. Deng hung in the wooden frame like a battered puppet, held upright only by the cords around his wrists.

Gao's expression was impassive as he gestured at Deng's bonds. Instead of loosening them, the guards pulled them taut. Deng's body was yanked higher until his feet could barely touch the platform, putting immense strain on his shoulders.

Zhen took a reflexive step forward, but Qing caught his wrist.

"Don't," she said in a low voice. "Let's go."

Zhen's heart was pounding, but he forced himself to walk away.

Chapter 18
ZHEN

"It's your turn," Xian said.

Zhen's attention snapped back to the wéi qí board. His feet prickled with pins and needles, and he uncrossed his legs on the straw mat. "Sorry, which stone did you just put down?"

Xian pointed at one of the black stones. "You seem distracted tonight. Is something wrong?"

Zhen couldn't stop thinking about what he had witnessed in the outer court earlier that day.

"I was there when they carried out Deng's punishment this afternoon." Zhen took a deep breath. He knew he should let it go. It wasn't his place to speak up. "If you had wanted, you could've asked that he be given a less brutal sentence."

"Deng committed a serious crime." Xian's tone was flat. "He got what he deserved."

"He's a courtesan. Those scars will do more than just stay with him for a long time. They will diminish his worth."

Xian's eyes glinted. "If you must know, I pardoned his more serious wrongdoing against me. If I had not, he would've received eighty strokes with the heavy stick instead of forty with the light one. Forget scars—he might not walk upright for a few weeks." He paused. "The forty strokes were for what he did to you. I made sure he received the full punishment for that."

Xian had probably expected Zhen to be comforted by his explanation, but knowing that the beating that Deng received was solely on his account had the opposite effect.

"I forgave him too!" Zhen blurted out before he could stop himself. "Does my forgiveness have less value than yours because of who I am?"

Xian looked taken aback. "He hurt you, Zhen. He has to pay for what he did. The law exists for a reason. I can't ask the court to let him off easy just because you feel sorry for him."

"You can do anything you want," Zhen replied. "You're a prince."

"Yes, I am." Xian leaned forward, his expression intense as he held Zhen's gaze. "And what kind of prince would I be if I didn't protect the ones I care about?"

Zhen blinked. He hadn't been expecting the fervor in Xian's tone or the sharp flutter that carved its way through his own chest.

"I chose to grant mercy to Deng because of you," Xian continued. "I specifically told Governor Gao not to dismiss him from the palace, because you'd somehow found it in your heart to forgive him. But I'm a prince of Wuyue. I am here representing my father. The Changle court is scrutinizing my every move, and I can't allow myself to be viewed as weak—or, worse, unjust."

Zhen had seen the volatile hierarchy within wolf packs. If the dominant wolf wavered, he risked losing his power. Older wolves would savagely attack younger challengers to assert their control and ensure obedience from other members of their pack.

"My eldest half brother is waiting for me to make a mistake and prove that I am unworthy of my father's favor. If you thought forty strokes of the light stick were brutal—" Xian let out a humorless sound. "You should see what rival consorts in the palace are capable of."

Especially since Xian's mother was a commoner—he had mentioned that she was from a family of tea farmers. Each decision Xian made affected not just him but his mother's standing in the royal court. She was yet another reason he couldn't afford to lose his father's approval.

"The amulet around your neck," Zhen said. "I've never seen you take it off. Is it a gift from your mother?"

Xian nodded. He reached into the front of his shirt and took out the amulet on its chain.

"She once told me that the longer a piece of jade has been worn, the stronger its protective powers." He smoothed the dull jade between his thumb and forefinger. "Their colors have different meanings: White jade is a symbol of love and clarity of mind, while dark green jade, like this one, means strength and resilience."

Unlike Qing, whose mother had named and cared for her, Zhen had never met his mother. Pythons laid eggs, and their young were left to fend for themselves after they hatched. He would never truly understand the connection between a mother and her child. But from the way Xian spoke about his mother— his fierce protectiveness, how he would do anything to find her cure—it was clear that he would, without hesitation, destroy anyone who stood in his way . . . including Zhen.

Zhen lowered his gaze to the board and pretended to contemplate his next move to avoid meeting Xian's eyes, but when he picked up a white stone, the small pebble felt as heavy as lead.

That night, Zhen waited until Xian's breathing next to him gave way to snores before he sat up. He paused to study the other boy's sleeping face. A faint line creased the space between Xian's brows and the shadows softened his features, making him look younger than his seventeen years.

Zhen swung his legs over the side of the platform bed, silently crossed the room, and unlatched the laticed window near the empty cot where he was supposed to sleep. Climbing out was the only way to leave without alerting the guards standing watch by the chamber doors.

Outside, the courtyard was dark and silent. The trees stood still and ominous, skeletal arms raised to the sky. Zhen stealthily made his way to the back of the compound where an elm tree grew close to the outer wall, its spreading branches reaching over the top.

He shut his eyes and concentrated. This time, the transformation hurt more because of his healing internal injuries from Deng's beating. His bones re-formed and his body lengthened while his limbs retracted . . .

When he had completely changed, he turned his serpentine head from side to side. Behind him, his white dorsal scales gleamed, pearlescent in the darkness.

Something pricked at Zhen's senses; he felt as if he were being watched by an unseen gaze. But when he checked his surroundings, he couldn't see anyone. As a python, his eyesight in the dark wasn't sharp, and in the past year, Qing had helped him navigate at night. Pit vipers were nocturnal hunters, and Qing could locate prey through their body heat.

He began climbing the trunk. Unlike lizards, Zhen didn't have feet to help him ascend vertically. But his scales clung to the rough bark, allowing him to push himself upward. He halted briefly at the top of the wall, listening for vibrations and movement. His forked tongue flicked out, detecting the faintest scents in the air: woodsmoke, crushed grass, night dew.

He descended the wall outside the royal manor. The white marble terraces of the palace camouflaged him well, and he kept close to the shadows that fringed the buildings as he slithered to the southern gates that led to the outer court.

Even with his poor vision, he saw the towering wooden frame stark against the night sky. A limp figure sagged between the upright posts, his tied wrists hanging from the overhead beam. His flayed back gleamed black with dried blood.

Zhen glided around the platform. Deng's face was contorted in a grimace, and his shoulders were rotated at an unnatural angle. The painful pressure seemed to compress his chest, making his breathing shallow, labored.

Deng's eyes opened—and filled with horror when he saw Zhen. He let out a high-pitched, keening noise but didn't cry out, perhaps fearing more punishment for causing a disturbance.

The quickest way for Zhen to reach Deng's bound wrists was by climbing up his body—but it would be pointless if Deng died of fright after surviving forty strokes. Zhen slithered up one of the posts instead. He slid along the top beam and coiled around the rope that led to Deng's wrists.

Deng gazed up at him, whimpering and shaking.

Zhen sighed. It came out as a hiss, which seemed to terrify Deng even more.

Zhen bit at the knots, tugging them loose. He couldn't risk untying them, since Deng might try to escape, which would get him into worse trouble. Zhen only hoped to relieve the strain on Deng's arms and chest, making it easier for him to endure until dawn.

As the rope slackened by a fraction, Deng finally appeared to realize what Zhen was doing. His expression changed from fear to disbelief to confusion. His arms twitched—they had probably gone numb from hours in that agonizing position.

Zhen glided down from the platform. He couldn't linger. The

outer court was vast and bare, with no trees or bushes for cover. He had to get back before Xian woke up and realized he was gone.

He returned to the royal manor, scaled the wall, and transformed into his human form behind the elm tree, where he had left his clothes. He quickly got dressed, fastening the sash around his waist as he crossed the courtyard toward Xian's chamber—

"Going somewhere?"

If Zhen had been a snake, he might've literally jumped out of his skin.

Fahai was seated on a stone bench in the courtyard. Zhen had been so preoccupied that he hadn't noticed his silent presence.

"Oh—I needed to, um, relieve myself." Zhen's heart was hammering so loudly he was sure Fahai could hear it. "I didn't want to disturb the prince, so I, uh, climbed out the window instead."

He realized, too late, how ridiculous that excuse was. He squinted at Fahai's face, but the shadows masked the older man's expression.

"Next time, use the door. You might be mistaken for an intruder." Fahai's tone gave nothing away. "It's good to see that you seem well enough for the hunting trip the prince has planned for tomorrow."

Zhen nodded despite the trepidation that roiled in his stomach.

"The prince is worried about your health," Fahai added. "I have some knowledge of herbs, and he asked me to look into preparing a decoction that might help you."

"Thank you, Counselor Fahai." Zhen hastily offered a small bow. "Good night."

As he hurried inside, he could still feel the taciturn court adviser watching him.

Chapter 19

ZHEN

The plum rain—the heavy downpours in the fourth and fifth months, when the plums turned yellow—cleared up by late afternoon the next day, and they set off. Zhen had seen hunting parties before, and they usually took dogs or even hawks and eagles. But that was when the game was stag or deer. Stalking snakes required silence and stealth.

"Lead the way," Xian told him.

Zhen rode ahead on one of the horses from the Changle stable. Xian followed on Zhaoye, and Feng and Fahai brought up the rear. Zhen and Qing had recently spent time in these forests as snakes; he was familiar with the lay of the land and knew which areas were too rocky and treacherous to attempt because of erosion or landslides.

Zhen led them to a creek with crystal-clear water where they could stop to rest and the horses could drink. He handed out meat buns he had brought along in a basket made from braided willows.

"Join us," Xian said.

"Thanks," Zhen replied. "But I'd like to scout the terrain to make sure it's safe to pass."

He swung up into the saddle and rode a distance ahead. The sun was beginning to set, and some snakes would be waking from their daytime slumber, hungry and ready to feed. He listened keenly to the murmur of the forest around him—crickets chirped in the bushes, squirrels skittered up tree trunks, and starlings and blackbirds bickered on the branches.

He raised his head and let out a low, sibilant sound beyond the realm of human hearing. It echoed off the canopy of leaves above him, a warning that only other snakes would understand:

Danger. Stay away.

The restive stillness was the only reply. But if he shut his eyes and concentrated hard, he could sense dozens of snakes responding to his urgent call, uncoiling and slithering into rocky streams or hiding beneath the cool mulch of fallen logs—

"See anything?"

Zhen's head snapped around as Fahai pulled up next to him on his mount. The man's expression was unreadable, the way it had been last night when he surprised Zhen in the courtyard. A flicker of panic rose in Zhen's chest, and for a moment, he wondered if Fahai had overheard his warning. But that was impossible. Fahai wouldn't be able to hear, much less comprehend the language of snakes. No human could.

Zhen gave a slight nod. "It's all clear."

Xian and Feng came up alongside them on their horses.

"We haven't sighted a single snake so far." Feng gazed up at the darkening sky. "I think I saw deer tracks back there. Let's just get one and call it a day."

"We aren't here for deer, Feng." Xian couldn't hide the exasperation in his tone.

"I know. But it would look bad going back to the palace empty-handed—"

"Wait." Fahai suddenly raised a palm. He gestured toward a cluster of shrubs. "I saw something white moving in the grass over there."

To Zhen's dismay, a snake darted out of the bushes and slithered across the clearing. Its scales gleamed pale in the fading light.

"There!" Xian dismounted and grabbed a steel hook and a pair of tongs from the rattan case tied to the back of Zhaoye's saddle. "Don't let it get away!"

The frantic snake tried to escape the way it had come, but Fahai blocked its path. Xian moved forward, trying to catch it with the tongs. The snake hissed, rearing up and showing its fangs; Feng drew his sword, but Xian quickly held out a hand.

"No! We need it alive." He pointed at the pole with a noose in the rattan case. "I'll drive the snake toward you. If I can't get it with the hook, you snatch it with the noose—"

A roar from behind them made Zhen spin around.

A leopard burst out of the thicket, leaped a startling distance, and landed several feet from Xian. It growled, baring its teeth.

The snake vanished into the underbrush, unscathed.

Zhen's senses had been so focused on the snake that he hadn't detected the leopard's approach. Xian had a hook in one hand and a pair of tongs in the other—effective against a snake, but useless against this predator. Leopards were one of the strongest wild cats, and Zhen had seen one dragging a carcass heavier than itself up a tree.

Feng moved first, stepping in front of Xian. He brandished his weapon, the look in his eyes as deadly as the leopard's. He swung his sword just as the animal leaped at him.

Zhen's stomach lurched. Even before the leopard's paw knocked the sword out of Feng's hand, Zhen knew the prince's bodyguard didn't stand a chance.

Feng fell backward under the crushing weight of the animal. He let out an anguished yell as the leopard's teeth sank into his left shoulder. If he hadn't put up such a spirited fight, that first bite would've punctured his throat. But the next one could.

"Feng!" Xian rushed forward.

Fahai caught his arm. "No!" The adviser had his bow in hand, but he couldn't hold Xian back and fire an arrow at the same time.

Zhen picked up a thick fallen branch, ran toward the leopard, and, with all the strength he could muster, swung at the leopard's left hind leg. The leopard howled and whirled around.

"Zhen, watch out!" Xian shouted as the leopard released its grip on Feng and advanced toward Zhen.

Zhen stood his ground, stared into the depths of the leopard's eyes, and spoke in its language:

Leave the humans alone. Run before they kill you.

He wasn't sure what kind of sound emerged from his mouth, but the recognition in the leopard's eyes was unmistakable. It raised its head and looked balefully at Xian, who had picked up Feng's fallen sword, and Fahai, who had pulled an arrow from his quiver—

With a frustrated growl, the leopard sprang away just before Fahai's arrow whistled past, narrowly missing its head. It bounded into the bushes and disappeared.

"Feng!" Xian hurried forward and dropped to his knees next to his injured best friend. "How bad is it?"

Feng grimaced. His bleeding shoulder looked dislocated. "I'm fine."

"No, you're not. You just got mauled by a leopard!"

Feng looked at Zhen, mystified. "That beast swept my sword away like a toy. How did you hit it hard enough to knock it back?"

"When it jumped at you, it landed awkwardly, favoring its left hind leg," Zhen replied. "I assumed it had been injured earlier, so I struck its most vulnerable spot. It probably ambushed us because it couldn't run fast enough to catch its usual prey—"

"We need to get Feng back to the palace," Fahai interrupted. "An animal bite must be cleaned and covered with a poultice as soon as possible to prevent festering."

"I know the shortest route," Zhen said.

Their horses hadn't spooked and run off when the leopard attacked, proof of the quality of their training.

Xian helped Feng to his feet. "You'll ride with me."

"I'll have to turn down that honor, Prince." Feng gritted his teeth and managed to climb onto his steed without jarring his injured shoulder. "The only time you'll bring me in on your horse is if I'm dead."

"Don't say such things, you idiot." Xian glared at him as he swung up into Zhaoye's saddle. "We've had enough bad luck for today."

Chapter 20
ZHEN

Dusk had fallen by the time they arrived back at the palace. Xian accompanied Feng to the infirmary; Fahai started to follow, but he paused and turned to Zhen.

"Well done," he said. "Your swift reflexes out there saved the day."

Zhen was surprised at the compliment. "Thank you. I did the best I could."

"It was strange," Fahai mused, his gaze fixed on Zhen. "The leopard escaped just as I nocked my arrow. And the white snake seemed to know we intended to capture it . . . almost as if they could understand us."

Zhen inwardly tensed but managed not to show it. "I suppose that's why it's called instinct."

When Zhen returned alone to the royal manor, Qing was

waiting with the dinner dishes. "Where's everyone? The food's getting cold."

"We were ambushed by a leopard while out hunting," Zhen told her. "Feng defended the prince, and the leopard attacked him instead. He's in the infirmary now."

Qing looked worried. "Is he going to be all right?"

"I think so. The leopard bit his shoulder, not his throat." Zhen sighed. "I should've been more alert. But I was distracted by a white snake and didn't hear it approaching—"

"You met another white snake? Was it a python as well?"

Zhen shook his head. "It was a krait. Smaller, but very venomous. I rode ahead and tried to warn off as many snakes as I could, but this one must've panicked and darted out."

"Hey. You can't save them all." Qing reached out and rubbed her thumb over a smudge of dirt on Zhen's cheek. "I keep telling you that, but you never listen."

Zhen had to do everything he could to prevent more bloodshed—even if that meant putting himself in danger by working against the prince's purpose. "I have to try."

"I know." A smile lifted the edges of Qing's mouth. "I wouldn't be here if you hadn't."

After Qing left, Zhen washed up and changed into a clean robe. He went around the chamber refreshing the incense sticks and ensuring the tea leaves were fresh, but it didn't make him feel any less restless. Or helpless.

Qing was right. He couldn't save everyone. Like that dead snake on the shore of the islet with the fishhook in its mangled mouth. The old tortoise spirit had told him that day about yin and yang, about how the equilibrium always found itself. But that harsh truth of the universe didn't make the crushing sense of futility any easier to bear.

Finally, just before midnight, the doors slid open and Xian stepped in, his face drawn. The front of his leather hunting tunic was stained with traces of Feng's blood.

Zhen quickly walked to him. "How is Feng?"

"They fixed his dislocated shoulder, but he was running a high fever," Xian replied. "The physicians were afraid that some kind of disease had entered his blood through the bite. Fahai prepared a decoction of herbs to draw out any toxins. We'll have to wait and see if that helps."

Zhen remembered the food Qing had brought. "You must be hungry. Dinner has gone cold, but I can go to the kitchen—"

"There's no need." Xian sounded weary as he rubbed the back of his neck. "They brought me something to eat at the infirmary. I'll check on Feng again in a few hours. Hopefully his fever will have broken by then."

Zhen dropped to his knees. He glimpsed Xian's surprise.

"I was supposed to be the guide." Zhen bowed his head. "I should have been more alert. What happened to Feng was my fault. I'll accept any punishment you choose."

"Don't be ridiculous." Xian took Zhen's arm and pulled him to his feet. "You were the only one who noticed the leopard's weak leg and managed to drive it off. You saved Feng's life."

If the leopard had attacked Xian instead, and if it had

refused to listen to Zhen's warning to flee, Zhen would've done much more than strike its leg. Pythons were powerful constrictors and could coil their bodies around their prey in the blink of an eye, cutting off blood circulation and blocking airways. Zhen couldn't do that as a human, but if he'd had to, he would have gone down fighting. He owed Xian that much.

"I was so close." The quiet anguish in Xian's voice was almost more than Zhen could bear. "The white snake was right there— and I let it slip out of my reach."

"That leopard attacked out of nowhere." Zhen tried to keep his voice neutral. "We had to help Feng. You made the only natural choice."

"Cùn cǎo chūn huī." A sad smile ghosted across Xian's mouth. "A child can never repay a mother's love, just like a blade of grass cannot repay the spring's sunlight. I carry my mother's hopes in my name, but I have failed her again. I am an unworthy son."

In that moment, Zhen wanted to tell him the truth. The truth about the pearl, his real identity, everything.

"Your mother doesn't believe that," Zhen whispered instead. "She gave you a name that means 'immortal' for a reason."

"You remembered." An unidentifiable emotion flitted across Xian's face. "What about you? Which character is your name?"

Zhen was caught off guard. "I'm . . . not sure. I don't know how to read or write."

Before he became a snake spirit, other creatures had called him Little White One, for his unusual color. The first time he had transformed, as he lay shivering and naked on a muddy riverbank, he distantly heard a boy's laughter, a woman calling, "Zhen! Zhen!"

"Maybe it's this one." Xian went to the dresser table, picked up a brush, and wrote a single character on a piece of parchment: 貞. "It means 'virtue and loyalty.'"

An inexplicable feeling bloomed inside Zhen's chest as he stared at the character in Xian's handwriting. He had chosen the name because he liked the way it sounded and it was the first name he had heard as a human. But now, he felt as if Xian had given him not just the meaning of his name but another piece of who he was.

Xian walked to the copper basin and splashed some water on his face. Zhen glanced at the gilded bathtub that stood in one corner of the chamber. Steward Chu had said his job duties included drawing a bath for the prince.

He spoke. "Would you . . . uh, like me to draw you a bath?"

There was a pause. Zhen held his breath, hoping he didn't look as flustered as he felt.

Xian met his gaze. "I would like that."

Zhen's heart was beating faster than usual as he prepared the bath, first boiling water on the stove and then pouring it into the bathtub with a jug. Xian walked to the wooden clothes rack and, facing away from Zhen, stripped off his tunic and undershirt. It wasn't the first occasion Xian had disrobed in his presence, but this time would be . . . different. Xian would be naked for a long while, and Zhen would be right there. He wasn't sure whether he regretted offering the bath or that Xian had said yes.

Then Xian turned around, and the handle of the jug nearly slipped from Zhen's hand.

Zhen had never paid close attention to the details of the human physique, but now his eyes drank in the lean muscles in Xian's arms, the taut angles of his abdomen, the tracery of dark hair trailing downward from his belly button . . .

Zhen tore his gaze away. The heat on his cheeks had nothing to do with the steam rising from the water. He tried to focus on the soap powder, the washcloth, and the pumice that was much smoother than the one Zhen had been scoured with in preparation for his first night as the prince's attendant. But his hands were unsteady, and he accidentally added too much soap to the bath, creating a thick layer of bubbly lather on the surface.

Xian walked toward him. He seemed unperturbed by being naked . . . and by the effect he was having on Zhen.

Zhen swallowed past the knot in his throat. "Please be careful. The water is a little hot."

Xian raised his foot and tested the water with his toes before he gracefully stepped into the tub. Zhen was almost relieved when the lower half of Xian's body disappeared beneath the bubbles. Xian closed his eyes and leaned against the tub, his elbows resting on the edge.

Zhen ran the pumice over Xian's shoulders and the back of his neck, careful not to tug at the strands of hair that had come loose from his bun. He took the opportunity to admire the ridge of Xian's collarbones, the line of his jaw, the plane of his chest where the jade amulet rested.

Xian let out a soft, satisfied sound when Zhen began massaging his shoulders, kneading his tight muscles in slow circles to unknot the tension. Pressure built between Zhen's thighs, and he shifted uncomfortably. He had never been so attracted to anyone before. How many more times could he clean the upper half of Xian's body without venturing beneath the water?

Zhen ran the washcloth over Xian's chest—without warning, Xian's hand darted out and caught Zhen's wrist.

Zhen froze.

"My name." The droplets on Xian's lashes gleamed like tiny pearls. "I want to hear you say it."

The space between them was everything and nothing at the same time. The air was thick and heavy, like in the woodlands before a thunderstorm, sharp with the scent of petrichor. Zhen was sure the other boy could hear his heart pounding inside his rib cage, the same way pythons could feel the ebbing pulses of their prey . . .

"Xu," Zhen began, but Xian shook his head.

"No." He leaned forward, his gaze intense. "Call me Xian."

Zhen stared at him wide-eyed, like an animal pinned by a brilliant light.

"Xian," he exhaled. He let the name roll off his tongue again, and it was the most natural thing in the world. "Xian . . ."

Raw emotion coalesced in Xian's eyes at the sound of his name, and a sharp coil of yearning tightened inside Zhen's lower abdomen. But the other boy didn't move forward, as if he were consciously holding himself at the brink of an invisible line that he was waiting for Zhen to cross.

You're the one who has to make the first move, Qing had said.

Zhen kissed him. The rush was dizzying, overwhelming, like the time he had swallowed the pearl, except now it was Xian's mouth moving against his, the pleasurable scrape of his stubble grazing Zhen's lips—

Xian abruptly rose from the tub, sending water sloshing over the edges, rivulets streaming down his limbs. Zhen pulled back, dazed, and automatically reached for a towel, but Xian stopped him.

"You'll catch a cold—" Zhen began.

Xian stepped out of the tub and drew him close against his naked body. "I don't care."

This time, Xian's mouth was hard, searching, his tongue flicking against Zhen's, teeth tugging at his lower lip. The roughness was startling, but Zhen couldn't get enough of it.

Xian urged Zhen to the platform bed and maneuvered him onto his back without breaking their kiss. He straddled Zhen's waist and leaned over him, the jade amulet around his neck swinging like a pendulum.

Zhen took Xian's face in his hands and pulled him down until their mouths met again. He wanted Xian so badly he could hardly breathe. His fingers tangled in Xian's hair, loosening more strands from his bun. Xian slid a hand between their bodies—even through the layer of clothing Zhen wore, a shock went through him, and he jolted in response.

Xian immediately stopped. "Are you all right?"

"Yes." Zhen sucked in a shuddering breath. "It's just that I've never . . ."

He trailed off, expecting a flash of impatience from the other boy. But instead, Xian stroked Zhen's cheek, brushing a lock of hair away from his face.

"It's all right," he told Zhen. "We don't have to do anything."

Xian's fingertips were calloused, likely from hours of gripping sword hilts and drawing arrows. A reminder of his future as the leader of a kingdom, someone who expected to be obeyed without question. Yet here he was, refusing to demand that right when they were alone. He didn't want anything from Zhen that he wasn't willing to give.

A stone on the wéi qí board couldn't be moved unless it was captured. The boy who had shared an apricot with him in the stable, who had made a pot of pu'er tea and taught him how to savor it, who hadn't hesitated to wipe his bleeding nose with his own sleeve . . . he had captured Zhen's heart.

Zhen didn't look away as he loosened the front of his own robe. Surprise flickered in Xian's eyes, which swiftly darkened with desire that mirrored his own.

Zhen took the small bottle by the bed and pressed it into Xian's palm.

"I want to," he whispered.

Chapter 21
ZHEN

They lay in a tangle of limbs, catching their breath.

They had done it twice—once last night and again in the early morning. Zhen's body was pleasantly sore, and the invisible imprint of Xian's touch still lingered on his arms, his torso, his thighs.

Despite all the occasions he had transformed, his human body always felt like a second skin that was ready to be shed. But Xian had changed that. For the first time, Zhen had discovered sensitive places he didn't know he had, sensations he never knew his body was capable of. He tried to memorize everything, the pleasure, even the pain, because Xian had been right there, murmuring reassurances every step of the way.

He started to get up, but Xian caught his hand.

"Stay," he said.

Zhen acquiesced, nestling his head on Xian's chest. The steady vibrations of Xian's heartbeat against his cheek suddenly reminded him of how, when coiled around his prey as a snake, he felt their faltering heartbeats until they faded to nothing. He forced the unwanted sense memory aside.

Xian idly caressed his hair. "Worn out?"

Zhen brushed his lips over Xian's clavicle. "I'm ready for the third time when you are."

Xian let out a breathless chuckle. "Give me a moment to recover."

His hand slid down Zhen's torso and drew circles on his skin. Zhen shivered, although he stiffened when Xian's fingers found the smooth, raised scar above his left hip.

Xian halted. "What happened here?"

If the old tortoise hadn't found him in that snake trap and helped him get free . . .

"I don't remember," Zhen replied. "It was a long time ago."

That was a lie, and he was sure Xian knew it. Pain that left a mark that deep wasn't something you could ever forget. But he couldn't tell Xian how he had gotten the scar any more than he could tell him the truth about who he really was.

Xian moved, rolling Zhen onto his back. He bent forward and kissed a languid trail down Zhen's chest and across his abdomen until he reached the scar. Zhen gasped as Xian's tongue darted over the knot of healed flesh. The intimacy, the tenderness—Zhen felt a stirring between his legs again.

Zhen reversed their positions, planted his knees on either

side of Xian's body, and captured the other boy's mouth in a fervent kiss. Xian's pleased grin when they pulled apart, both of them panting and flushed, confirmed how much Xian relished seeing that bold side of him.

"You said you were born in Wuyue," Xian said, smoothing his thumb over Zhen's cheekbone. "I want you to come home with me."

Zhen's breath caught in his throat. "Are you—are you serious?"

Xian nodded.

"The palace in Xifu is right by the West Lake," he said. "Standing on the Broken Bridge and watching the sun set behind Leifeng Pagoda . . . it's unforgettable. And I can introduce you to my mother. I think she'd really love to meet you."

The mention of Xian's mother was like an avalanche crashing down on Zhen.

He drew back. "I don't think that's a good idea."

Xian sounded puzzled. "Why not?"

"I'm sure you have more capable courtesans to serve you in Wuyue."

"You're not a courtesan. And I don't want any of them. I want you." Xian's brow furrowed. "Why is that so hard for you to believe? What are you afraid of?"

Zhen wanted more than anything to go back to Wuyue with him. But he couldn't.

He wordlessly pulled Xian into a kiss. This time it was slow, deep, lingering. Like the melted snow on the sunny side of the Broken Bridge, he just couldn't let go of the illusion, even if it couldn't last. Even if it was never real.

When they broke apart, Xian tucked a loose strand of hair behind Zhen's ear.

"The oracle led me to Changle to heal my mother," he told Zhen. "I will not return to Wuyue without the cure." He leaned in until their noses bumped. "And I know, deep in my heart, that I won't be going back without you either."

Zhen averted his eyes so Xian wouldn't see the expression in them.

"The sky is getting light." He swung his legs over the side of the bed. "Shall we go to the infirmary to see if Feng is feeling better?"

When they arrived, Feng was sitting up, his left shoulder bandaged and his arm in a sling. Qing was by his side, holding up a spoonful of congee. Was she feeding him?

"If I'd known you had this young lady for company," Xian said, walking to Feng's bed, "I wouldn't have come visit so early."

Feng blushed. So did Qing as she lowered the spoon. Zhen arched an eyebrow at her, and she gave him a quelling glance.

Zhen still didn't feel entirely at ease around Feng. "I hope you're feeling better, my lord."

"Hold on, Zhen." Xian turned to him. "When you stop a leopard from biting Feng's head off, you earn the right to call him by his name. It's one of the royal decrees of the kingdom of Wuyue."

Feng shot Xian a mock-affronted look. "Biting my head off is an overstatement, don't you think?"

Xian touched the back of his hand to Feng's forehead. "Has your fever broken? Any chills?"

"I'm fine," Feng replied. "The physician said I should be out of the sling by the Duanwu Festival."

Xian looked at Qing. "Tell the kitchen to make a special soup of pork ribs double boiled with white peony, lotus seeds, ginseng, and cordyceps at every meal for the next couple of days. That's the recipe for my mother's special healing tonic. Serve it to him personally."

"Yes, Your Highness," Qing replied. "I'll ask the chefs to start preparing the soup right away."

"I'll go with her and have your breakfast brought here, Your Highness," Zhen volunteered. He was quite sure Xian wanted some time alone with his best friend.

When he and Qing stepped out of the infirmary, Zhen gave her a grin. "Didn't expect to see you here."

Qing shrugged. "My job is to bring meals to the Wuyue delegation. Since Feng's in the infirmary, I delivered his breakfast there instead."

"I see. Does your job also include feeding him?"

She turned red. "His arm is in a sling! How's he supposed to hold the bowl and the spoon at the same time?"

"Well, he seemed pleased." Zhen gave her a fond nudge. "Almost like he thought getting mauled by a leopard was worth it."

Qing smiled furtively. "He's all right, I suppose. A lot less uptight than I thought."

Zhen glanced around them to make sure no one was within

earshot. "Listen, there's something I need to tell you."

"Yeah, I know." Qing smirked and pointed at his neck. "Your prince left a pretty obvious clue."

Zhen's cheeks flushed. He'd been walking around the palace with a bite on his neck. Feng must've seen it too.

Qing leaned in conspiratorially. "So how was it? Did it hurt a lot the first time?"

Zhen waved her off. "That wasn't what I wanted to talk to you about. He told me that when he goes back to Wuyue . . . he wants me to come with him."

"Are you going to?" Qing sounded astonished. "Wait—what about me? You'll ask him if I can come too, right?"

"No. We need to leave Changle before he does. We've already stayed far too long."

Qing blinked. "I thought you liked the prince."

Zhen shut his eyes. The hurt was like a wound left by a serrated hook that had been yanked out of his chest. "I do."

Qing frowned. "Then is this because he's hunting snakes? Humans have been hunting us for a long time, for all kinds of reasons. Our skins. Our meat. Our gallbladders—"

"I was the one who stole the cure from him," Zhen blurted out.

Qing looked startled. "What? How could that be? You only just met him!"

Zhen couldn't keep this bottled up any longer.

"I first met Xian seven years ago, when I was an ordinary snake," he said. "He was only ten years old at that time. He fell into the West Lake and almost drowned. Something drew me to him, and I pulled him out of the water. He was holding a spirit pearl in his hand, and I . . . took it."

Understanding dawned in Qing's eyes. "The pearl turned you into a snake spirit?"

"The same pearl that was meant to cure his mother of her snakebite." Zhen rubbed his forehead, thoroughly miserable. "I didn't know until he told me a few days ago."

"You can't blame yourself," Qing said. "You had no idea what the pearl was for. You were a snake. You saw something shiny, and you swallowed it. That's what animals do."

"I knew exactly what it was," Zhen replied. "An old tortoise spirit once told me that these pearls were so valuable to them because consuming one added hundreds of years' worth of cultivation and they could ascend to heaven sooner. I didn't care about all that; I just wanted to become a snake spirit so I could transform and live as a human. I took the pearl, and . . . I just left Xian there on that islet in the middle of the lake. He might've died if no one had rescued him."

"He's a *prince*. The palace wouldn't have stopped searching until they found him. You saved his life, Zhen. He wouldn't be here now if it weren't for you."

Zhen had never thought about it that way. Even though the strong taking from the weak was the law of nature, all these years he had lived with the guilt, the persistent reminder that he was an impostor living a life that wasn't his.

He slipped his hand into the sleeve of his robe and withdrew a small piece of parchment. He had surreptitiously taken it from the dresser table while Xian wasn't looking.

贞. *It means "virtue and loyalty,"* Xian had said.

Zhen gazed at his name in Xian's handwriting, and something sharp and bittersweet twisted through his chest.

"What's that?" Qing asked.

Zhen folded the piece of parchment and put it back into his sleeve pocket. Zhen was a snake, and Xian was a snake hunter. There was no way anything between them could end well.

"We will leave Changle the day after the Duanwu Festival," he told Qing.

Chapter 22
XIAN

Duanwu, one of the four most important festivals of the year, marked a change in seasons that could bring a year of prosperity—or of disaster. The beginning of summer coincided with the arrival of plagues such as sickness, crop-destroying insects, and drought. To ward off evil, people hung mugwort and calamus on their doors and nailed eight-sided coin charms to the gates of their houses.

As Xian stood in front of the mirror in his chamber dressed in his lóng páo, the same feeling churned inside his chest: They were on the brink of a change of fortune—good or bad, he did not know.

The doors of the adjoining room opened and Feng emerged, sharply attired in his uniform. The bold white cross collar set him apart as a royal bodyguard. His sword hung by his waist in an ornate black-and-gold scabbard worn only during official occasions.

Xian winked. "You look good."

"Careful." Feng flexed his left arm, freshly liberated from its sling. "Your lover might be jealous."

"He's gone off to get ready. They made him a special robe for the celebration."

Feng scoffed. "The only difference to you is how quickly you can get him out of it tonight."

Xian smirked. The past few nights, Zhen had been mortified each time the bed creaked under them as their rhythmic sounds grew louder, more feverish.

"Sorry. I know you're a light sleeper." Xian paused. "I want to bring him with us when we return to Wuyue."

Feng seemed surprised. "What?"

"Don't worry, I'll make sure his sister comes along too. I have no doubt you will be entirely honorable and marry her before you sleep with her."

"Don't try to change the subject." Feng shot him a look. "I wouldn't give the poor boy false hopes like that. You might get tired of him before we reach Xifu, and then what?"

Xian raised an eyebrow. "Is that concern I detect? For the one you vehemently argued should not be allowed to sleep in my chamber? Is this your way of thanking him for saving your life?"

"He acted bravely that day." Feng's tone was grudging. "But I think you're moving too fast. You barely know him."

Feng's objection mirrored Zhen's reaction when Xian talked about bringing him back to Wuyue. Like Feng, Zhen didn't seem to believe he could hold Xian's attention for long.

Well, they were both wrong. Zhen hadn't hidden the fact that he hadn't been with anyone else, but this was also a first for Xian. The way he felt about Zhen was different from any other boy that came before, and Xian didn't want him to be just an enjoyable fling in a distant land. He intended to bring him back to the palace in Xifu, and once they found the cure and his mother was healed, he would have time to win the other boy's heart.

"I had a long talk with Fahai earlier," Xian said. "Hunting snakes got us nowhere, and we're running out of time. We need a more efficient way to capture the white snake."

"And what's that?" Feng asked.

Xian showed him a coin charm with a square hole in the middle, the kind widely sold in marketplaces before the festival. One side of the coin was engraved with symbols of the wǔ dú, the five poisons: the centipede, the lizard, the scorpion, the toad . . . and the snake.

"'Even a powerful dragon struggles to overcome a snake in its native haunt,'" Xian said. "The priest's words are the clue we've been missing. The oracle said the key to finding the cure lies *in* Changle—not just the place, but the people. We need them to bring the white snake to us."

"Your father didn't want anyone else knowing the real reason for us coming to Changle," Feng pointed out. "How can we enlist the help of the population without raising suspicion?"

The corners of Xian's mouth curled up. "I have a plan."

The palace in Wuyue was located right next to the West Lake, where the annual dragon boat race was held. But Changle's palace was about an hour's ride from the Min Jiang, the venue of their dragon boat race.

When Xian and his entourage arrived, the celebrations were already in full swing. Families milled around, laughing and chatting, while children chased one another with egg pouches swinging around their necks. Vendors sold food as well as silk handkerchiefs, five-colored bracelets, and incense sachets. The fizzle of firecrackers filled the air, and the river shimmered with sunset hues of vermilion and violet as the dragon boats gathered downstream.

A sheltered dais with tables, couches, and a stage for the evening's entertainment had been set up on the riverbank for the senior court officials and the most honored guests from Wuyue. A herald of horn blasts welcomed the royal entourage, and everyone stopped and bowed as Xian walked past, followed by Feng, Fahai, and Governor Gao.

Xian's gaze searched for Zhen and found him on the dais, standing next to the grandest cushioned couch. Zhen looked beautiful in an embroidered white robe that reached to his ankles. A silver filigree band encircled his forehead, and the top half of his long hair was braided elaborately while the rest flowed down his shoulders.

As Xian ascended the steps, Zhen knelt gracefully, his hands folded in front of him. Then he rose and offered Xian a cup of steaming tea.

"Your Highness," he said, a glimmer of mirth in his eyes.

Xian took the cup and drank the tea. Then he reached out and tucked a stray strand of hair behind Zhen's ear. That was something he never did to any of the other boys he slept with. He'd kissed them, touched them, but he had never stroked their hair away from their faces or felt such affection as he ran his fingertips over the curves of their ears.

Qing appeared with a tray of dumplings wrapped in bamboo leaves. She wore a high-waisted green dress with long white sleeves, the formal attire of palace maids. She smiled at Feng, who had taken a seat on the other couch with Fahai. Feng beamed back.

Drumbeats signaled that the dragon boat race was about to begin. The setting sun had touched the horizon, and a handful of longboats festooned with flags and banners were waiting at the starting line. Each wooden watercraft had a carved dragon head in front, a tail at the end, and brightly colored scales painted on the sides. The hull was exceptionally narrow, with just enough space for a crew of twenty men seated in pairs with oars.

Xian unwrapped a triangular dumpling and bit into the filling of chestnuts, jujubes, red beans, and minced pork mixed with sticky rice.

"This can't compare with the zòng zi my mother makes," he told Zhen. "Her secret ingredients are dried red dates and pine nut kernels. My father likes to joke that Qu Yuan would've written poetry about them."

"Who's Qu Yuan?" Zhen asked.

Xian was surprised. What kind of isolated childhood had Zhen had to be unfamiliar with the people and stories behind the popular festivals?

"Qu Yuan was a poet and a court official who lived in Chu during the time of the Warring States," he replied. "He was a good man, but jealous rivals slandered him, and he was exiled by the king. When he heard of Chu's defeat by its enemies on the fifth day of the fifth month, he threw himself into the river in grief. The villagers were so touched by his love for his homeland that they went out on boats to search for him."

"Did they find him?" Zhen asked.

"No. But they threw sticky rice dumplings into the water to stop fish from eating his body, and they continued to remember the day of his death by going out onto the river on boats decorated with fierce dragon heads, beating loud drums to drive away the river monsters."

At the sound of the horn, the dragon boats shot off the starting line and sliced through the water like wooden blades. The race was a sprint across five hundred yards, a burst of raw power fueled by cheers from onlookers thronging the banks. Oarsmen rowed in perfect, furious synchronicity to the thunderous, frenetic beat of the drummer at the head of the boat.

Xian stole a glance at Zhen. The fascination on the boy's face as the winning vessel sailed across the finish line was more interesting than the race itself.

At festivals, it was customary for the highest-ranked official to give a short speech before feasting began. Xian walked onto the stage. This was the first time the prince of Wuyue was publicly addressing the people, and the crowd fell quiet, eager to hear what he had to say.

Xian spoke, his voice clear in the crisp evening air.

"When I was a young boy, my beloved mother would scrupulously follow all the traditions of the Duanwu Festival," he said. "She would bathe me in water that had been left out in the sunshine. She would boil an egg in tea, dye it red, and hang it around my neck in a small bag woven with colorful string. She would dip her finger into white wine mixed with realgar powder and write the character 王 on my forehead to drive away evil spirits. I see many of you fathers and mothers have done the same."

The crowd listened, rapt. Parents hugged their children close.

Xian raised the reverse side of the coin charm he had shown Feng earlier, which was carved with the characters 驅邪降福.

"Qū xié jiàng fú—'Expel evil and send down good fortune,'" he said. "In this Year of the Snake and on behalf of my father, the king of Wuyue, I am announcing a bounty: I will award one silver tael to every person who brings a white snake to the Changle palace by the end of tomorrow."

There was stunned silence. A silver tael was two months' wages for most workers.

"The snake must be white, and it must be alive and unharmed,"

Xian continued. "No reward will be given otherwise."

Applause broke out, and some people immediately departed, likely to get a head start with the hunt. Xian stepped back, pleased. Hopefully by this time tomorrow, they would have at least one white snake in their possession, and he would find an excuse to leave for Wuyue immediately.

The banquet dishes served were similar to what Xian ate back home during the festival: Green bean sprouts, leek, and shredded meat wrapped in wheat flour pancakes so thinly rolled, they were as translucent as silk. Eel, in season and particularly fatty and tender, stewed with tofu and mushrooms. Boiled salted duck eggs with a liquid white and a firm, orange-red yolk.

As Xian and his entourage dined, musicians played bowed strings, woodwinds, cymbals, gongs, and the qín, favored instrument of emperors. Courtesans came onto the stage and danced, twirling multicolored silk fans. Deng wasn't among them.

Next to Xian, Zhen looked very pale, and he barely touched the food. Before Xian could ask if he was all right, a few drops of fresh blood landed on Zhen's white robe.

"Your nose is bleeding again." Xian reached for Zhen's hand as another crimson spot fell. "Your palms are freezing! Are you ill?"

"I don't feel well." Zhen's voice was constricted. "May I be excused? Qing can accompany me back to the palace—"

"This may help." Fahai approached with a ceramic goblet in both hands. "Prince, I prepared this herbal decoction as you instructed."

"Perfect timing." Xian took the goblet and offered it to Zhen. "I asked Fahai to prepare this medicine for you. It will help your nosebleed. Here, drink it."

Zhen looked stricken, like a cornered animal. Blood continued to trickle from his nose. Xian took a handkerchief and dabbed his upper lip.

"Give Fahai's medicine a try," he urged. "The palace is an hour's ride from here, and you look like you might pass out if you take more than a few steps."

He brought the goblet to Zhen's mouth, but the other boy recoiled. Qing and Feng came over, looking anxious.

"What's wrong with him?" Qing asked.

Xian didn't know why Zhen was so reluctant to drink the decoction.

"Tell you what," he said, "I'll drink the first mouthful, and you finish the rest." That was how Xian's mother used to coax him to take medicine when he was little. Xian sipped from the goblet and suppressed the urge to gag. These decoctions always tasted terrible. "Now your turn."

Zhen seemed to blanch even more, turning his face away from the goblet.

"Xian," he whispered, just loud enough for him to hear. "Please . . ."

Fahai spoke sternly. "It is not proper to refuse the concern of the prince, especially in the sight of so many of his subjects."

Zhen looked distraught. His lips finally parted, and he shuddered as he gulped down the acrid-smelling decoction. When he finished, he remained unnaturally still, his eyes closed. His hands were clenched so tightly that his knuckles turned white.

"Zhen?" Qing hurried to his other side. "Are you all right?"

Zhen caught Qing's wrist; his fingers dug so hard into her flesh that she gasped. When he opened his mouth, an unintelligible noise emerged—a guttural breath that sounded almost feral.

Xian jumped to his feet. "Zhen? What's wrong?"

Zhen's eyes rolled back in his head. He twitched like a puppet jerked by invisible strings and toppled to the floor, convulsing with violent spasms. Patches of scaly white bloomed across his face and neck, spreading over his skin.

Xian rushed forward, but Fahai caught his arm. "Stay back, Prince."

Zhen let out a bloodcurdling, inhuman shriek. His limbs began shrinking; it looked as if his bones were melting from their marrow. His torso lengthened with the same frightening speed that his arms and legs vanished. His body grew longer, narrower, and his embroidered robe pooled around his limbless, writhing form. His face contorted as if it had been splashed with acid, altering from human into something grotesque, something reptilian—

Xian stared in horror as a large white snake reared up where Zhen had been. Its scales gleamed, and when it raised its serpentine head, it was more than half the height of a man, its bulky body as thick as a huge pipe. On its left side was a deep, pitted scar several inches in length.

Chaos erupted. People screamed and fell over one another trying to get away. Guards drew their weapons, but even they seemed too afraid to come close.

The white snake's forked tongue flicked out. Its unblinking, brilliant green eyes fixed on Xian.

Feng swung out with his sword. The tip of his blade grazed the snake, leaving a thin line of blood against its bone-white body. The snake hissed and opened its jaws, revealing two rows of sharp, backward-curving teeth.

Feng drew his arm back for another strike—

"No!" Xian wrenched himself out of Fahai's grip and leaped in front of the snake. "Don't attack!"

Everyone froze. Feng looked shocked; his arm halted in mid-air, his blade inches from a fatal stroke across Xian's neck.

Xian felt as if he were underwater again, drowning in the West Lake, the white snake's coils around his body squeezing the last breath from his lungs—

"Don't kill him," Xian blurted out. "I need him alive."

Chapter 23
XIAN

Xian stood alone in the darkness of his chamber. He was still dressed in his lóng páo, which was streaked with dirt from the ride back to the palace. His pulse hammered inside his skull, pounding so hard that his head hurt and he had to shut his eyes.

The oracle had directed him to Changle. The priest had warned that danger was close by. But the white snake had been even closer than Xian realized.

By his side. In his bed.

The signs had all been there: the healed wound on Zhen's left hip, which matched the scar on the white snake that had pulled him out of the West Lake. How Zhen had said he was born in Wuyue and his reluctance to go back there with Xian. His uncanny connection with animals, including Zhaoye and the leopard that had attacked them during the hunting trip.

Back on the dais, Fahai had unleashed a tranquilizer-laced dart that found its mark between the white snake's dorsal scales. The creature had arched and screeched, its body undulating, its powerful tail knocking over footstools even as its movements grew feebler.

When the snake finally stopped moving, the guards locked it inside a large rattan cage.

"Bring it back to the palace," Xian had commanded.

Now Xian opened his eyes. Everything in his chamber was a reminder of Zhen. The teapots Xian had used to show him how to make a cup of pu'er tea. The wooden rack where Zhen had meticulously smoothed out the creases of Xian's lóng páo, the one he was wearing now. The wéi qí board where he had taught Zhen to play. The platform bed where their bodies had tangled with breathless laughter and drawn-out kisses.

With a roar, Xian swept the tea ware off the table. Porcelain cups flew over the edge and shattered on the floor. Teapots smashed, sending shards of purple clay in all directions. He upended the low table with the wéi qí board, which struck the floor with such force that it cracked in half. Black and white stones scattered to the corners and skittered under the bed.

Xian held out his shaking hands and stared at a bleeding cut on his knuckles.

He had found the white snake, but there was no sense of victory. Just the taste of betrayal, bitter as bile in the back of his throat.

When he looked up, Fahai and Feng stood in the open

doorway, their faces somber. Their knocking had probably been drowned out by the sounds of his rampage. They were the only two who would be forgiven for entering without permission.

Xian clenched his hand. The sting of pain was oddly calming. "Has the prisoner been secured?"

"He's locked in the dungeon," Feng replied. "He had transformed into a human again by the time we arrived at the palace, but he's still unconscious."

"I put a collar around his neck," Fahai said. "It's made of bīn steel that has been quench-hardened and tempered until a spiral pattern emerged. The collar has the power to stop him from changing back into a snake and escaping."

Xian let out a sharp, unhinged laugh. "You just happened to have a magical collar up your sleeve, Fahai?"

"No. I procured one when I first had suspicions about Zhen." Fahai's tone was level. "But I didn't want to accuse him until I was absolutely sure. That's where the realgar powder in the decoction came in."

Xian understood. "Snakes cannot tolerate sulfur. That's why he recoiled when we offered him the medicine."

"I added many strong-smelling herbs to mask the realgar, but snakes have an excellent sense of smell," Fahai said. "He must've detected the scent—however, at your insistence, and with all of us watching, he had no choice but to consume the decoction."

"When did you start suspecting Zhen wasn't who he said he was?" Feng asked.

"There was something strange about him from the start," Fahai replied. "What he said about his past, his family . . . something didn't add up."

His family—

"Where's Qing?" Xian demanded.

A flicker crossed Feng's face. "We searched but couldn't find her. Guards are scouring the forests as we speak."

Qing was very likely a snake spirit as well. Zhen hadn't been lying when he said she was his sister. Two snake demons living as humans in the Changle palace. Xian's hands tightened into fists. What a mockery.

"The other day, when he went hunting with us as our guide," Fahai said grimly, "I had a feeling he was actually warning the snakes off."

"But we almost caught one," Feng pointed out.

"It must have panicked and crossed our path by accident." Fahai cut a sidelong look at Xian. "I would not be surprised if Zhen was the one who summoned that leopard to attack Feng as a diversion to allow that snake to escape."

"What does Zhen want?" Feng sounded mystified. "Why did he go to such lengths to infiltrate the palace and get close to Xian?"

"If I didn't know better, I would say it was an act of bad faith by the Min court," Fahai replied. "But Zhen wasn't among the courtesans offered. They couldn't have known the prince would select him. There must be something else the snake is after."

Xian pinched the bridge of his nose. Feng and Fahai didn't

know about the connection forged between him and Zhen that fateful day years ago.

But what about Zhen? At what point had he realized Xian was the boy from the lake?

He must have recognized Xian from the start. And he had used that to his advantage, stealthily charming his way behind enemy lines . . . and Xian had been so besotted that he let his guard down. He hadn't realized he'd been played until it was too late.

Xian looked at Fahai. "Can a white snake spirit be used to create the antidote for my mother?"

Fahai nodded. "If anything, its supernatural abilities will increase the effectiveness of the cure. Possibly the only silver lining in this regrettable situation."

"There is nothing to regret. We finally have what we came for." Xian's tone was implacable. "Fahai, please let Governor Gao know that we will depart for Wuyue at dawn. Feng, make the necessary arrangements so that our delegation is ready to leave with the prisoner in tow. Double our guard for the journey back to Xifu."

"Shall I ride ahead to inform your father?" Fahai asked. "He will be eager to know that we have found what we need for the antidote."

Xian nodded. "Arriving earlier would give you more time to make preparations in your laboratory. You shall leave tonight."

Fahai held out a pair of cuffs. "These will ensure the prisoner does not escape."

Xian eyed the long, fragile chain linking the fetters. "I'd be more comfortable with something sturdier."

Fahai smiled. "Appearances are deceiving, Prince Xian. These are the most secure bonds you can find. They, too, are crafted from bīn steel and reinforced with a dragon-claw lock. No weapon can cut through the metal, and only one key in the world can open the lock."

Xian took the pair of cuffs and their key. So they had magical properties, like the collar. Fahai's knowledge of the arcane served them well.

"The snake spirit may try to bargain for freedom by offering to heal your mother," Fahai continued, his tone grave. "He knows very well that you are seeking a cure above all else, and he may attempt to exploit that. But you must not trust him. If he gets close to her and tries to perform any kind of dark magic, it could cost her life. Do not allow him to deceive you again, Prince."

"I would be a fool to make the same mistake twice," Xian replied, his tone as hard as bīn steel.

Feng cast Xian a concerned glance before he and Fahai exited the room, leaving Xian alone.

Xian stood where he was for a long time, staring at the white and black stones strewn across the floor. The wéi qí board wasn't the only place Zhen had found a weakness in Xian's defenses.

He had to stop thinking of Zhen as a boy he once cared about. That boy never existed. The white snake was his captive, and it would have to pay its debt in flesh and blood. And by the end, it would be crystal clear which of them had really won this game.

Chapter 24
ZHEN

Zhen's eyes cracked open.

Where was he? Was he a snake or a human? Or something else? He didn't know. He had no sense of place or time. His body felt boneless; if he had limbs, he couldn't feel them.

The memories burned like the sulfur in the decoction going down his throat. The excruciating pain of his joints unlocking against his will—the first time he'd had no control over his transformation. Each bone had felt like it was being ripped from its socket, and all he could do was scream and writhe and beg for everything to stop, to end.

He had shouted to Qing in the language of snakes, which humans could not understand, and told her to run. He hoped that, for once, she had listened. He couldn't bear to imagine what they would do if they captured her. He prayed that, by now, she was far, far from wherever he was.

His surroundings gradually materialized from the shadows. He was lying on a cold stone floor, facing a wall. A sickly glow slanted through thick vertical bars. He didn't take long to guess which side of those bars he was on.

He was human again. He shivered, a reminder that he was naked. A threadbare blanket had been thrown over his lower body. His throat felt like he had swallowed briars, and his skull felt as if it had been split apart and fused back together. Probably because it had.

Don't kill him—I need him alive.

A terrible prickle rose over Zhen's bare skin. The chilling tone in Xian's voice as he spoke those words was something he would never forget.

Xian finally knew who Zhen was. *What* he was. Not just a snake, but the monster he had been hunting all these years. The one he blamed for taking away his mother's cure.

When he lifted his head, something cold and hard pressed against his neck. He reached up and brushed his fingers against the metal band that encircled his throat. He could sense the ore's unnatural power suppressing his own. With this collar, he would not be able to change back into a snake.

The equilibrium always finds itself.

As a snake, he'd wanted nothing more than to experience everything human life had to offer . . . and Xian had given him that. Every touch, every breath, every sensation had imprinted on his soul, and each time Xian held him close, their bodies fitting together like two halves of a whole, he wished they could stay that way forever.

That illusion had shattered the moment Xian announced the bounty. A silver tael for every white snake brought to the palace alive. The edict had made the blood in Zhen's veins turn to ice, just like the night when Xian had opened his rattan case of steel instruments reeking of snake blood. Only that horror would be multiplied a thousand times as citizens of Changle swarmed the forests around the capital hunting for snakes, indiscriminately killing those that weren't of the color they were seeking. The shock and dread had been too overwhelming, and Zhen's nose had started bleeding again.

A rustle of footfalls made him stiffen. Instead of a burly guard coming down the flagstone steps, a slender silhouette appeared at the far end of the dungeon. The figure sidled along the wall and halted in front of the cell, revealing a familiar face.

Recognition dawned. "Deng?"

Deng spoke with quiet awe in his voice. "It really was you."

It took Zhen a moment to realize that Deng was talking about what had happened in the outer court on the night of his punishment, when Zhen had transformed into a snake and bitten through his ropes to make his ordeal more bearable.

"What are you doing here?" Zhen climbed to his feet, holding the thin blanket around his waist as he limped toward the bars. "How did you get past the guards?"

"They open the underground tunnels during the summer in case of flooding. I know where they intersect with the dungeon."

Deng moved closer. "I came as soon as I heard what happened at the festival. Are you hurt?"

Was Deng actually here to help him? Zhen could hardly believe it. But he didn't have much of a choice. The number of people in this palace on his side at that moment could be counted on the number of fingers he'd had as a snake.

Deng pointed at Zhen's right side. "You're bleeding."

Zhen looked at the linear cut on his rib cage. The blood had already crusted over. He vaguely remembered a sting of pain when Feng attacked him with his sword on the dais.

"It's just a scratch," he replied. "Did you see Qing, my sister? Did they capture her as well?"

Deng shook his head. Zhen's heart sagged in relief.

"The guards are searching the surrounding forests, but I don't think they've found her," Deng said. "Is she a snake spirit too?"

Zhen ignored his question. "You have to leave now. If the guards find you here, you'll get in serious trouble—"

"I know you put in a good word for me with the prince," Deng interrupted. "It's the only way I could've gotten a lighter punishment. You did that even after I beat you brutally. I owe you a debt of gratitude." He paused. "They said you transformed in the middle of the feast. What happened?"

Zhen grimaced, pushing his long, tangled hair away from his face. "There was sulfur in a tonic the prince asked his adviser to prepare for me." He had detected the scent even though it was heavily masked by other herbs. "Snakes cannot tolerate sulfur."

"People like to mix realgar with white wine during the Duanwu Festival," Deng said. "Wait—did you say that the prince's adviser prepared the tonic for you?"

Zhen nodded. "That's why I couldn't refuse, even though I was afraid of what the sulfur would do to me."

He had thought the sulfur would make him pass out or become seriously ill. He'd never imagined it would set off an uncontrollable transformation.

Deng's brow furrowed. "His adviser came to me the day after my punishment. He demanded to know about the white snake that had appeared in the outer court the night before."

Zhen's heart skipped a beat. "What did you tell him?"

"Nothing. I didn't even know it was you at that time. I just told him a white snake showed up, scared the hell out of me, and slithered off."

Fahai had discovered his secret. He must've seen Zhen transforming back into a human that night. He'd probably figured out that Zhen was warning off the snakes during the hunting trip, and he had added sulfur to the decoction to expose Zhen's true nature in front of everyone.

"Come on, we don't have much time," Deng said. "The tunnels divert floodwaters to the underground canals, and you can follow them to reach the Min Jiang." He started in the direction he had come before glancing back at Zhen. "What are you waiting for? Change into a snake and follow me!"

Zhen pointed at the band of metal around his neck. "I can't transform with this thing on me. It's a magical collar."

Deng looked crestfallen. "Then how do I get you out of here?"

"I don't think you can," Zhen said. "They made sure of that."

Men's voices made them both whirl toward the stairs. Deng's eyes widened in panic.

"You need to go," Zhen told him. "If anyone catches you, I won't be able to help this time."

Deng bit his lip. "I'm sorry. I tried my best."

"I know," Zhen replied. "Thank you."

As Deng vanished like a ghost, Zhen pressed his forehead against the cold metal bars. His former nemesis was the last person he would've expected to come to his aid.

Boots descended the flagstone steps, and the prince's bodyguard came into view. Feng had been distrustful of Zhen from the start, but now his misgivings had been proven right beyond all expectations. Zhen's treachery was, more than anything else, a slap in the face for Feng as the prince's bodyguard.

Xian appeared behind Feng.

Zhen's stomach clenched. Xian's expression, half cast in shadow, was a perfect visage of calm. A true leader did not flinch in the face of anything, not even betrayal. Anyone else would have seen a prince with the power to sentence him to death, but Zhen saw the boy he had never intended to hurt.

As Xian stepped forward, Zhen's fingers tightened around the bars that separated them. "Xian, please—"

"Don't you dare speak the name my mother gave me." Xian's tone was a knife that found its mark between Zhen's ribs, sending excruciating pain through his chest—like he hadn't fully transformed, like he was a human trying to survive with a snake's heart.

"I'm sorry," Zhen whispered.

"Open the cell," Xian ordered the guards.

They unlocked the cell door and roughly dragged Zhen out. The threadbare blanket fell away, exposing his naked, bruised body. A body that Xian had once tenderly touched and kissed. But given the dispassionate way Xian stared at him now, that was all in the past.

A guard thrust a rough gray tunic into his hands, and Zhen lowered his gaze as he clumsily put on the garment. He had nothing left to salvage, not even his pride.

Feng spoke. "I can secure the cuffs on him."

"No," Xian replied. "I want to do it myself."

Xian took out a pair of cuffs connected by a deceptively thin chain, but Zhen could sense the supernatural quality of the metal. Like the collar they'd put around his neck, these cuffs were no ordinary steel.

"Hold out your hands," Xian commanded.

Zhen did as he was told. His fingernails, neatly trimmed and buffed just hours ago, were now caked with dirt and his own dried blood.

Xian snapped the cuffs around his wrists before lifting hard eyes to meet Zhen's. "I did say I wouldn't be going back to Wuyue without you."

Those words were a cruel mockery of what Xian had said to him the morning after they'd made love for the first time.

He should've left immediately after, saved them both from this inevitable outcome. Even snakes knew when to back down from a lost cause.

Such hubris, to think that his deception wouldn't come at a terrible price.

Xian turned on his heel and strode up the flagstone steps without a backward glance.

After the guards had fastened a set of ordinary manacles around Zhen's ankles, Feng moved forward. The steely glint in his eyes was more terrifying than any sword. Zhen was sure Feng would have slain him on the dais if Xian hadn't intervened.

Feng's tone was grim as he spoke. "Take this unworthy creature out to the wagon."

Chapter 25
XIAN

Xian stood alone in front of the Spirit Hall. The sky was still dark, but in the distance, he could hear the neighing of horses and the grind of wagon wheels, the clamor of his delegation preparing to leave at the first light of dawn.

He entered the temple through the dragon door, and the noises from outside fell away. The silence was a knell as resonant as the three-pronged sān qīng bells that Daoist priests tolled during rituals to beckon deities and banish demons.

The cruel words he'd spoken to Zhen in the dungeon rang in his mind with the same copper clarity. Xian had wanted so badly to change his hurt into hate. After Zhen had deceived him, made him a laughingstock in front of the entire Min court and his own entourage . . . he'd thought saying the words out loud right to Zhen's face would extinguish the connection between them.

A prince does not cry, his father had sternly told four-year-old Xian when he ran to the throne chamber in tears after Wang wrestled him to the ground and pulled down his pants while his other half brothers laughed. *A prince does not show weakness.*

A prince should not feel heartbroken.

But seeing Zhen locked inside the cell, shivering and bereft . . . it had almost undone him. Despite everything, Xian still couldn't bring himself to hate the boy responsible for his mother's suffering. How pathetic. How unfilial—

"Prince of Wuyue."

He turned. The priest had emerged from the inner shrine.

"Dao Zhang." Xian bowed. "I am leaving Changle. I have come to give thanks and petition the gods for a safe journey back to my father's palace."

His words were hollow, dutiful, and he had a feeling the priest could tell. The priest, his crinkled eyes unblinking, studied Xian as if he were gazing into his soul. Xian glanced away, unused to feeling so exposed, as if the unseen wound inside him that had ripped wide open when he saw Zhen transform into a snake was clear for all to behold, a badge of shame and dishonor.

"You came in search of the cure for your mother's illness," the priest said. "Are you leaving with what you hoped to find?"

A pang went through Xian.

"Yes," he replied. "At a price."

The priest gave a solemn nod. "You have been betrayed."

Xian blinked. Was it that obvious?

The priest took two jiǎo bēi—crescent-shaped bamboo blocks painted red—and pressed them into Xian's hands. "Perhaps this will give you some clarity of mind."

The jiǎo bēi were always used in pairs. The concave side of each block represented yang, the convex side yin. A pilgrim would ask the gods a question and throw both blocks to the floor. If one came up yin and the other yang, it was shèng jiǎo, the answer of sagehood—the deities were in favor. If both were yang, it meant xiào jiǎo, the answer of derision—the deities were laughing in scorn. If both fell to yin, the deities were displeased—nù jiǎo, the answer of fury.

The priest spoke. "Your doubts may seem insignificant now. You may dismiss them like water disappearing through cracks. But over time, the water will freeze and then thaw, becoming strong enough to break massive rocks apart."

Xian stared at the blocks. A part of him still desperately wanted to believe that he hadn't fallen for the enemy. That the undisguised emotion in Zhen's eyes when he gazed up at Xian as they made love was real . . .

No. None of that was important. The only person who mattered now was his mother. He shut his eyes, his fingers tightening around the two curved bamboo blocks as he silently asked:

Is Zhen the one who will save my mother's life?

He threw the blocks into the air. When they clattered to the floor, the sound echoed sharply through the chamber.

He opened his eyes.

One block was facing up, and the other was facing down.

Xian's heart constricted. Shèng jiǎo. The gods had given their approval.

Zhen was the cure that the oracle had predicted. Fahai would find a way to use him to create the antidote. His mother would live.

A rush of relief went through him as he touched the front of his shirt, where the jade amulet was hidden. But at the same time, there was something else, a spasm of pain deep inside his chest, like a reverse heartbeat that pushed his blood backward, against nature.

Xian forced his misgivings aside. He put his palms together and bowed. "I am eternally grateful for your guidance, Dao Zhang."

As he turned to leave, his heart was as heavy as the gilt bronze statues of deities that surrounded the pilgrims' hall.

You have been betrayed.

The priest was referring to Zhen, but in another way, Xian was a traitor to himself. He had to root out the last treacherous feelings for Zhen that still lingered. But it was as impossible as trying to draw out water that had already slipped through the cracks in his heart.

He walked toward the tiger door, but he was so preoccupied that he almost forgot which leg he was supposed to step with. He halted on the threshold just in time and crossed over the red plank with his right foot.

Chapter 26
XIAN

Dawn broke across a flurry of activity in the outer court as the Wuyue contingent prepared to depart. Fahai had already left the night before. For the return trip, Xian eschewed his official armor in favor of a lighter brigandine that was more comfortable to ride in. The homeward journey would be much faster as they weren't hauling wagons filled with gifts, and Xian wanted to cover as much distance as possible every day. His mother's condition must have deteriorated in the intervening time, and he hoped he would not be too late.

The guards snapped to attention as Xian and Feng inspected the delegation. Their numbers had been doubled as Xian had instructed. In their midst stood an armored wagon built for the transfer of prisoners. The structure and wheels were made of sturdy wood reinforced with metal spikes. A guard sat on a bench in front to drive the two horses.

Xian walked to the barred iron door at the back of the wagon.

Inside, Zhen was curled up in a corner, his knees drawn up to his chest. He looked nothing like the ferocious creature with gleaming white scales and blazing green eyes that had reared up during the festival yesterday. It was almost impossible to believe they were one and the same.

Now Zhen's eyes were morose, hooded with more than just exhaustion. The bīn steel collar glinted around his neck, and his wrists were shackled by the matching cuffs Fahai had provided. His dark hair was a messy tangle framing his pale face, and he was clad in a gray cotton tunic.

I am still unsure exactly what part of the white snake will complete the antidote, Fahai had said, *whether it's its venom, organs, or perhaps even its beating heart.*

When they arrived at the palace in Xifu, Zhen would be brought to the secret laboratory in Leifeng Pagoda where Fahai would find the answer. Which meant this was very likely the last time Xian would see Zhen alive.

An ache rose inside Xian's heart, but he pushed it down. The deities had spoken. The crescent-shaped blocks were fate's answer.

Governor Gao and the senior officials of the Min court bade Xian farewell with the formal fist-and-palm salute. Xian acknowledged their greeting before walking to Zhaoye, who waited at the helm of the delegation. In Fahai's absence, Feng would ride on Xian's left, the most favored position.

At Xian's signal, they rode forth, leaving Changle behind. Xian vowed never to return.

They passed hillsides covered in shrubs and ferns, then plains where herds of water buffalo and elk grazed. The terrain grew rugged and steeper as they entered the forest, but the plum rain had passed and the ground was dry and firm beneath their horses' hooves. The canopy of interlocking branches above their heads shielded them from the midday sun, and the air was cool and crisp, although Xian could detect the faint hint of wood-smoke.

The smell grew stronger as they rode along, and when they rounded a bend, they saw up ahead a massive, hollowed-out log lying in the middle of the clearing, blocking their way. Thick, white smoke rose from holes in the log. There wasn't any chemical odor, just the smell of smoldering wet grass and damp wood.

Zhaoye and the other horses slowed, neighing and hanging back nervously. The path through the forest was flanked by dense walls of pines, and going around the obstacle would be difficult with the armored wagon.

"Get that log off the road," Xian ordered. They didn't have time to waste.

Feng and a few others in the vanguard dismounted and approached the obstruction, and Xian slid from Zhaoye's saddle, his gaze cutting from side to side. Something was off. This wasn't just a fallen tree that had been ignited by a lightning strike or a stray spark. The hollowed-out log had several holes carved along its length, and there wasn't any fire, only copious amounts of smoke that sharply reduced visibility. The wind was blowing toward them, engulfing their delegation in thick clouds.

"Wait," Xian called out, but Feng and the other guards were too far ahead to hear him. Through the haze, he could barely see their silhouettes.

The forest had gone peculiarly still. It was the opposite of the frenzy of hunting—baying of dogs, shrill cries of deer, beating of wings as birds frantically took to flight—and Xian had the distinct, unpleasant feeling that *they* were the ones being stalked.

A man's bloodcurdling scream made Xian whirl around just in time to glimpse what appeared to be dozens of cords falling from the branches over their heads.

But they weren't cords.

They were snakes.

Pandemonium broke out. Horses shrieked and reared as battle-hardened guards howled and threw themselves to the ground as countless snakes latched onto their bodies.

A reddish-brown snake with black stripes landed on Xian's shoulder. He twisted and knocked it away; undeterred, the snake slithered up his left foot, opened its jaws, and sank its fangs into his shin.

Xian yelled and slashed with his sword at its limbless body, drawing blood. The snake hissed and retreated. But more snakes materialized from the underbrush—coiling, limbless waves that swarmed over their entire company. It was the most horrendous battle Xian had ever witnessed, and one side clearly overwhelmed the other.

The horses harnessed to the armored wagon kicked their forelegs off the ground, eyes wild and nostrils flaring as snakes encircled their necks and legs. One horse slammed into the other, causing both to fall over, dragging the wagon along with them—it hit the ground with a resounding crash of splintering wood.

Dread flooded through Xian, colder than the tingling sensation spreading up his leg that the snake had bitten.

Zhen. Xian couldn't let him escape.

"Secure the prisoner!" he yelled, but his words were drowned out by the frantic shouting all around. A panicked horse came out of nowhere and charged toward Xian, and he had to throw himself to the side to avoid being trampled. His sword flew from his hand and landed out of reach.

One of the guards staggered toward Xian, vomited blackish blood, and collapsed. Xian jumped up and rushed to his aid, but the man's eyes rolled in his head and he went still. There were two puncture wounds in his neck.

Xian shouted for Feng; through the fumes and chaos, he couldn't find his bodyguard. He coughed, his eyes watering as he ran to the toppled wagon, which lay on its side. Its barred door had cracked wide open, and the cage was empty.

Zhen was gone.

Xian's heart sank. He looked around desperately, but smoke wreathed his surroundings, making it impossible to see beyond a few feet. Suddenly a paralyzing cramp gripped his left leg; his knee buckled without warning and he fell forward into the dirt.

A hand touched his arm. "Xian?"

He rolled over and found himself looking into Zhen's face.

"Are you all right?" Zhen's gaze traveled down to Xian's leg, twisted at an unnatural angle. "Did you get bitten?"

Xian stared at him in disbelief. Zhen's hands and feet were still shackled, but he didn't appear to be harmed—of course not. This ambush was his doing. Although the collar Fahai had placed on him stopped him from transforming, he must have still been able to summon the snakes as they passed through the forest, calling on them to rise up in terrifying numbers and attack.

But why was Zhen still here? Why hadn't he fled?

The pain in Xian's leg gave way to an icy numbness, which was even more frightening. He couldn't move or feel anything below his left knee. He couldn't stand up. Couldn't defend himself. The only weapon he had was a concealed dagger in a sheath on his right ankle.

Zhen knelt next to him. "Can you walk?" The concern in Zhen's eyes was unmistakable as he took Xian's arm. "Here, let me help you—"

Xian's first instinct was to jerk his hand away from Zhen, but instead he grabbed Zhen's right wrist and dragged him closer. He dipped his other hand into a small pouch on his belt and took out the key to Zhen's cuffs. His fingers were shaking so much that he managed to unlock the cuff only on the second try.

Zhen seemed confused. "Xian, what are you—"

Xian put the open cuff around his own left wrist and snapped it shut. Then he drew back his arm and flung the key as hard as he could. The key sailed through the air and disappeared into the bushes.

Zhen's jaw dropped as he stared at their wrists, now chained together.

Xian glared at him with as much vehemence as he could muster. "I'm not letting you get away again."

Before Zhen could respond, a tall figure in a hooded cloak leaped out from a dense thicket of trees. His face was obscured by a black mask over his nose and mouth, and in his hand he wielded a scimitar.

"Come with me," he said, his voice deep and gruff.

It took Xian a moment to realize the masked man was talking to Zhen, who seemed just as mystified as Xian.

The man's gaze fell on their cuffed hands. His eyes narrowed as he turned to Xian.

"Foolish move, Prince." He sounded like an old man, yet from his agility, he was clearly anything but. "Chaining yourself to your enemy with unbreakable cuffs—I don't think that's what Master Sun Tzu meant by keeping your friends close but your enemies closer."

"Who the hell are you?" Xian demanded.

"Wrong question." The masked man uttered a sharp laugh. "You should be asking yourself how attached you are to your cuffed hand, because it won't be connected to your body for much longer. Perhaps your fate will be closer to another of Master Sun's axioms: If you wait by the river long enough, the bodies of your enemies will float by."

The man drew back his blade. Xian felt his blood draining from his face.

"Wait!" Zhen jumped forward, putting himself between Xian and the man. "Don't!"

Xian blinked.

Similar surprise crossed the masked man's eyes as he looked at Zhen. "You must've hit your head when the wagon crashed. This prince intends to torture you to within an inch of your life when he brings you back to Wuyue as his prisoner."

"I know." Zhen remained where he was. "But I still can't let you hurt him."

Xian couldn't believe his ears. Was Zhen *protecting* him?

"I'm here to take you to a safe place." The masked man's reply was terse. "Can't do that with his arm connected to yours." He gestured at Xian's leg, folded uselessly under him. "He can't walk. The only way to be rid of him is to cut off his hand—"

"No!" Zhen threw himself across Xian's body, shielding him. "I . . . I'll carry him."

Xian was too shocked to react.

"No," the man said flatly. "He can't come with us."

Zhen faced the masked man squarely. "Whoever you are, thank you for trying to rescue me. But if you truly have good intentions, then you will respect my wishes. I cannot let you harm him."

There was exasperation in the man's expression, along with something else that Xian couldn't decipher.

"Stop right there!" One of the guards stumbled toward them.

He was holding a bleeding bite on his shoulder, but he still drew his sword. "Back away from the prince, you brigand!"

The masked man didn't hesitate. He stepped forward and, in a smooth movement, plunged his scimitar into the guard's chest.

The guard's eyes went wide. The masked man pulled out the blade. Bright red blood spewed out of the guard's mouth and dribbled down his chin before he keeled over, dead.

The masked man nonchalantly stepped back as if he had just swatted a fly. Xian's gaze cut toward Zhen, whose face reflected the horror that Xian felt.

"Xian!" came Feng's voice through the smoke. "Xian, where are you?"

Before Xian could call out to his bodyguard, the masked man leaned down and stabbed two fingers to a specific point on Xian's neck. Feng had told him about the diǎn xuè techniques he had learned in Shaolin—an advanced martial arts skill that an attacker could use to immobilize a person from head to toe by simply striking precise acupressure points on his body. Now, not only could Xian not feel his leg, he couldn't move any other part of his body except his eyes.

"We need to get out of here now," the masked man said. In a swift stroke, he brought the blade of his scimitar down onto the ordinary chain that connected the manacles around Zhen's ankles. The iron links shattered, liberating Zhen's feet.

I'm here to take you to a safe place, the masked man had told Zhen.

Zhen seemed genuinely bewildered by the ambush, so if he

wasn't the one who planned everything, who had? Who was this masked man, and how had he managed to marshal the support of the multitude of snakes?

Zhen bent down and slid one arm under Xian's shoulders and the other beneath his knees. The chain between their linked wrists clinked as Zhen lifted him off the ground with surprising strength.

Xian's head lolled to one side. He could hear Feng calling his name as if from a great distance away. But he couldn't shout back.

The masked man plunged headlong into the forest. Zhen followed, carrying Xian in his arms.

Xian caught a last hazy glimpse of the carnage around the overturned wagon. Some guards held their snakebitten limbs and groaned in pain while others lay motionless, like stones in a wéi qí game that had been completely defeated by the enemy.

Chapter 27
ZHEN

Zhen's heart hammered as he weaved between the trees. The broken chains of the manacles around his ankles dragged through detritus of dead leaves on the ground. Every sensation was amplified—the bristle of moss underfoot, the whisper of wind through the leafy dome, the earthy scent of blooms mingled with decay.

Up ahead, the cloaked figure darted swiftly and silently through the forest. He clearly knew not only the terrain but also how to avoid leaving tracks; he stayed off dirt trails, vaulted over fallen logs, ducked under low-hanging branches, and took short-cuts through thickets.

Who was he? There was something strangely familiar about the masked man's voice, his eyes . . . but Zhen couldn't place it. The more important question: Why was he helping Zhen?

Zhen was too out of breath to wonder any further. He huffed under Xian's weight; he seemed to grow heavier with each step Zhen took. The other boy didn't—couldn't—move, but his accusing eyes bore into Zhen. Zhen wanted to reassure him, but he knew nothing he could say could convince Xian.

The masked man halted in front of a thick curtain of vines that hung from a rocky escarpment and almost completely concealed the entrance to a grotto. He pushed the vines aside and gestured for Zhen to go first.

Zhen ducked inside, still carrying Xian. The air in the tunnel was cool, filled with the damp scent of lichens and minerals. Stalagmites protruded from the ground, their tips flat and blunted, while stalactites hung overhead, their pointed edges like daggers.

They ventured deeper until the underground passageway opened into a large cave. Gaps in the overhead rock crevasses allowed shafts of sunlight in. In the center was an impressive column made of a massive stalactite that met a huge stalagmite rising from the base to form a natural pillar.

Qing leaned against the pillar, still wearing the high-waisted green dress from the festival, although her long white sleeves were now streaked with dirt.

Zhen stopped. "Qing?"

"Zhen!" Qing's wide grin promptly vanished when she caught sight of Xian in his arms. "What is *he* doing here?" Her head snapped toward the masked man. "You let him bring *the prince*?"

"I didn't have a choice." The masked man waved his scimitar at Xian's and Zhen's linked wrists. "I wanted to set him free by cutting off the prince's hand, but your gallant friend here refused and insisted on bringing him with us."

Zhen lowered Xian to the ground, their wrists still connected by the cuffs. Qing came forward and threw her arms around Zhen.

"I was so worried," she whispered, burying her face in his neck. "Are you all right? Did they hurt you?"

"Don't worry, I'm still in one piece." He embraced her with his free arm. "Why didn't you leave Changle like I told you?"

"I did," she replied. "I hid in the forest and cried out to the snakes. I told them a white snake spirit was in terrible danger." She nodded at the masked man. "Some of the snakes went to him for help, and he found me in the middle of the night. We came up with a plan to rescue you, and our friends agreed to help."

Zhen was again overwhelmed by that feeling of recognition. He had seen the masked man somewhere before—

"The equilibrium always finds itself, Little White One," the man said.

Zhen's jaw dropped.

"Hei Xing?" he breathed.

The man's eyes crinkled in a smile that was hidden behind his mask. "You remember my name."

"I could never forget," Zhen replied. The name meant "black star"—for the star-shaped design on the shell of the old tortoise from the West Lake. "You saved my life. Again."

"Tortoises and snakes have a close affinity, after all," Hei

Xing said. "The forest was alive with chatter that a white snake spirit was in grave peril at the hands of humans, and I thought to myself, *Could that be the same young white snake I knew in the West Lake? Has he also traveled south to Changle, as I have?* When I met your friend Qing, she told me everything that had happened."

Qing looked at Zhen. "There was something poisonous in the decoction that the prince's adviser made, wasn't there?"

Zhen nodded. "Realgar powder. I could smell it."

Qing frowned. "Then why did you drink it?"

"I thought the skills I cultivated in the past seven years as a snake spirit would be able to counteract the toxin, at least for a short while," Zhen replied. "I never imagined the sulfur would be potent enough to make me transform uncontrollably right there in front of everyone."

Hei Xing spoke. "You need many more years of cultivation before you're strong enough to withstand something so lethal to snakes."

Xian made a scratchy sound in his throat, catching Zhen's attention. He lay on the ground, stiff as a scarecrow, and his face was contorted like he was trying to cough but couldn't.

Zhen looked at Hei Xing. "Can you release the prince's diǎn xuè point?"

"No," Qing said immediately. "I prefer him this way. Silent. Powerless." She stepped forward and glared down at Xian. "Doesn't feel so good, does it, when you're the one at someone else's mercy?"

Xian's eyes stared daggers up at them.

"Qing, he was bitten by a snake," Zhen said. "If he can't move, the toxin in his bite might stagnate and fester. I don't think he's any kind of a threat against the three of us."

"First, I'll take this," Hei Xing told Xian, leaning down and removing the concealed dagger in Xian's ankle sheath. Zhen hadn't even noticed the weapon was there.

Hei Xing tapped two fingers against an acupressure point on Xian's neck. A jerk went through Xian, and his entire body shuddered. His rigid posture relaxed, and his mouth opened in a quiet exhalation. Zhen wondered if he would attempt to fight. But Xian seemed to know there was no use, especially with Hei Xing ready to immobilize him again.

Zhen looked at the chain between their cuffed wrists. "Any idea how to get out of these?"

"That's easy," Qing said. She picked up a twig. "Just transmute this into a skeleton key, like you did when we were locked up by those constables."

"I can't." Zhen pointed at his neck. "This collar suppresses my powers."

Qing turned to Hei Xing. "Can you do something?"

Hei Xing shook his head. "These cuffs are made of unbreakable bīn steel. They have powerful magical properties and can't be unlocked by a transmuted key. Only one key in the world can open the lock, and our smart prince here very helpfully threw it into the forest."

Zhen turned his attention to the snakebite on Xian's leg. The prince wore thick leather boots, which protected his feet, but the snake's fangs had penetrated his riding breeches. There were two swollen puncture wounds on his shin. The fact that Xian wasn't dead right now meant the bite was likely a dry one. Venom glands took time to replenish, and snakes had to be careful not to waste their venom when they weren't hunting. But even the minuscule amount of residual toxin in the dry bite had been enough to disable Xian's leg, which meant the snake that had bitten him was highly venomous. Healing Xian with his spirit powers would have been easy, but with the collar suppressing Zhen's abilities, he'd have to try the human way.

Xian recoiled as Zhen brought his mouth closer to the snake-bite. "What the hell are you doing?"

"I need to get as much of the venom out before it spreads further." Zhen couldn't help thinking of the times his lips had touched other parts of Xian's body, under entirely different circumstances, eliciting a completely opposite reaction . . .

Now he just hoped Xian wouldn't kick him in the face.

He sucked the puncture wound and spat out the bitter copper taste; he repeated the process a few more times before pulling back. Qing looked chagrined. Hei Xing handed him a gourd-shaped water vessel. Zhen rinsed out his mouth, then poured some water onto the snakebite. He tore a strip of fabric from the hem of his own tunic and tied it around the wound. The injury would need a proper poultice, but this would have to do for now.

Qing crossed her arms, narrowing her eyes at Xian. "You don't deserve him."

The expression that flitted across Xian's face was hard to decipher, like trying to count dozens of butterflies in flight.

Zhen looked at Qing and Hei Xing. "Can you two give us a minute?"

"I'll climb to the vantage point above this cave to see if they've picked up our trail," Hei Xing said. "We should leave as soon as possible. I know a safer hiding spot deeper in the mountains."

"I'll ask the snakes to search the forest for the key so we can get rid of this unwanted baggage." Qing shot Xian a hostile stare. "And if you try anything funny while we're away, I'll use your intestines to make one of those decorative knots they sell in the markets."

Xian glowered at her but said nothing. Zhen was sure no one had dared to speak this way to Xian in his entire life.

Qing and Hei Xing exited the cave, leaving Zhen alone with Xian. Some water remained in the gourd-shaped vessel, and Zhen held it out to Xian. "Here. You must be thirsty."

Their fingers brushed briefly as Xian took the bottle. There was no spark, only a bitter reminder of the thrill that used to go through Zhen each time they touched.

Xian drank the last drop before he lowered the vessel. His shoulders sagged, and somehow he seemed . . . smaller, like the boy Zhen had left behind on the islet in the West Lake all those years ago. But his eyes were still fiery when he met Zhen's gaze.

"Did you take the pearl as some kind of payment for saving me from drowning?" he asked.

A pang went through Zhen's chest. "Of course not."

"Then *why*?" Xian's voice echoed off the roughened rocks above and around them. "For once in your life, tell me the truth: Why did you take the pearl?"

Telling the truth would expose a shameful side of the reckless young snake that Zhen once was. But after everything he had put Xian through, Zhen owed him this much.

"I wanted to experience what it was like to be human," he replied. "As a snake I watched humans from the lakes and canals, and I envied your carefree lives, the way you could sing, dance, laugh, and . . . love."

The silence was barbed, sending a chill across Zhen's skin.

"That pearl was meant to heal my mother." Xian's tone was dangerously soft. "And you took it because you wanted to know what it was like to walk on two legs and screw boys?"

Zhen flinched. Xian was their captive, but the deadly flash in his eyes made Zhen feel like he was the one at Xian's mercy.

"If you hadn't stolen the pearl, my mother would have been cured seven years ago," Xian continued. "Because of you, she has suffered far longer than she had to, and now she's dying. I want you to remember this: Nothing, *nothing* in this world can ever make up for what you've done."

If only Zhen could turn back time—if he had never taken the pearl that day, Xian would've had it with him when he was rescued, and they would've used the pearl to heal his mother. Zhen would have continued to live as an ordinary snake in the West Lake, gazing wistfully at the people walking across the Broken Bridge, and Xian would have lived the past seven years without guilt and anger over his mother's illness. He and Xian would never have met in Changle, would never have drunk pu'er tea together or played wéi qí or kissed . . . Zhen's life would not have been so unforgettable, yet he would have made that exchange in a heartbeat. The sacrifice would've been worth it.

Qing burst into the cave, breaking into Zhen's thoughts. "Found it!"

She waved a key triumphantly. Xian looked stunned.

"How did you find it so quickly?" Zhen asked.

"One of my fellow pit vipers saw the key sailing through the air and watched it land in the bushes," Qing replied. "She figured it had to be important, so she got it and brought it straight to me. Hunter's instinct."

She gave the key to Zhen. With a smooth click, the cuff around his wrist fell open. Before Zhen could do anything else, Qing reached out and snapped the open cuff around Xian's other wrist, chaining his hands together.

"We have a problem," Hei Xing's voice called.

They turned as Hei Xing appeared from the opposite end of the cave, looking grim.

"The prince's bodyguard is coming our way with reinforcements," Hei Xing reported. "Some guards must have escaped, gone back to Changle, and raised the alarm. They're armed with sulfur powder, which they're spreading along the forest trail as they advance. The snakes won't be able to help us this time."

Qing looked panicked. "What should we do?"

Hei Xing pointed at the opening in the rocks through which

he had just come. "This is the only way out. It leads through the heart of the mountain and emerges on the other side."

"Let's go," Zhen said. "We'll leave Xian here for his bodyguard and their men to rescue—"

"Are you out of your mind?" Hei Xing retorted. "You were the one who wanted to bring him along, and he's the reason they're so close on our heels. Now you want to let him go?"

"He can't walk with that snakebite!" Zhen replied. "I'm not sure how far I can carry him."

Hei Xing let out an exasperated noise. He dropped to his knee and put a hand on Xian's injured leg—from the dawning incredulity in Xian's eyes, Zhen realized that Hei Xing was using his spirit powers to heal him.

"He's the only leverage we have." Hei Xing grabbed Xian's collar, dragged him roughly to his feet, and shoved him forward. "If they catch up to us, we will need to barter him for our freedom."

Xian stumbled, still unsteady on his newly healed left leg.

Zhen immediately caught him. "Are you all right?"

Xian jerked his arm out of Zhen's grasp. "Don't touch me."

"I'm not going to ask as nicely as him." Hei Xing leveled his scimitar in Xian's face. "Move. *Now*."

They escaped through the narrow archway in single file. In front of Zhen, Xian walked with a slight limp, as if he hadn't fully regained feeling in his leg. Snakes lived in burrows and dens, so Zhen was used to navigating in cramped underground spaces, but Xian kept bumping his head on the low ceiling as the passage rose and dipped, veering this way and that.

They finally emerged into another cavernous subterranean chamber, this one bisected by a wide chasm that was bridged by a thin neck of rock. They stopped at the brink of the divide. Zhen's foot knocked over a small stone, which echoed several times as it fell before abruptly fading out.

Hei Xing spoke. "I hope none of you are afraid of heights."

Qing and Zhen exchanged dubious looks. There was no way out but through.

Hei Xing went first, holding a torch, followed by Qing, then Xian. Zhen brought up the rear. The bridge was about three feet wide, although it felt a lot narrower with the sheer drop on either side.

Halfway across, Xian suddenly tripped. He stumbled forward, but his left leg wasn't strong enough to bear his weight—

Zhen's stomach lurched. "Xian!"

Xian teetered at the edge just before falling over.

Zhen threw himself forward and grabbed both of Xian's cuffed hands. Everything happened fast; if Zhen hadn't possessed the reflexes of a snake, Xian would've plunged too far for Zhen to reach him.

Qing spun around. "Zhen!"

From the direction of the cave they had left behind came the rumble of boots and men's voices. Their pursuers had found them and were gaining ground—

"Let him go!" Hei Xing called out from his position in front. "We don't have time for this!"

Xian's eyes were wide with horror as he clung to Zhen's hands. "Zhen—"

Zhen looked at Qing and Hei Xing. "Both of you, go ahead without me."

"No!" Qing yelled. "I'm not going anywhere without you!"

"Listen to me, Qing!" Zhen's voice was labored from the effort of holding Xian's full weight. "Run. Don't look back."

A small stone whistled through the air and struck the back of Zhen's hand like the bite of a flying serpent. The sharp pain made him loosen his grip a fraction.

One of Xian's palms slid out of his grasp.

"Xian!" Zhen's head snapped toward Hei Xing as another stone was fired at him. It narrowly missed his other hand, the only thing stopping Xian from plunging into the infinite, empty depths. "Hei Xing, what are you doing?"

Hei Xing's eyes blazed in his masked face. "Drop the prince!"

"No!" Zhen shouted. "I left him behind once—I won't make the same mistake again!"

"I'm not leaving you!" Qing rushed forward, but Hei Xing grabbed her arm. She snarled, trying to extricate herself from his grip.

"Over there!" came Feng's voice behind them. Running footsteps approached the bridge.

"Take Qing and *get out!*" Zhen roared.

Hei Xing let out a frustrated growl. He hoisted a struggling Qing over his shoulder and sprinted toward the other end of the bridge, where a trace of daylight lit the route to freedom. With a swish of his dark cloak and a last glimmer of Qing's green dress, they were gone.

Xian stared up at Zhen, his legs swinging wildly over the abyss that yawned below. Their joined palms were sweaty, and Xian's hand was slipping out of Zhen's—

"I've got you," Zhen whispered. Below him, Xian strained to clasp Zhen's other hand—their fingertips touched, but neither of them could manage a firm grip. "I won't let you go—"

Feng finally reached them. He leaned forward and grabbed Xian's arm, and together, with a grunt of effort, they hoisted Xian back onto the bridge.

"Xian!" Feng caught his best friend's shoulders in both hands, and Zhen could see the worry and relief shining in his eyes. "Are you all right? Are you hurt?"

Xian's face was ashen, his gaze filled with disbelief as he looked at Zhen.

Before either of them could say anything, the guards accompanying Feng grabbed Zhen and dragged him away from Xian. They slammed him facedown, and one of them shoved his knee painfully into Zhen's back. Zhen didn't resist as they twisted and bound his arms behind him.

He had been given a second chance to make the right choice— and this time, he had stayed by Xian's side.

Chapter 28
XIAN

Xian brought the cup of bái jiǔ to his lips and drank, letting the liquid blaze a trail down his throat. White liquor was strong and meant to be taken with food, not on its own, but the dishes on the table were still untouched. He had dismissed everyone, and they left him alone in the finest room in the inn at their first way station.

Five guards were dead, fourteen injured. But instead of returning to Changle to regroup, Xian had chosen to press on with the journey. They had already lost enough time that day. The goal remained unchanged: reach Wuyue as soon as possible.

There was a comfortable wooden armchair in the room, but he had opted to sit on the floor. He stretched out his bandaged left leg. A mild tingling of nerves was all that remained of the snakebite healed by the masked man. A physician had pronounced the wound clean and applied a salve of herbs.

An image of Zhen's mouth drawing out the venom from his snakebite flashed in Xian's mind. There was nothing romantic or titillating about the dark blood on Zhen's lips as he spit, but somehow it had meant more than any of the kisses Zhen had given him.

I left him behind once—I won't make the same mistake again!

Zhen had saved his life. When his masked accomplice shot stones at him to force him to let Xian fall, Zhen had refused to leave Xian's side even if it meant being recaptured. Even when it meant being separated from Qing, the only family he had. A choice as inexplicable as the tangle of feelings that Zhen still evoked in him.

Xian stood, gingerly putting weight on his injured leg. He grabbed the handle of the jug of bái jiǔ and walked to the door. The guards outside his room stood at attention as he left and made his way out of the inn.

Next to the barn where their horses were stabled was a new armored wagon that Feng had requisitioned from Changle. Feng himself was standing watch; after the debacle earlier that day, the royal bodyguard was taking no chances.

Feng looked resigned when he saw Xian, as if he'd known he would show up sooner or later.

"You should be resting." His brow furrowed as his gaze fell on the jug in Xian's hand. "And you certainly shouldn't be drinking."

"I want to talk to him," Xian said.

Feng uttered a small sigh. He stepped aside, and Xian approached the barred door.

Zhen was curled up in the corner of the cage. Back on the

underground bridge, Zhen had surrendered without a fight and handed over the key to unlock Xian's cuffs. They now encircled his own wrists, glinting like the collar around his neck that forced him to stay in human form.

Zhen blinked when he caught sight of Xian. He was clothed in a clean gray tunic, although his long, dark hair was still disheveled. His forearms and elbows were covered in scrapes, probably chafed raw by the rocky edge where he had held on to Xian and promised not to let him go.

Xian spoke in Feng's direction. "Open the door."

"What?" Feng sounded appalled. "Xian—"

"You were there," Xian said. It didn't matter that Zhen could hear them. "He could've escaped. He didn't."

Feng still looked incredibly put-upon, his bodyguard's instincts clearly warring with Xian's order. Xian raised his chin, as if challenging his best friend to defy his command. A moment passed before Feng took out the key to the wagon. Its hinges creaked as he opened the door.

Zhen emerged, his expression wary as he set his shackled feet on the ground. Even as a prisoner, he still possessed a kind of grace, a sort of dignity that refused to be crushed.

Xian nodded toward a stone bench a distance away. Feng's disapproving stare followed them as they walked toward the bench. Zhen's bonds clinked as he moved, the new set of manacles around his feet stopping him from taking more than small steps.

Xian wasn't sure why he had asked for Zhen to be let out

of the wagon. Maybe it was the recklessness of the alcohol. Or maybe he knew that he just couldn't have this conversation with Zhen through iron bars.

They sat side by side on the bench. Out of the corner of Xian's eye, he could see Feng standing guard several feet away, his hand poised on the hilt of his sword. The dim outline of woodlands lay ahead, demarcated by the watershed of mountains. Was it a mockery to bring Zhen to this spot, within view of his forest home, knowing he could not return?

Zhen broke the silence. "You're drunk."

Xian let out a humorless sound. He brought the jug to his lips and drank straight from the mouth. His father would've been appalled.

"You should try some." He shook the jar of bái jiǔ—there was about half left—and held it out to Zhen. "Don't worry, there's no realgar in it."

Zhen didn't move for a long time. Just as Xian was about to withdraw his hand, Zhen reached out and took the jug by its neck. Their fingers touched—a sense memory of something that was now beyond reach.

Xian watched as Zhen drank deeply, like a condemned man on the eve of his execution. He was surprised that the other boy could stomach the strong, burning liquor without coughing. Perhaps he had learned to drink, on other prior occasions when he had taken on human form. It occurred to him, now, how little he really knew about Zhen, about the life he had lived in these past seven years. Before their paths had crossed again in

Changle, had Zhen already experienced as a human everything he wished for?

Zhen passed the jug back to Xian, who surreptitiously touched the rim of the jug to his lips. Maybe it was his imagination, but the warmth of Zhen's mouth still lingered, like the ghost of a kiss.

Zhen looked down at Xian's bandaged leg. "Are you all right?"

Xian turned to face him. "Your friends wanted you to choose your freedom over my life. Why didn't you?"

They were close enough to touch, but the distance between them felt vast, uncrossable.

"What you said was true," Zhen replied quietly. "Nothing will ever make up for what I took from you. I don't expect what I did to change anything."

A knot formed in Xian's throat. He wanted to believe that everything Zhen said were lies—but as he had dangled over the edge, his legs kicking a thousand feet above nothingness, he had stared into the other boy's eyes and seen only honesty.

Xian drew a breath and steeled himself. "Before we left Changle, I went to the temple. I asked the gods to give me a sign, and they did. I have to bring you back to Wuyue. You are the cure that will save my mother's life."

Zhen's expression became earnest. "You saw how Hei Xing cured your snakebite so you could walk." He dropped his voice so Feng wouldn't hear. "Our spirit abilities allow us to heal. I once healed Qing when she was badly injured. I could try to do the same for your mother—"

The snake spirit may try to bargain for freedom by offering to heal your mother. Fahai's warning echoed in Xian's mind. *But you must not trust him. If he gets close to her and tries to perform any kind of dark magic, it could cost her life. Do not allow him to deceive you again.*

"No," Xian said.

A shadow of hurt crossed Zhen's face. "You think I'm a monster."

"I don't," Xian replied. "You saved my life even though you didn't have to. But I can't let you near my mother. Don't make this harder than it has to be."

As Xian got to his feet, he felt a tug on his sleeve.

"Xian—"

Zhen broke off, and Xian blinked at the glint of a blade at Zhen's neck.

In a split second, Feng had moved forward and leveled his sword at Zhen's throat. "Take your hands off him."

Zhen swallowed hard and stepped back, holding up his shackled hands. His eyes shone in the darkness as they met Xian's.

Xian held the other boy's gaze.

"Goodbye, Zhen." He glimpsed the other boy's shattered expression before he turned to Feng. "Summon the physician to tend to the injuries on his arms."

Xian had to muster every ounce of willpower not to look back as he walked toward the inn.

He returned to his room and sat heavily on the floor, letting the empty jug fall from his hand. The vessel landed on its side with a dull thunk and rolled a couple of feet away.

Xian had wanted so badly to bring Zhen back with him to Wuyue. But he had never imagined it would be like this. Caged in a wagon. Chained hand and foot, a shameful collar around his neck to keep him from reverting to his true nature.

A prince should not feel heartbroken.

He raised his scratchy voice. "Guard."

One of the guards came into the room with a brisk bow. "Yes, Your Highness?"

Xian pointed at the empty wine jug lying close to his out-stretched leg.

"Get me another," he said.

They arrived at the palace in Xifu at dusk on the eighth night of the journey. By then, the town was already buzzing with news about the white snake the prince was bringing back to Wuyue, which in human form had been his attendant and likely also his paramour.

Xian wasn't concerned. Let them talk. This wasn't the first time people had gossiped about his love life, and it certainly wouldn't be the last. The important thing was that no one knew the truth about what really happened after the ambush. The attack on their delegation was too major an event to obfuscate—but in the official version, Xian had pursued Zhen through the forest and cornered him in the underground cave while his accomplices had fled.

No one except Feng, who had reached them first on the bridge, knew that Zhen was recaptured only because he had stayed behind to save Xian's life.

Most people speculated that Xian had brought the snake spirit back to the palace to be subdued by the priests or sacrificed to the gods. Only a handful knew where the white snake was really being imprisoned.

Feng escorted the wagon to Leifeng Pagoda, where Fahai would be waiting, and Xian headed back to the palace on the pretext of needing to speak to his father. The truth was that he couldn't bear to personally hand Zhen over to the fate that awaited him.

When Xian arrived at the palace, General Jian informed him that his father had invited monks from Goryeo to seek blessings from their ancestors and pray for his mother's recovery. The king was observing their rites behind the closed doors of the Ancestral Temple and had given strict orders that they were not to be disturbed.

Since Xian would have to wait until the morning to see his father, he headed straight to his mother's quarters. Her handmaids bowed as he entered her bedchamber. When he stepped around the folding screen, he saw his mother lying in bed instead of sitting against the headboard.

"Niang Qin," he greeted her. "I have returned."

In a month, she had grown visibly weaker, like the waxy green leaves of a lotus starting to shrivel at the edges. But her smile still shone like the elegant petals of a lotus flower.

She held out her thin arms. "Xian'er."

Xian hugged her. She seemed so fragile in his embrace. But not for long. She would recover. The gods had decreed it. He had brought back the cure . . . even though he felt as if he had lost as much as he had found.

"How are you feeling?" he asked.

"I promised I would stay in good health to wait for you to come home," she replied. "Was your journey to Changle a success?"

Xian pushed down a sharp pang. "Everything went as planned."

"That's wonderful. Your father will be pleased." She beamed. "And I am, as always, ever so proud."

He took her hand in both of his. "Did you make zòng zi for the Duanwu Festival?"

"Not this time," she replied. "I wasn't in the mood without you around to help me."

Xian guessed she had been too weak.

"Just as well," she added. "I would've missed chiding you for denting the dumplings as you tied them."

Xian smiled in spite of himself. "I give you my word that I will help you next year. And I solemnly promise I will eat all the dumplings that I dent."

His mother chuckled. "Mischievous boy. That will only give you incentive to dent more of them!" She stretched out her hand, her bony fingers trembling, and touched his cheek. "There's something different about you. Did anything unusual happen in Changle?"

I fell in love with the one responsible for prolonging your suffering for seven years, Xian couldn't say. *And I still can't bring myself to hate him.*

His mother's expression turned furtive. "Ah . . . I know that look. Did you meet someone special?"

Xian wished everything were so simple. That Zhen was just

an ordinary boy he had met in Changle and fallen in love with, someone he could bring back to the palace and introduce to his mother as his beloved. Instead, Zhen was imprisoned under Leifeng Pagoda, and his mother would never meet him or know his name.

She squeezed his hand. "Oh, all right. Keep your secrets. I know you'll tell me when the time is right."

If his mother knew the true price of her healing, it would grieve her. They would always have to keep this secret from her.

"The hour is late." Xian leaned forward and kissed her forehead. "I'll come and visit you again in the morning."

When he exited her bedchamber, Feng was waiting in the corridor. The handmaids stole surreptitious glances at him. Xian signaled toward the garden, and they stepped outside.

"Were there any problems?" Xian asked.

"Everything went smoothly," Feng replied. "Fahai was waiting for us at the pagoda. Zhen didn't put up any resistance when we handed him over." He hesitated. "What's Fahai going to do to him?"

"I don't know." Xian wasn't sure he wanted to. "Whatever he needs to do to make the antidote." Out of the corner of his eye, he caught a flash of a topknot darting from behind a jujube bush at the far end of the garden. "Who's there?"

The figure ducked into the shadows, slipped into a side corridor, and vanished.

"The gardeners should not be working at this late hour," Feng said with a frown. "I'll have a word with your mother's guards to be on the lookout for any intruders."

Xian looked at Feng. "Did Zhen say anything before you left?"

Feng shook his head.

After the first night at the inn, Xian had not gone to see Zhen again. There was nothing left to be said, and he couldn't afford to drink himself into a stupor every evening when he had to ride from dawn to dusk the next day.

Feng spoke. "You still care about him."

It wasn't a question but a statement. Xian turned away so Feng wouldn't see through him, even though his best friend knew him too well.

"It doesn't matter," he replied. "Not anymore."

Chapter 29
ZHEN

Zhen opened his eyes. A strange, dull pressure throbbed inside his head. The gray stone ceiling swam above him—it took him a moment to realize it was actually the floor.

He was suspended upside down in the center of a vast, windowless chamber. The manacles and cuffs were gone; instead, chains around his ankles were attached to a hook, which was rigged to a complicated pulley system anchored to the ceiling. His arms were bound by his sides with rope.

He turned his head to get a better look at his surroundings. A narrow flight of steps led down from a level above, and flickering oil lamps threw shadows across the bas-reliefs of deities carved on the walls. This place must have been used by Daoist monks as some kind of meditation hall. Probably underground, judging from the stale, musty scent.

Directly beneath him was a perfectly circular pool, like a black moon sunk into the stone floor. The surface of the pool was faintly disturbed even though the air in the chamber was oppressively still, which meant the agitation had to be coming from within its depths.

The sound of hinges grinding made Zhen look up. Footsteps descended the flight of stairs, and Fahai came into view.

Zhen remembered Feng's stoic expression as he had handed him over to Fahai at the base of the pagoda. Fahai had waited for Feng to leave before he clamped a handkerchief soaked in some kind of acrid chemical over Zhen's nose and mouth. Zhen had choked as burning fumes filled his nostrils and throat . . . then he had woken up here.

Fahai's eyes glittered as he waved at the stone chamber around them.

"Monks used to spend hours, days, even weeks down here, cultivating martial arts skills." It was as if the court adviser had removed his mask of geniality, and beneath lay something ruthless. "A snake spirit like you would be familiar with xiū liàn—the mystical practice of cultivation that can lengthen one's life, increase one's powers, and, finally, bestow immortality."

Fahai pulled a lever on the wall. The contraption on the ceiling, which was rigged to the chains around Zhen's feet, began to move. Cogs turned, pulleys creaked, and Zhen's stomach lurched as he found himself being slowly lowered . . .

"Seven years ago, you took something very precious that didn't belong to you," Fahai said. A chill coursed up Zhen's spine.

Xian must have told his court adviser everything. "The pearl you consumed has immense power that is worth five hundred years of cultivation. You foolishly squandered some when the pearl turned you into a snake spirit, but there should be at least three hundred years left, which is more than enough."

More than enough for what? Was there a way to give back the pearl's power after it had been swallowed? Is that what Xian meant when he said Zhen was the cure that would save his mother's life?

"The pearl is divine, and once consumed, its purity and strength cannot be forcibly taken from the person who possesses it," Fahai replied, as if guessing the questions running through Zhen's mind. "You must surrender its power willingly, which obviously you will not do. That's where this cultivation pool comes in."

A dark, ancient aura seemed to emanate from its depths, a cold whisper of sinister power that made Zhen's skin prickle.

"This cultivation pool is one of only a few that exist in the world." Fahai watched Zhen's descent toward the pool, now unnaturally calm. "It has the ability to accelerate the cultivation process, which is why monks built the pagoda above this underground chamber—to keep the pool secret from all except those who are worthy."

Zhen raised his eyes as the pool steadily drew closer. Its surface gleamed opaquely, like the inverse of a mirror, drawing in light and reflecting none.

"I've spent a lot of time and energy altering the fundamental nature of this pool," Fahai continued. "Now, instead of enhancing cultivation, the waters will gradually draw out the pearl's power—and by the end of seven days, the essence of the pearl will have been fully extracted from your body."

Zhen was just a couple of feet above the pool—panic set in and he struggled, but it was useless.

"I had to remove the bīn collar inhibiting your abilities, otherwise the pool would not be able to absorb your power," Fahai added. "But once you have been submerged for the first time, you will not be able to change form."

Up close, the pool glinted like black ice. Zhen sucked in a sharp breath and squeezed his eyes shut as he plunged headfirst into the water.

Except it wasn't water. Zhen had never experienced anything like this. His entire being was swallowed up by something intense, unspeakable, empty—like falling into another universe, another eternity. The darkness seemed to enter his nostrils, reaching deep into his core and siphoning away a sliver of his soul—

He felt a distant jerk at his ankles and was yanked out of the pool, gasping and convulsing like a fish struggling on a hook. He shivered uncontrollably, as if he had been submerged in a frozen lake. His teeth were chattering and he couldn't speak, could barely breathe . . .

When he raised his head, Fahai was standing by the lever, wonderment on his face, as if Zhen were an experiment that showed great promise.

"The mechanism is steam-powered by the furnace in the

laboratory above us," he told Zhen. "It will immerse you in the pool at regular intervals. Not long enough for you to drown, of course. We certainly wouldn't want that."

"Does Xian know?" Zhen's voice was hoarse, his breath still coming in harsh stabs. "What you're doing?"

Fahai uttered a laugh. "Why do you think he didn't bring you to me personally?"

Don't make this harder than it has to be.

Cold realization crystallized in Zhen's heart, jagged as hoarfrost. Xian knew. That was why he hadn't come to see him during the rest of the journey after the first night. Why he'd sent Feng to deliver him to Fahai.

Goodbye, Zhen.

The pulley system on the ceiling began to move, lowering him again. Zhen shut his eyes in dread as he sank closer to the pool. He braced himself just before he touched the surface and let the blazing dark engulf him whole.

Chapter 30
XIAN

The next morning, Xian entered the king's chamber dressed in his golden-yellow court robe. Fahai was already there. The incense that wafted from the burners on either side of his father's throne made Xian recall standing in the temple just before he left Changle, inhaling the same sweet, woody scent while he had asked the question inside his mind.

Is Zhen the one who will save my mother's life?

Fate had given its answer in the form of two crescent-shaped blocks lying on the floor, one facing up and the other down.

As Xian approached the throne, he raised his eyes to the wooden plaque, behind which was the sacred box with the name of the king's chosen heir.

"Father." He bowed low. "I have returned."

"General Jian reported that your delegation was attacked by

snakes on the journey back from Changle." His father leaned forward, looking concerned. "You were brave but foolhardy to single-handedly chase after the snake spirit and its allies before Feng and the other guards caught up."

"Royal Bodyguard Feng deserves special commendation for the way he handled the situation," Xian replied. "We did not allow that delay to deter us from bringing the captive back."

Fahai dipped his head in Xian's direction. "I'm relieved to see that you are well, Prince."

"Fahai has just finished giving me a detailed account of your decisive actions in the Min court." The king gave Xian an approving nod. "Despite various unexpected events, you carried out your mission to bring back the cure that the oracle had predicted."

"Thank you, Father," Xian replied. "I could not have succeeded without Counselor Fahai's wisdom and guidance."

Fahai spoke. "Your Majesty, I have already begun the process of creating the antidote. It will be ready seven days from now."

Xian's stomach churned. He should be gratified that his mother's healing was finally within reach. But the thought of whatever Zhen was going through now—what he would have to endure for the next seven days—

One day for each year that his mother had unnecessarily suffered, he tried to remind himself.

"The monks from Goryeo are leaving tomorrow, and they have been asking to meet you," Xian's father said to Fahai. "A lavish feast is at odds with their ascetic vows, so arrange for the best vegetarian dishes to be served to them in my dining chamber."

Fahai bowed. "Yes, Your Majesty."

The king turned to Xian. "You should rest after the long journey. You are excused from the meal tonight. Wang will attend as the representative of the princes."

After the meeting ended, Xian and Fahai exited the king's hall together. Fahai halted on the terrace and looked at Xian somberly.

"I was shocked to hear about the ambush," he said. "Zhen's accomplices should be brought to justice for daring to attack a royal delegation. I'm relieved to see that you emerged from the ordeal unscathed."

Xian glanced over his shoulder to make sure no one was within earshot.

"Extracting the cure . . ." Xian hesitated. "Will it hurt him?"

Fahai tilted his head. "You're still concerned about his welfare?"

"I just don't want him to suffer more than he has to."

Fahai put a hand on Xian's shoulder. "I give you my word."

"Well, if it isn't the golden boy returned from Changle," a sneering voice said behind them.

Xian turned. Wang stood there, arms crossed over the front of his yellow robe. His hair was tied in a bun crowned with his guān lǐ headpiece. On the outside, he seemed the consummate future crown prince, the tall, handsome firstborn who excelled in studies and swordsmanship.

"Hello, Wang," Xian said. "Father told me that while I was

away, you acquired several priceless sutras for his collection from a merchant from Nihon."

Wang flashed a simpering smile. "In addition to hosting the monks from Goryeo and holding meetings with magistrates from Huzhou prefectures."

"Yes, I heard about that too," Xian replied. "The magistrates reported having problems with cattle husbandry, didn't they? Farmers are refusing to castrate bull calves with undesirable traits? Good to hear you had your hands full with cattle balls while I was gone."

Anger flared in Wang's eyes. If they were younger, he would have dragged Xian off somewhere and pummeled him. But they weren't children anymore. Not since Xian defeated him, by the narrowest of margins, in the sword-fighting championships in front of the entire royal court, including their father and Wang's mother. Xian had been fifteen, Wang eighteen. That was when his eldest half brother had stopped seeing him as a child to bully and as a challenger for the throne.

Fahai shot Xian a look that said, *Stop baiting your brother.* "I shall take my leave. Prince Wang, we will see each other this evening at the farewell meal for your father's guests."

As Fahai walked away, Wang stepped forward, getting right up in Xian's face.

"A prince cavorting with a boy who turned out to be a snake demon." Wang's voice was filled with contempt. "Everyone is talking about it. What a disgrace you are. Father must be so ashamed."

Xian stiffened but stood his ground. "Fahai and I just met with

Father, and he declared the diplomatic mission to Changle a success. So perhaps you should mind your own business."

"What's that saying again? Gè huā rù gè yǎn?" Wang's mouth twisted. "'Different flowers catch different eyes' . . . and you've always had the most sordid preferences. One can overlook your choice of gender, but species?"

Xian's hand darted out and shoved Wang's shoulder. He instantly regretted letting his half brother know he had touched a nerve, but it was too late.

Wang made a show of stumbling a couple of steps back before breaking into a knowing grin.

"They say the travesty of nature you brought back was taken to the palace prison." He gazed pointedly in the direction Fahai had gone. "But I think I know where your reptile lover is really being held."

The hairs on the back of Xian's neck stood on end, but he forced down the flicker of panic that rose within him. Wang couldn't possibly know about Fahai's secret laboratory in Leifeng Pagoda. But Xian's lack of swift retort was telling, and Wang was too smart to miss it.

"I suppose one must excuse your poor taste in bedmates." Wang dusted off the shoulder that Xian had pushed. "After all, no one would expect the son of a lowborn concubine to have any standards."

Rage ignited inside Xian's head like saltpeter exploding in a hollow bamboo firecracker. Feng had taught him how to hit his opponent's nose hard enough that it would be crooked for life.

Every time Wang looked in the mirror, he would remember he never should've dared to speak that way of Xian's mother—

Xian clenched his jaw. There was no use lashing out. Few rules in Confucian teaching were more sacred than showing honor to older relatives—which included siblings.

Xian raised his chin, his eyes lethal as they met his half brother's. Then he turned on his heel and strode in the opposite direction, his boots echoing sharply on the white marble.

Xian entered the martial arts training hall alone, still fuming. Feng had told him never to practice from a place of anger; progress could only come from a calm, focused mind, and he wouldn't improve if he used negative emotions as fuel. But Xian needed to vent, to act out what he'd wanted to do to his smirking half brother's face earlier.

He changed into a sparring robe and walked to the mù rén zhuāng, a wooden training post invented by a master from Shaolin. The post had four protruding slats at different heights and angles, meant to represent the position of a person's arms and legs. The slats were springy, absorbing and returning the energy of each blow to mimic an opponent's blocking movements.

The truth was, it wasn't just anger. Anger was straightforward—a wildfire blazing skyward, destroying everything in its path and dying out when all the wood had turned to ash. What burned inside Xian's chest was more complex, like a peat fire—spreading unseen beneath the surface and consuming fossils of dead things as it continued to smolder even under snow-covered ground.

Xian struck the training post with ferocity, pivoting seamlessly from one stance to another. But his concentration was fragmented, like a sea of broken ice. He hit the wooden targets harder than he should have, even though he knew he would either injure himself or tire himself out.

"Stop. Your form is way off."

Xian paused as Feng walked into the training hall.

"What are you doing here?" Xian wiped the sweat from his brow. "We're not supposed to have a practice session today."

"I've been searching all over for you," Feng replied. "Wang is unwell, and your father wants you to take his place at the farewell meal for the monks from Goryeo. It starts in less than an hour, so you should clean up and get ready."

Xian frowned. Wang had looked perfectly fine earlier. That pompous ass would not want to miss such a prestigious event, especially when he knew his place would go to Xian.

Feng must have caught his expression. "What's wrong?"

"I think the person eavesdropping on us last night outside my mother's chamber was Wang," Xian replied. "He confronted me today, acting smug, and he seems to know more about Zhen than he should."

"Why would Zhen matter to him, though?" Feng asked. "We both know your brother isn't the type to get caught up in anything unless he can twist it to his own selfish purposes. Even if your father knew that you and Zhen were together in Changle, I doubt it would affect your chances of being chosen as his heir."

Gossip about Xian's dalliances with boys had probably reached his father's ears long before he traveled to Changle; Wang would've made sure of that. Fulfilling one's royal duty while still cherishing one's true love—his father would understand that better than anyone else. Zhen's gender wouldn't affect Xian's standing as a potential heir as much as the embarrassment of the way Zhen had deceived him would.

"Wang is up to something, and I need you to find out what that is," Xian said. "I have to attend the meal—it would be a disgrace to my father if neither of his most favored sons showed up. But Wang clearly wants me occupied tonight so he can do something without interruption. Follow him. I'll come up with an excuse to leave early. Meet me at my chamber half an hour after the meal begins."

Chapter 31

XIAN

Feng was waiting inside Xian's chamber when Xian showed up nearly fifteen minutes later than they were supposed to meet. He arched a brow at the soy sauce stain splashed on the front of Xian's lóng páo. "This is what you meant by finding an excuse to leave early?"

"Wang already took the sickness excuse, so I had to improvise." Xian shut the doors. "Did you manage to follow him?"

"He left the palace alone shortly after the start of the meal," Feng reported as he helped Xian remove his lóng páo. "He rode down the southern road along the lake. I followed for a short distance before coming back."

A jolt went through Xian. The southern road led to Leifeng Pagoda. Wang had hinted that he knew Zhen wasn't locked up in the palace prison. Could he have discovered that he was being kept in Fahai's underground laboratory in the pagoda?

"He's going after Zhen," Xian said. "It wasn't just me he needed to keep occupied at the meal. He knew Fahai would be there too, which would leave his laboratory unguarded for a few hours."

Feng looked puzzled. "I still don't understand what Wang is after. How does he intend to use Zhen against you?"

"Maybe he just wants to spite me. To hurt someone I care about who can't fight back." Xian pulled an outer robe over his undershirt. "Whatever it is, I don't intend to stand by and let him get away with it."

"If you're going to Leifeng Pagoda, I'll come with you," Feng said.

"No," Xian told him. "I need you to stay behind. Make excuses for me to my father."

Feng looked aghast. "You're asking me to lie? To the king?"

"I don't want to give Wang any chance to implicate you or get you in trouble." Xian glanced around and picked up a purple clay teapot. "You tried to stop me, but I hit you on the back of the head with this." He hurled the teapot to the floor. Clay fragments scattered around their feet. "By the time you came to, I was long gone."

"Why don't I just say you splashed me in the face with soy sauce?" Feng grumbled, but he relented. "If you're not back in an hour, I'm riding out there to look for you. I don't care about Wang."

Xian clapped him on the shoulder. "You'll probably be in time to scrape whatever's left of him off the pagoda floor."

As Xian approached the pagoda, his suspicions were confirmed: Wang's horse was already there, its lead rope tied to a tree. The night was silent except for the chirp of crickets and the occasional sleepy hoots of orioles. He didn't want hoofbeats to alert Wang to his arrival, so he slowed and dismounted a distance away. Zhaoye let out a dissatisfied neigh but acquiesced to being hidden behind a thicket of weeping willows.

Xian stealthily made his way around to the back of the pagoda—the iron door leading to the laboratory was unlocked. Wang must have discovered it while Xian and Fahai were in Changle; he'd had weeks to learn how to pick the lock and get inside.

Xian slowly pushed the door open so the creak of hinges wouldn't give him away. The light of flickering oil lamps emanated from within, along with the crackling of firewood. He drew his sword as he crept down the steps.

Fahai's laboratory was lit but empty. The fireplace was burning brightly, and his worktable was in its usual state of organized mess. Xian's ears detected a low, mechanical whirring that he hadn't heard all the previous times he had been here. When he pressed his ear to the wall, the gear-like noise hummed louder, as if it were coming from *within* the stones.

Xian ran a palm along the wall and halted in front of one of the bookcases. One thick tome had fallen to the floor, its pages splayed open. As he picked up the book, its empty spot on the shelf caught his eye. There was a wooden knob in the back of the bookcase that the book had concealed.

He reached inside and turned the knob. There was a click—then the bookcase began to shift, rotating to reveal a stairway that led down to a deeper level. The whirring grew louder, echoing from somewhere below.

Xian frowned. Fahai must have been aware of this secret entrance within his laboratory—so why hadn't he said anything to Xian or his father? What was going on down there?

Xian cautiously descended the jagged steps, which terminated in another underground chamber. Its sparse furnishings and the bas-relief carvings of deities on the stone walls were similar to the pilgrims' hall in a temple—except for the circular black pool in the middle of the space, above which a familiar figure was suspended upside down from a system of pulleys and ropes rigged to the ceiling.

Xian's heart plummeted. "Zhen?"

Zhen's eyes fluttered open—their gazes met, and neither of them could hide their shock. Zhen's arms were bound to his sides, and his long hair was wet, hanging in limp strands, which meant he had already been immersed in the water.

"Zhen," Xian heard Wang say. "So this abomination of nature has a name."

Xian's head whipped around as his half brother emerged from behind one of the pillars. He didn't look at all surprised that Xian had shown up. Xian had been so stunned to see Zhen hanging upside down from the ceiling that he momentarily forgot that he had tracked Wang there.

"What the hell are you doing to him, Wang?" Xian demanded.

"Me? You give me too much credit." Wang gestured at the underground chamber. "I've always wondered where Fahai went when he left the palace in the late evenings. He must have been working on this little torture chamber of his. No wonder you two get along so well—both of you have such deviant inclinations."

A chill coursed through Xian's veins. Wang wasn't the one who had tied Zhen in this cruel position—it was Fahai. He had volunteered to ride ahead of them and arrive a day earlier to make arrangements, but the court adviser had clearly been preparing this chamber for far longer.

Wang looked up at Zhen, who was shivering as he hung upside down above the pool.

"Bet you hoped that you would be more than just another one of his conquests." Wang let out a scornful sound. "Well, congratulations, you got your wish. I'm pretty sure he's never done this with any of the other boys he screwed."

"Shut up," Xian hissed. His hand tightened around his sword as he stalked toward his half brother. "Don't you *dare* speak to him—"

"Or what? You're going to save him?" Wang sneered. "You're the one who brought him back from Changle shackled and caged like the animal he is—"

Xian drew back his fist and hit Wang. The other prince staggered back but caught himself a few feet from the wall. He held his jaw as he stared at Xian, his expression darkening.

"This place wasn't the only secret I uncovered while you were away in Changle," he said. "I also opened the box behind the plaque."

Xian's jaw dropped. "What? You know that's punishable by death—"

Wang's face twisted as he threw an unfolded piece of parchment at Xian's feet. "*This* should be punishable by death."

The wax seal with the king's stamp, which kept the contents secret, had been broken. Xian stared at his own name in his father's handwriting: 許仙.

His father had chosen him to be his successor.

"*I* am the rightful crown prince." Wang drew his sword and leveled the blade in Xian's face. "Did he ever think about the humiliation I would be put through when everyone finds out he chose the son of a concubine over his firstborn?"

Xian didn't understand why Wang had lured him all the way down here to have this confrontation.

"If you want to duel to the death to decide who gets to be the crown prince, fine." Xian gripped his own sword by his side. "But leave Zhen out of this. He's nothing to you."

Wang laughed. "But anyone with half an eye can see that he's something to *you*."

He moved toward a lever on the wall connected to the rope that suspended Zhen above the pool.

"No!" Xian shouted, rushing forward.

Wang swung his sword, severing the rope.

The pulleys rattled as the tension abruptly slackened. Above the pool, Zhen lurched. The rope caught in one of the riggings, slowing his drop—but before Xian could get close enough, the rope pulled loose and slipped free.

Zhen plunged headfirst into the water with a loud splash.

Xian dropped his sword as he reached the edge of the pool. Zhen had disappeared beneath the surface.

He jumped in.

After falling into the West Lake, Xian had learned to swim. But this felt nothing like water—it was cloying, unnatural, like oil. He waved the bubbles away from his face and forced his eyes open. Zhen, bound hand and foot, was steadily sinking, as if he were being sucked toward the bottomless depths by some kind of magnetism.

Xian dived deeper after Zhen. But the water slowed his movements, like invisible fingers tugging at his wrists and ankles, holding him back while dragging Zhen farther from him. He surged forward, kicking his legs harder until he managed to grab hold of Zhen's shoulders. He pulled Zhen's body against his own, wrapped his arms tightly around the other boy's waist, and propelled them both upward. The glimmering light above seemed like a universe away; his lungs were on fire, screaming for air, and with Zhen weighing him down, he didn't know if he could make it—

He finally broke the surface, gasping for breath, his head spinning.

"Zhen?" He shook the unmoving boy in his arms.

Zhen didn't respond. His eyes were closed, and his lips, slightly parted, were tinged blue as if from frostbite.

Wang was nowhere to be seen. Xian swam to the edge and,

with effort, heaved Zhen onto the side of the pool and climbed out after him. The water temperature hadn't been uncomfortably cold, but Zhen, though unconscious, was shivering uncontrollably.

During his palace lessons, Xian had studied emergency rescue techniques written down by physicians from the Jin dynasty more than five hundred years ago.

He laid Zhen flat on his back and tilted his head up to open his airway. He should also lift his arms, but they were bound to his sides and he had no time to untie the ropes. There was an empty ceramic urn nearby, and Xian put it under Zhen's feet— elevating them would help to return blood to his heart.

Zhen wasn't breathing. The ancient medical texts prescribed blocking the nostrils and breathing into the other person's throat through a reed pipe or bamboo tube. He didn't have any of those, so Xian leaned forward and pressed his mouth directly to Zhen's. It was nothing like the other times their mouths had touched; now the other boy's lips were cold, almost lifeless, and all Xian could feel was panic and desperation.

He couldn't let Zhen die, and not because of the antidote.

Xian alternated between blowing air into Zhen's mouth and pressing down with both palms on his chest. Finally, a guttural noise emerged from Zhen's throat, and he let out a shaky, wheezing breath.

Xian exhaled in relief as Zhen's eyes fluttered open. His unfocused gaze met Xian's—disbelief shaded his pale features, as if he thought he had to be dreaming.

"Xian?" he whispered.

At the sound of his name falling from Zhen's lips, something cracked wide open inside Xian's heart. He embraced Zhen and held him tightly, stroking his palm over Zhen's damp hair. He could feel Zhen trembling.

"Don't worry." He spoke in Zhen's ear. "I've got you."

A stab of pain lanced through the back of Xian's shoulder. He reached around and pulled out a two-pronged dart, its twin metal points stained with his blood.

"I have to thank Fahai for being so organized." Wang stepped in front of Xian with a mocking grin. "Shelves stocked with different kinds of venom, all neatly labeled."

An icy, burning sensation spread through Xian's left scapula. The dart had been laced with snake venom. Suddenly he understood why his half brother had lured him there: to poison him and frame Zhen for it.

"You son of a whore," Xian gritted out.

Wang laughed. "Who wouldn't believe a vengeful snake spirit would fatally attack the prince that had captured and imprisoned him? The two puncture marks in your shoulder will be all the evidence they need."

Xian tried to stand, but a wave of dizziness hit him and his knees buckled. The pain in his shoulder had changed to numbness, creeping down his left arm and up his neck. He stumbled and fell close to his half brother's feet, his body jerking involuntarily as the toxin took hold. Copperhead venom, judging from the potency. It wasn't called the hundred-pacer for nothing.

"Don't exert yourself, brother." Wang picked up the incriminating dart and slipped it into his sleeve pocket. "The venom is taking effect. It'll be easier if you don't try to fight it."

Wang turned to Zhen, who was still bound. A prickle of dread went up Xian's spine.

"Lay a hand on him and I'll destroy you," Xian blurted out. "If not in this life, then I swear, I'll find you in the next."

"I have no intention of killing him," Wang replied, heading to the stairs. "When they find him alive next to your body, you can be sure that Father, grieving the loss of his favorite son, will sentence him to the most terrible death imaginable." He cocked his head. "Do snake spirits go to the same afterlife as humans? Probably not. What a shame . . ."

Xian lay helplessly sprawled on the floor as Wang's footsteps faded. His heart was racing, pumping the venom more swiftly through his veins. Cold sweat broke out across his skin, and his muscles went rigid; paralysis was setting in.

A shuffling sound made him turn his head.

Zhen had rolled over to Xian's sword, which he had tossed aside before jumping into the pool. Zhen vigorously rubbed his bonds against the blade until the ropes frayed. He disentangled himself and rushed over to Xian.

"Zhen," Xian croaked. "You need to get out of here before they—"

"Don't try to talk." Zhen tilted him onto his side, exposing his injured shoulder. "Just concentrate on breathing."

Zhen pushed down the collar of Xian's robe and pressed

both palms to the puncture wound. A familiar weightlessness entered Xian's body—he had felt the same thing when Hei Xing touched his leg in the cave and healed it so he could walk. But this was different. Hei Xing's power had been like a black storm surge in a turbulent sea, but Zhen's energy was like white, luminescent waves warring with the venom in his blood—

Xian shut his eyes and clung to Zhen's light, his lifeline in the darkness.

Chapter 32
ZHEN

Zhen lowered Xian to the floor of the chamber. Thankfully Fahai had removed the bīn collar around his neck before submerging him. His spirit powers were greatly weakened by the cultivation pool, but he had somehow mustered enough healing energy to divert blood from Zhen's meridians and prevent the toxin from reaching his heart. Xian had lost consciousness, but his breathing was stable.

He had to get Xian out of there as soon as possible. It was only a matter of time before Wang returned with the palace guards in tow. He would not stop until he saw his half brother dead. Which meant the best way to ensure that he wouldn't come after them was to make him think he had succeeded.

There was an empty urn close by, and Zhen put it next to Xian. Then he shut his eyes, focused his mind, and passed his palm over the ceramic vessel. When he opened his eyes, the urn had disappeared—and in its place lay a faceless human body. A dummy.

Transmutation was one of the most difficult skills he had learned through cultivation, and the biggest challenge was prolonging the length of time the objects would stay in their transmuted form. The year before, the items he changed could last for only a couple of hours, like the blade of grass he had turned into a coin and given the old man in exchange for Qing. With more practice, the transmuted objects could now keep their form for a day. Hopefully that would be long enough to fool Wang.

Zhen took the ornately carved bronze hairpin from Xian's bun and laid it above the dummy's head. That should be enough proof of the body's identity.

He hoisted Xian onto his back and tied Xian's wrists in front of his own chest with a cloth cord so he wouldn't accidentally slide off. A large barrel of stone-lacquer oil stood near one of the pillars, and Zhen tipped it over; the flammable liquid spilled, raced across the floor, and flowed around the dummy, filling the chamber with a sharp, stinging scent.

Zhen took a lit torch from its wall bracket and tossed it onto the oil. Flames sprang up, wreathing the dummy. As the fire spread swiftly across the chamber, Zhen cast one last glance at the cultivation pool. Its perfectly round surface absorbed the glare of the flames and reflected nothing.

He rounded his shoulders to bear Xian's weight more comfortably and ascended the uneven steps into Fahai's laboratory on the level above. The doors of a wooden cabinet had been thrown open, revealing neatly labeled bottles of venom inside.

This was probably where Fahai experimented on the snakes Xian had captured. Empty bamboo cages were stacked at the other end of the room. Several contained silvery gossamers of snake skin sheds. Snakes shed their skins every three to six months, which meant some of the former occupants of these cages had been kept there for longer. Were they released . . . or killed?

The acrid scent of smoke wafting up the stairwell from the chamber below was a warning that he couldn't linger. He turned away from the gruesome laboratory and made his way up the last flight of steps that led out of the pagoda.

He burst through the iron door and breathed in deeply, letting his lungs fill with the familiar, unforgettable scent of the West Lake. All these years, he had longed to return, but his guilt over the boy he had left behind on the islet in the middle of the lake had kept him away.

Now he carried that boy on his back, and he would stop at nothing to keep him safe.

Something rustled in the distance, and Zhen spun around, tensing. A moment later, Zhaoye trotted out of the shadows, shaking his dark mane as he came toward Zhen.

Zhen couldn't suppress a smile as he put a hand on Zhaoye's flank. "Hello, my friend."

The prince's horse stood obediently still as Zhen climbed into the saddle with Xian behind him. Xian didn't stir, but Zhen could feel his heartbeat against his back.

Zhen still remembered the terrain around the West Lake, especially the secret paths through the woodlands that only animals knew. The forest he had come from would remember its own, and it would watch over them.

He guided Zhaoye up the steep, unmarked trail that led to the top of Feilai Peak, its majestic limestone bluffs towering over the surrounding sandstone mountains. They halted briefly on the ridge, and Zhen looked back.

In the distance, the base of Leifeng Pagoda glowed, a fiery ember on the southern shore, spirals of smoke rising like incense in the night.

He faced front and rode on.

They arrived at the small hut in the middle of the forest two hours later. The walls were made almost entirely of bamboo, which kept the interior dry during heavy rains and cool during humid summers. After Zhen had become a snake spirit, he had spent several months living there on his own. He didn't know who had built the hut, but the spartan furnishings within hinted at someone who had sought frugal seclusion. The table and bed had weathered from their original teak color to a faded silver-gray.

Both his clothes and Xian's were still wet from being in the pool. The wind at this altitude was chilly even during the summer, and he couldn't let Xian catch a cold. Zhen transmuted two hemp sacks into two plain white robes. He changed into one and carefully dressed Xian in the other. The twin punctures on the back of Xian's left shoulder where the dart had found its mark had already begun to heal.

A cold draft blew through the open window, and Zhen coughed. A single drop of crimson fell onto his own sleeve. Zhen blinked; his hand went to his mouth, where copper wetness clung to his lower lip.

Nosebleeds were a sign of rising imbalance in the body, but coughing up blood was a serious warning that internal illness had already taken hold. The pearl's power was the only way to save Xian from the venom—but rescuing Qing last year had weakened him considerably, and being immersed in the cultivation pool had further drained his strength. Fahai had said the pearl was worth five hundred years of cultivation, which meant its power was not infinite. Zhen was dangerously close to overusing whatever remained.

He would worry about that later. Right now, he was more concerned about Xian. He touched two fingers to Xian's wrist—his pulse was weak and threadlike, and he still hadn't woken up. As Zhen laid him on the bed, the jade pendant around Xian's neck slipped out from the folds of his robe.

Xian had said that his mother had given it to him as a protective stone. A swell of emotion rose inside Zhen's chest. Maybe this was his purpose . . . his penance. He owed Xian's mother that much. He would stay by her son's side and be his protector.

He stepped out of the hut. Overhead, the stars were distant and remote, and the waning moon looked like someone had taken a knife and sliced off a crescent. He had missed the kind of dense night that existed only out in the woods, far beyond the reach of lamps and torches.

He went to the well behind the hut and drew water for Zhaoye to drink before leading him to a grassy clearing. While Zhaoye grazed, Zhen ventured farther into the woods to forage for what he needed. As a snake, Zhen instinctively knew which plants to avoid, such as marigolds and azaleas. As a human, Zhen had met a kindly apothecary who had taught him how to identify healing herbs.

He collected various herbs and brought them to the front yard of the hut, where a firepit was sunk into the ground and lined with stones. He soaked the ingredients in water, crushed them, and put them into a round cauldron that stood on three legs above the fire. The bitter scent of the herbs in the rising steam brought back visceral memories of the decoction of realgar that Fahai had made for him on the night of the Duanwu Festival, but he pushed the unwanted thoughts to the back of his mind. Right now, Xian needed his full attention.

Once the medicine had cooled enough, he ladled some into an earthenware bowl and brought it inside. When he halted by Xian's bedside, the other boy's eyes opened.

Zhen's heart leaped. "You're awake."

Xian looked very pale, and his gaze was unfocused as he took in his new surroundings.

"Where are we?" he asked, his voice raw and scratchy.

"We're in a small hut deep in the highland forests of Feilai

Peak," Zhen replied. "We'll be safe here, at least for now." He gestured at the bowl of soup. "Here. Drink this first. It will help you feel better."

Xian sniffed at the contents and grimaced at the smell from the honey locust plant, which was so tart and pungent that it was often used to revive people who had passed out. "You cooked this?"

"I searched the forest and found zào jiǎo, huáng lián, huáng qín, and a bunch of other medicinal herbs," Zhen replied. "An apothecary once told me they can improve blood flow and draw out toxins."

Whether Xian drank the medicine or not would prove whether he trusted Zhen . . . or still viewed him as a traitor. Zhen wondered if he should volunteer to take the first sip, as Xian had done with the decoction that Fahai had prepared.

A long moment passed before Xian leaned forward and brought his lips to the edge of the bowl. Zhen held the bowl in one hand and supported the back of Xian's head with the other as Xian drank the entire bowl of soup.

When he finished, he wiped the back of his hand over his mouth and raised his eyes to Zhen.

"What happened?" he asked. "I don't remember much after pulling Wang's dart out of my shoulder. Did you carry me out of that underground chamber?"

Zhen nodded. "I also set the place on fire before leaving so they'll think you're dead and won't send out search parties looking for you."

Xian frowned. "But when they put out the fire and don't find any burned bodies, they'll know we both managed to escape."

"I, uh, transmuted an urn into a human dummy that's supposed to be you."

Xian's brows jumped. "You can do that?"

Zhen winced. "Sorry, I know that sounds terrible. But in that moment, I couldn't think of anything else. The dummy should keep its form for at least a day. I also left your hairpin behind to convince them it's really you."

Xian's brow creased. "I remember now." He reached around and touched the puncture wounds on his shoulder. "The light . . . that was you healing me."

Before Zhen could respond, Xian's gaze cut toward Zhen's arm. To Zhen's horror, a patch of white scales had bloomed on his forearm. Using the pearl's powers to heal Xian had taken a heavier toll on him than he'd thought. He rotated his arm and tried to hide the scaly patch against his body, although he knew Xian had already seen it.

"Are you going to turn back into a snake?" Xian's tone was hard to decipher.

Zhen's cheeks burned in shame. "I can't transform even if I wanted to. Fahai took off the collar, but once I was submerged in the pool, I became locked in my current form."

"What does that pool do?"

"It was meant to enhance cultivation," Zhen replied. "But Fahai altered its purpose so that when he immersed me into the waters, it would draw out the essence of the pearl instead."

Xian's eyes darkened. "Fahai obviously isn't the person I thought he was. He never told me or my father about the chamber or the cultivation pool."

"I'm sorry," Zhen whispered. "For everything. I shouldn't have lied to you."

Xian was quiet for a moment before he took Zhen's hand, prying his arm away from his side.

"When I found out the truth, I wanted to hate you," he said. "I tried so hard. But I just . . . couldn't. And when you sacrificed your chance to escape to stay with me . . . I knew the part of me that couldn't stop caring about you was right all along."

Then he ran a finger lightly over the pale tracery of scales on Zhen's forearm.

Zhen froze, too stunned to pull back. Xian held his gaze.

"I'm not afraid of who you are," he said intently. "Not anymore."

Who you are. Not *what*. Zhen couldn't believe his ears. He didn't realize tears had spilled onto his cheeks until Xian reached out, brushed them away with his thumbs, and closed the distance between their mouths.

The kiss was tentative, almost chaste, as if they were discovering each other for the first time. An explosion of warmth filled Zhen's heart. He'd never imagined in this life that he would get another chance to hold Xian, to kiss him again . . .

Zhen wrapped his arms around Xian's neck, pulling him closer and deepening the kiss. When they were in Changle, he had tried to cling to these moments because he knew they wouldn't last—but now he wanted to memorize every single one because they were finally real.

When they pulled apart, neither of them moved back.

"I'm sorry too." Xian held Zhen's face in his hands, a shadow of pain crossing his features. "When I saw you in that chamber, hanging above the pool . . ."

Zhen pressed their foreheads together. "I wish you didn't have to see me like that."

Xian shook his head. "It was my fault you ended up that way. I was the one who handed you over to Fahai." He tucked a loose strand of Zhen's hair behind his ear. "I won't let him lay a hand on you again, I promise."

Zhen glanced down at the blotch of white scales on his forearm that betrayed his true nature. For the first time, he didn't feel the instinct to hide who he was. He reached out shyly, taking Xian's hand in his; without hesitation, Xian's fingers entwined with his own.

"In the underground chamber, Fahai told me the pearl's power could be changed into five hundred years of cultivation, and he reckons there are three hundred left." Zhen bit his lip and drew a deep breath. "I healed you of the venom from Wang's dart . . . if you'll let me, I want to use the power from the spirit pearl to try to heal your mother as well."

Xian nodded. "I trust you. But we both need to recover before we return to the palace." His expression hardened. "I have a score to settle with my half brother—and it's worth coming back from the dead for."

Chapter 33

XIAN

When Xian opened his eyes, it took him a moment to remember where he was. The events of the night before came back in snatches and fragments: Wang's treachery. The cold bite of venom, followed by Zhen's healing. Only a lingering stiffness remained in his injured shoulder.

Outside, dawn had broken. Next to him, the bed was empty, and Zhen was nowhere to be seen in the small hut. As Xian sat up, the chain around his neck shifted. His hand went to the jade amulet that he had promised his mother he would keep close to his heart.

Seven years ago, I nearly lost you, his father had told him. *Both of you—in your mother's fragile state, grief would have overwhelmed her. I will not let that happen again.*

He hoped his father would keep the news of his supposed

death from his mother, at least long enough for him to return. He needed time to regain his strength, figure out how to thwart his vicious half brother, and, most important, convince his father that Fahai could not be trusted.

Concealed danger lurks nearby . . . You have been betrayed.

The priest was referring to Fahai. All these years, the court adviser had been hiding his true intentions from the king. Zhen said that Fahai had immersed him in the cultivation pool to extract the power of the pearl. Xian had told no one about what happened in the lake seven years ago—so how did the court adviser know that Zhen had consumed the pearl? What did he want with the pearl's energy? And now that his secret cultivation chamber had been discovered and set on fire, what would he do next?

When Xian stepped out of the hut, Zhaoye let out a whinny from the post where his lead rope was tied. He walked to his horse and stroked his shiny coat. "Thank you, my loyal friend."

Zhaoye nuzzled his neck and launched into a body search, checking his pockets for hidden fruit.

Xian chuckled. "Some things never change."

When he raised his eyes, he saw a familiar figure standing in a clearing a distance away. He inhaled, and his breath caught in his throat.

Zhen was dressed in a white robe identical to the one Xian was wearing, and he was hanging Xian's robe and his own to dry on a line he had tied between two trees. Zhen's dark hair on his shoulders was freshly washed and combed, and with his white robe backlit by the morning sunlight, he looked almost ethereal.

Xian walked toward him, and Zhen glanced around at the sound of approaching footsteps.

"You're awake," he said with a smile. "I wanted to let you rest for a little longer."

Xian put his hand on Zhen's lower back. "When you said you'd take me riding in the forest for our first date, I didn't know this was what you had in mind."

Zhen's laugh lilted above the tinkle and hum of the forest around them.

"I washed your robe so you can wear it when you go back to the palace tomorrow," he told Xian. "A robe transmuted from a hemp sack is not befitting a prince of Wuyue. It won't keep its form until tomorrow, anyway."

"Ah." Xian drew back a little and let his gaze travel down Zhen's body. "So at some point both of us will suddenly be . . . in a completely naked state?"

Zhen nudged Xian lightly in his side. "Flirting is highly inappropriate at this time, since you're in no condition right now to follow through."

Xian grinned in spite of everything that had happened. Even though the rest of the world thought he was dead, standing here with Zhen, he felt more alive than he ever had.

He and Zhen ventured through the forest, picking a variety of seasonal fruits for breakfast—lychees, kumquats, hawthorn berries, and goji berries. Zhen insisted on harvesting herbs to cook more medicinal soup for Xian. Xian managed to catch a large trout in a freshwater stream, and they roasted it over the fire in front of the hut.

"So have you thought about what you're going to do when we head back to the palace?" Zhen asked after they had finished eating.

"By now, they'll have discovered my charred 'body' in the wreckage of the pagoda, and Wang will have spun his story accusing you of causing my death by snake venom," Xian replied. "If the dummy you transmuted keeps its form for a day, hopefully they'll put my body into a casket before it turns back into an urn."

"Hei Xing and Qing might be able to help us," Zhen said. "Hei Xing is an old tortoise spirit—he has lived for hundreds of years, and he knows a lot about cultivation and mystical arts. He might be able to figure out what Fahai is really up to. I can get a message out to them."

"How? They could be anywhere by now."

"There's a secret way that animal spirits converse with one another." Zhen gestured at the trees. "We're standing right in the middle of it. The forest has its own huge, invisible communication network under our feet."

"You mean through their roots?"

Zhen nodded. "That's how trees talk to one another. When a tree dies, it sends whatever resources it has left back into the ground for its neighbors. Of course, not all trees are so selfless. Black walnuts are known to give out harmful substances to kill their competition."

"Pretty sure Wang was a black walnut in his past life," Xian remarked.

Zhen walked to a tall, weathered fir. He put his palm on its bark, and his lips moved a little as he spoke to the tree in its language.

"It's done." He let his hand drop and turned to Xian. "It might take some time to spread across the woodland. If Qing or Hei Xing puts a palm on a tree trunk, they'll get the message. Or they might hear it whispered in the rustling of leaves."

"What message did you send?" Xian asked.

"I told Qing and Hei Xing that you and I are on the same side now, that we're headed back to the palace in Xifu, and we could use their help. I didn't want to mention details, in case any unfriendly ears intercept the message. We'll fill them in when they meet us at the palace."

"Knowing Qing, she'll already be on her way to Wuyue to rescue you."

"You're probably right." Zhen sounded wry. "She never listens to me."

Zhen walked toward a broad ledge and gazed out across the breathtaking vista of mountain slopes cloaked with pines and firs. Xian followed, halted behind him, and wrapped his arms around Zhen's waist. The afternoon sun filtered through the branches overhead, speckling the ground at their feet.

They stood in comfortable silence, Zhen's back warm against Xian's body. Xian closed his eyes and breathed in. He never imagined that out here, in the middle of nowhere, he would finally find a place—no, a person he belonged with.

"I sheltered in this hut during my first winter as a snake spirit." Zhen nestled closer against Xian's chest. "Hei Xing told me there was no better place in the world to cultivate than the West Lake, that the qi in the environment was purer and more pristine than anywhere else he had cultivated. I was an ordinary snake back then, and I used to admire how he could stay perfectly still for hours, even days, on the shores of the West Lake as a tortoise."

Xian rested his chin on Zhen's shoulder. "Why did you leave, then?"

Zhen turned his face toward Xian's until their cheeks touched.

"You," he said softly. "I carried the burden of what I did to you every single day. You were the reason I didn't come back, and you're the reason I have returned." The edges of his mouth curled up. "I'm thankful, though. That we met again. That I had the chance to face up to what I did."

Xian hoped the other boy wouldn't hold on to the guilt any longer. After everything they had been through, they had earned the right to leave the past behind.

Xian pressed his lips to Zhen's neck. "I'm glad we have the chance to start over."

A soft intake of breath told Xian that his words had found their mark. Zhen's hands slipped into Xian's; they twined their fingers together on his abdomen.

"Do you believe in destiny?" Zhen asked.

"I believe destiny is an excuse people give not to fight for what they really want in life," Xian replied.

Zhen turned around in Xian's arms so they were face-to-face. "Will you fight for what you want?"

"Always." Xian leaned in and kissed him on the mouth. "I told you before: What kind of prince would I be if I didn't protect the ones I care about?"

Zhen's expression became furtive. "Do you believe that two people are meant to find each other and be together and nothing in the world can keep them apart?"

Xian smiled. "Zhī jǐ, you mean?"

"I've heard of that," Zhen said. "But I'm not sure what it means."

"It's a little hard to define," Xian replied. "It's someone who knows everything about you, maybe even knows you better than you know yourself, and who will stand by you no matter how dark or ugly you feel inside. You'll get mad at each other sometimes, but you can imagine spending the rest of eternity with this person, because you know the two of you will never get tired of each other . . . or stop loving each other."

Zhen tilted his head. "Like a soulmate?"

The intense feeling that flooded through Xian's chest was more than just attraction or affection.

"Yes," Xian said. "Something like that."

"I wish we could stay here for a little longer." Zhen sounded wistful. "Just the two of us, apart from the rest of the world."

Being out here with Zhen, with no one else for miles . . . the forest around them felt like a protective embrace. They had to leave tomorrow, but for now, he wanted to savor this stillness, this reprieve . . . this time he had with Zhen that was theirs and theirs alone.

"Me too," Xian said.

Moonlight slanted through the window, casting a faint glow across Zhen's face as they lay in bed. Zhen's head was pillowed on Xian's outstretched arm, and the long lashes of his closed lids fanned against his pale cheek.

"I can hear you thinking," Zhen said without opening his eyes.

A smile tugged at Xian's mouth. "Is that another of your skills?"

Zhen's eyes opened. "No." His dark, soulful gaze sent a twinge of yearning through Xian. "But I can sense it. You're worried about what will happen when we go back to the palace."

"Hmm, wrong." Xian shifted closer, nuzzling Zhen's neck. "I was actually thinking about how good you look in white. And when the transmuted robes will vanish off our bodies. Should be anytime now, am I right?"

Zhen raised an eyebrow. "Are you such a sweet-talker to all the boys you take to bed?"

"Only the ones that help me fake my death and thwart my evil half brother."

Zhen trailed a finger up and down Xian's arm. "All right, stop trying to evade the question. What were you really thinking about?"

Xian kissed him on the forehead. "I was thinking that when

all of this is over . . . I want you to be my consort."

Zhen's eyes widened. "Are you serious?"

Xian nodded. "I want to make it official. If you agree, that is."

"You're a prince." Zhen still looked incredulous. "You don't need to ask for anyone's permission."

Xian met his gaze. "I'm asking you."

Zhen smiled. He pushed himself into a sitting position and swung a leg over Xian's body, straddling him. He leaned in and claimed Xian's mouth in a deep kiss.

Xian grinned against Zhen's lips when they came up for air. "I'll take that as a yes."

Zhen responded by unfastening the front of his robe and pushing it off his shoulders.

Xian loved seeing Zhen take the initiative—more than anything, he wanted the other boy to see them as equals. It took all the effort he could muster to catch Zhen's wrists, stopping him.

Confusion flitted across Zhen's face.

"I know healing me has taken more energy out of you than you want to let on," Xian told him. "Earlier, you made an excuse to go outside so I wouldn't see you spitting up blood."

Zhen looked sheepish. "I'm fine. You already have so much to deal with. I didn't want you to worry."

"I'll worry even more if you don't tell me," Xian replied intently. "When we get back to the palace, I'll take you to the infirmary. No exertion until then."

Zhen groaned and rolled off Xian's body. "You are such a killjoy."

A slight flush had returned to Zhen's cheeks, and the faint sheen of sweat that gleamed on his neck was a good sign.

"We can still have a little fun." Xian slid a hand into the front of Zhen's robe and ran his palm over his bare abdomen. Zhen gave a shiver of pleasure, although he stilled when Xian's fingers settled on the scar on the left side of his torso.

"Someone hurt you?" Xian knew Zhen hadn't been ready to tell him how he'd gotten this scar the last time he had asked about it.

"I was caught in a snake trap," Zhen replied. "I was sure I would die there, but Hei Xing rescued me."

"Since he saved your life, I guess I'll have to forgive him for threatening to cut off my hand. Although asking you to drop me into the abyss was pretty heartless." Xian guided Zhen's hand to a healed mark on his own right thigh. "Here. I have one too."

Zhen's fingers circled the raised scar. "What happened?"

"Wang lured me into the armory and stabbed me in the leg with an arrow. He was nine, and I was six." Xian shook his head in disgust. "I swore I would never fall for his tricks again. And yet I still did."

"I'm sorry that he used me to get to you," Zhen said.

"You have nothing to be sorry for." Xian idly stroked Zhen's hair. "You know, after you've healed my mother, and when she's well enough to travel, I want to bring her to the smaller eastern palace in Yuezhou to recuperate over the winter. She could use some time away from the gossip and politics of the royal court. Yuezhou is close to her hometown, which is famous for lóng jǐng tea."

"Doesn't that mean 'dragon's well'?" Zhen asked.

Xian nodded. "Lóng jǐng is a special pan-roasted green tea grown only in that region. It's named after a legendary well with water that's unusually dense. When rain falls, the lighter rainwater floats on top, forming a coiling pattern on the surface that looks like a dragon twisting."

Zhen yawned and gave a sleepy smile. "You'll have to teach me how to brew lóng jǐng tea properly one day."

His eyes fluttered shut, and after a few minutes, his breathing grew steady.

Xian lay on his side, watching him. All his life, other people had stood guard while Xian slept. In the palace, he had grown up in luxury and had been the one waited on, surrounded by everything he could ask for.

But out here on their own, Xian and Zhen weren't a prince and a snake spirit; they were two boys who would risk their lives for each other, again and again, without thinking twice.

"Zhī jǐ," Xian whispered. "My soulmate."

Chapter 34

XIAN

They departed the hut at daybreak, the dawn at their backs as they rode westward toward the palace. Xian sat in front, holding Zhaoye's reins; Zhen sat behind him, his arms linked around Xian's waist.

They arrived at the town outside the palace, which was also named Xifu, just after eight in the morning. Along the streets, vendors sold steamed meat buns, roasted sweet potatoes, and loquats. People sat on benches and hungrily slurped noodles from earthenware bowls. Cobblers mended shoes, and a woman screamed curses at a group of children who had trampled all over the dyed fabrics she'd laid out on the ground to dry.

Xian had been able to slip out of the palace for trysts without being recognized; after all, most commoners had never seen the royal family up close. Now he listened intently to conversations around them, hoping to glean some news. People discussed the fire that had scorched the base of Leifeng Pagoda but had been put out before the upper parts of the structure were damaged. They were puzzled as to why the gates of the palace that separated the inner court from the outer had been shut for the day with no explanation. But to Xian's relief, there was no talk about the prince's death.

At the post station, Xian scribbled a brief, unsigned message, sealed the letter, and wrote Feng's name on the front. His best friend would recognize his handwriting. He used one of the silver fixings on Zhaoye's reins to pay for a courier.

When the courier left to deliver the letter, Xian turned to Zhen. "Come on, let's throw out these old clothes and get a new set of robes."

They entered a garment shop. Xian changed into an indigo robe and stood in front of the bronze mirror on the wall. He combed back his hair and secured the bun on top of his head with a gilded hairpin. Next to him, Zhen put on a white robe that Xian had picked out for him; its wide sleeves flowed elegantly by his sides.

"Come here." Xian ran a comb through Zhen's long hair, twisted the top half into a knot, and slid a jade hairpin through it. Then he picked up a white paper fan and put it in Zhen's hand.

"What am I supposed to do with this?" Zhen asked.

In addition to swords, martial artists sometimes liked to wield more unusual weapons—paper fans, ink brushes, even musical instruments. A fan was a useful weapon for a long-range attack; it could fly out in a wide arc, slice enemies, and return to the hand of its owner.

"With your powers, you could do some damage," Xian replied. "Give it a try."

Zhen unfolded the fan and threw it at an upward angle. The fan sailed through the air and reached the opposite end of the room, startling the shopkeeper, before it looped back toward Zhen, who deftly caught it.

Xian grinned. "Show-off."

He handed over a gold buckle from Zhaoye's halter to the shopkeeper to pay for their purchases. They pulled the hoods of their robes over their heads as they exited the shop. No one cast a second glance at the prince in commoner's clothing.

They left the busy marketplace and headed to a vacant farm at the outskirts of town. The abandoned grain silo's reinforced iron door hinted at the structure's true purpose.

"I'm guessing this passageway leads into the palace?" Zhen asked.

"It's one of the secret escape routes in case the palace is attacked," Xian replied. "The door is bolted from the inside—if it's locked, no one can get in from outside. Whenever I sneaked in and out of the palace at night to meet boys, I had to pray that a watchman wouldn't pass by and find it unlocked."

Zhen smiled. "I suppose none of those boys knew they were being romanced by the most eligible bachelor in the kingdom."

The groan of bolts unlatching made them stop and turn. Hinges squealed in protest as the heavy silo door swung open.

Feng stood in the doorway, his face a mask of disbelief as he stared at Xian.

Xian gave him a lopsided grin. "You look like you've seen a spirit."

A choked sound escaped Feng's throat as he enveloped Xian in a tight embrace.

"I almost couldn't believe it when I got your letter," he whispered hoarsely in Xian's ear. "I really thought we'd lost you."

Xian chuckled. "Easy, I need to breathe. Don't want to suffocate and die for real."

Feng released him.

"How?" Feng still couldn't hide his amazement. "I . . . saw it with my own eyes. Your . . . remains. Only your bronze hairpin survived the fire. Your father broke down when we brought it to him."

"Wang poisoned me with snake venom and tried to frame Zhen." Xian's tone became grim. "He broke into the box behind the plaque and found my name. He wanted me permanently out of the picture so our father would choose him instead."

Feng frowned. "Did he set the fire to cover his tracks?"

Zhen spoke. "No, I did." Feng looked at him, aghast, and he added, "I'm sorry, but that was the only way to fake Xian's death and give us a chance to escape."

"Does my mother think I'm dead?" Xian cut in. "Did my father tell her?"

Feng shook his head. "Only a few of us know what happened. Your father made each of us swear on our lives that we wouldn't say a word to anyone, especially your mother. The entire inner court has been sealed off to prevent the news from spreading. Your father is at the coffin home now, observing the monks performing rites for you. Wang is with him."

"Perfect." Xian's mouth twisted. "It's time to show my half brother that the living can be a lot scarier than ghosts."

They entered the underground passageway. Xian had used this tunnel so many times that he could navigate it with his eyes closed. They emerged from the hidden entrance behind the altar in the Pavilion of Benevolence. Xian glanced at Zhen; being in the palace was probably intimidating, given that he had been brought back to Wuyue in chains.

He took Zhen's hand in his own. "You're with me. I won't let anyone hurt you."

Zhen squeezed his palm. "I know."

The three of them made their way to the coffin home, where caskets were kept before the deceased were entombed in the royal mausoleum outside the palace. The building had a somber gray roof with white lanterns hanging from the eaves. Daoist verses hung vertically on the bone-colored pillars, and the wooden plaque above the doorway was inscribed with the epithet 義莊—"Mansion of Righteousness."

The double doors of the coffin home were open. Inside, a casket rested on two wooden stools; a small altar with burning incense and a lit white candle stood at its base. Daoist monks flanked the casket chanting prayers to the ear-piercing, discordant sound of the suǒ nà, a woodwind instrument.

Xian's father stood in the courtyard, facing the open doors. An older person was not allowed to pay their respects to someone younger, so Xian's father—and his mother—couldn't publicly mourn for him. They couldn't even attend the funeral procession, as it was believed that would bring more ill fortune and disaster to the family.

General Jian stood on his father's right. On his left was Wang. His half brother had wasted no time in claiming the most favored position. Fahai was notably absent.

Xian pushed back the hood of his robe and stepped forward. "Father."

His father turned. The shock on his haggard face sent a twinge through Xian. His father's grief was real. General Jian looked astonished; Wang's disbelief quickly changed into panic that he couldn't hide.

"Xian?" his father whispered. "Are—are you a spirit?"

"No, Father." Xian knelt and bowed with his forehead to the ground. "It is me. Your son. I am still alive."

"My son," his father echoed. He exhaled in a rush and moved forward, his hand outstretched; he swayed, and General Jian quickly steadied him. "Is it really you?"

"It's not possible!" Wang burst out. "General Jian and I saw his remains being put into the casket with our own eyes." He glowered at Xian. "Whoever you are, you're not my brother. You're an impostor. A charlatan!"

Xian remained calm. "There's a straightforward way to resolve this matter. Please allow me, Father."

He strode into the coffin home, and the startled monks inside broke off mid-chant. Xian walked toward the casket, put both hands on the wooden cover, and threw it wide open. The monks gasped and jumped back, shielding their faces with their hands—

"See for yourself," Xian said.

A ceramic urn lay in the casket, surrounded by joss paper and swathed in a yellow cloth that would've covered the corpse's face. More than a day had passed since the fire, and the dummy that Zhen had transmuted had changed back to its original form.

His father gripped the doorway, gawking at the empty casket.

Wang stared at the urn. He whirled around to face Xian.

"You have insulted us!" he snarled. "You have made a mockery of Father, of us all! Do you know how much he grieved when he heard of your demise?" He shot a hateful stare at Zhen. "What kind of son allies himself with the same breed of snake devil that poisoned his own mother, that poisoned him?"

"Poisoned me?" Xian countered. "With my body charred beyond recognition, how did you know I was poisoned before I supposedly burned to death?"

Wang's expression froze. Surprise crossed the king's and General Jian's faces.

"Your plan worked beautifully, for the most part." Xian pulled down the left shoulder of his robe, exposing the two healed puncture marks. "You lured me to the underground chamber where Zhen was imprisoned, and then you stabbed me with a poisoned dart, knowing Zhen would inevitably be blamed for the venom that killed me. But you didn't expect the whole place to go up in flames."

Wang's nostrils flared. He turned to their father.

"Certainly you will not believe this—this lying, heartless son who ran away with a monster and made you believe he was dead for an entire day and night! Such an unfilial prince does not deserve to be chosen as your heir!"

A long silence filled the air before their father spoke. "How did you know that I chose Xian to be my heir?"

Chapter 35

XIAN

Wang paled. His throat bobbed as he swallowed.

"I . . . didn't." He pointed a finger at Xian. "He . . . told me. That's all he's been bragging about! He's the one who broke into the box and found his name inside!"

"That's right—because pretending to be dead and running away is exactly what I would do if I knew I was going to be the crown prince," Xian replied.

Rage spasmed across Wang's face. He started toward Xian, drawing his sword—

Zhen moved forward, flicked open the white fan, and held it to Wang's throat. Wang skidded to a halt, startled. The sharp edge of the fan nicked his neck, drawing a thin line of blood.

General Jian's hand went to his own weapon, but Feng stepped to his father's side and stopped him. It was the first time Xian had seen his best friend standing up for Zhen. He had also never witnessed Zhen in fiery protector mode, which was incredibly appealing.

Their father's eyes blazed at his eldest son. "What devil emboldened you to commit this unspeakable deed, Wang?"

Wang dropped his sword, defeated.

"I succumbed to a moment of weakness!" He fell to the ground. "I am your firstborn, the son of your wife. All my life, I have done everything to gain your approval—"

"Yet you were brazen enough to defy the one command everyone in this kingdom knows!" his father thundered. "The box behind the plaque was deemed sacred by your forefathers. By opening it, you have offended not just me but your ancestors—a sin that is deserving of death!"

Wang crawled on elbows and knees to the king's feet. "Please, Father, forgive me! Surely you will show mercy to your own flesh and blood?"

No one in the courtyard spoke. Xian could see the pained expression on his father's face; despite Wang's malice, his first-born was still one of his favorite sons.

Finally, General Jian came forward.

"If I may intercede, Your Majesty," he said with a bow. At the king's assent, he continued. "The political situation at this time is especially delicate, and Southern Tang is watching us closely for any hint of weakness or disharmony. Other kingdoms do not have the same succession practice that Wuyue does; they follow the strict tradition of appointing the eldest son of the queen or empress as the crown prince. As such, they may not fully understand the significance of the box behind the plaque. If word gets out that you have executed your firstborn son for this crime, they may interpret it as a sign of internal discord within your court, which might spur them to attack our borders, hoping to catch us in a state of civil turmoil."

The king was silent. Xian held his breath. Wang lay facedown on the ground, his rib cage rising and falling as he awaited his fate.

"Very well." The king glared imperiously at Wang's prostrate form. "You stole something from me that you should not have. I will punish you in my capacity as your father rather than your king. For your lack of filial piety—the eighth of the ten abominations—instead of death, you will be given the next most severe penalty: ròu xíng, corporal punishment. You shall be dealt a severe blow to your right hand, which is the sentence given to a thief. I will grant you the dignity of receiving your punishment in private rather than in the outer court as other officials would have." He gave Xian a curt nod. "You shall deal the stroke to your brother using his own sword. Do it now."

Xian blinked. *He* would be the one to carry out Wang's punishment?

Wang stared up at Xian in dread. There was obviously no doubt in his mind that he would walk out of that courtyard permanently maimed.

Xian picked up Wang's fallen sword. The weapon had been his father's gift to Wang on his sixteenth birthday—the same sword he himself had wielded as a teenager, the one that had been given to him by his own father. Many in the royal court believed this sword was a kingmaker, a strong indication that Wang would be the chosen heir. Perhaps it had been true at that time—and Wang was willing to kill to reclaim the favor he once had.

"Hold out your right hand," their father ordered Wang.

Wang crawled to his knees and extended his trembling arm, tears streaming down his cheeks. As Xian stepped forward, he cast a surreptitious glance around; their father's expression was stoic, while General Jian's face was somber. Zhen had averted his gaze, as if he couldn't bring himself to watch. Feng met Xian's eyes and gave a barely perceptible dip of his chin. The king had spoken, and Xian was duty bound to carry out his command.

The tension in the air was palpable as Xian towered over Wang, the sword hilt gripped in his hand, its tassel swishing against his wrist. Cutting cleanly through a limb was harder than it appeared; equal measures of precision and force were needed to sever tendons, muscle, flesh, and bone in a single stroke.

Xian focused on Wang's quivering forearm—then he drew back his sword and brought it down in a swinging arc.

Wang let out an anguished scream as the blade made contact with his forearm. He twisted away, collapsed onto his side, and clutched his arm, his face scrunched as he sobbed piteously. Blood blossomed on his robe sleeve—but contrary to everyone's expectations, his hand was still attached to his body.

Their father frowned at Xian. "Did you deal a light stroke on purpose?"

"No, Father." Xian dropped to a knee and placed the blood-stained blade on the ground in front of him. "I dealt a serious blow to his hand as you ordered, completely severing an important tendon in his forearm. He will never be able to wield a sword again." Xian glanced at Zhen, who couldn't hide his amazement. "Someone I care about very deeply once reminded me that the small dot of the opposite color in each half of the yin-yang circle represents the choice to act not just to one's own advantage but to the other person's."

Zhen's forgiveness of Deng had left a deep impression on Xian—even though, knowing his own half brother, such compassion was probably misplaced. An old proverb warned that weaklings never forgave their enemies. But still, Xian wanted to choose as Zhen would have.

His father tilted his head, understanding crossing his stern features. He walked to Xian, who still knelt on one knee.

"A calligraphy master's gentle stroke is not a sign of weakness but of control. A man's mettle is revealed not by his strength but by his mercy." His father removed the signet ring on his right thumb and held it out to Xian. "I have chosen well, Crown Prince of Wuyue."

Xian couldn't believe his eyes. The incredulous expressions on General Jian's and Feng's faces confirmed that he wasn't the only one. His father bestowing the ring on him—this was even more binding than his name in the box behind the plaque. There would be no need to reveal a successor. The king had already publicly declared his choice.

"Thank you, Father. I will not disappoint you." Xian kowtowed, took the ring, and reverently slid it onto his thumb. He got to his feet. "I regret that my first action as your heir is to inform you that your—our—trusted counselor Fahai has betrayed us. He claimed to be researching a cure for Mother in Leifeng Pagoda, but that was just a smokescreen for his true objective: a secret cultivation pool in an underground chamber beneath his laboratory that he told no one about."

His father's forehead creased. "After the fire, Fahai explained to me that the underground chamber was a special prison he had prepared to contain the powerful snake spirit. When they found your hairpin along with a charred corpse, Wang testified that you insisted on riding to the pagoda to meet the snake spirit, against his advice. He was worried, and so he followed you and saw smoke billowing out of the basement."

Xian looked at his half brother in disgust. "Liar."

Wang cowered, as if afraid that Xian might decide to pick up the sword and take another swing at his bleeding arm.

"Summon Fahai." The king turned to General Jian. "Where is he?"

"He has gone to Leifeng Pagoda to salvage whatever he can from his laboratory," General Jian replied.

Xian took Zhen's hand and pulled him to his side. "Zhen isn't the enemy Fahai made him out to be. He healed me of the deadly venom that Wang stabbed me with—which means he has the power to save Mother too."

They were interrupted by the arrival of General Jian's

second-in-command. The chief guard looked stunned to see Wang writhing on the ground, cradling his bleeding arm.

"Your Majesty." The chief guard bowed to Xian's father. "Please forgive my discourtesy, but I have urgent news that cannot wait: The masked brigand who was involved in the attack on the prince's delegation on their journey from Changle has surrendered himself at the palace gates. He says he has an important message that he will convey only to Prince Xian and his companion."

Zhen's eyes widened. He looked toward Xian.

Xian swiftly stepped forward. "Father, please allow me to attend to this matter." At his father's nod, he turned to the chief guard. "Bring me to him."

Xian, Feng, and Zhen followed the chief guard to the department of military affairs, located to the west of the southern gate that separated the inner court from the outer. The chief guard led them to the underground prison, where a familiar figure was locked in one of the cells.

"Hei Xing!" Zhen rushed forward. "Where's Qing? Is she with you?"

For the first time, Xian saw Hei Xing's face unmasked. He had coarse gray hair, and despite the lines on his face, his features were strangely youthful.

"I'm sorry to be the bearer of bad news, Zhen, but Qing is in serious danger." Hei Xing's expression was grave. "I came without delay to warn you."

Zhen looked stricken. "What happened to her?"

"We both received your message through the trees asking for our help," Hei Xing replied. "We arranged to meet outside the palace; when we arrived in the early hours of morning, the gates were still shut. I wanted to stay hidden until daybreak, when we would find a way to send you a message. Qing refused and insisted on pestering the guards to let her speak to someone close to you. She told me to wait for her out of sight, but hours passed and she did not return."

"Who did she ask to talk to?" Xian demanded.

"I don't know. I never saw him." Hei Xing paused. "If I recall correctly, she said he was a scholar."

Zhen and Xian looked at each other in consternation.

"Fahai," Zhen said. "He has Qing. General Jian mentioned that he has gone to the pagoda. He must be holding her captive there. Please, Xian—we have to save her."

Xian nodded. "We will ride there at once."

"What about you?" Zhen said to Hei Xing. "Can you come with us?"

"Unfortunately not." Hei Xing gestured at the chains around his wrists and the cell he was locked in. "I had no choice except to surrender myself to let you know that Qing is in trouble. But if you are in time to save her, my arrest will be well worth the sacrifice."

Xian turned to Feng.

"Marshal the palace guard without delay." He raised his hand with the signet ring, which gleamed blue-green like malachite. "I will lead them to Leifeng Pagoda within the hour."

Chapter 36
ZHEN

Zhen stood at the window of Xian's bedchamber. In the horizon, ominous storm clouds had gathered, completely blotting out the sun. A foreboding rumble of thunder reverberated like a knell within his chest.

No! Qing's voice rang out in his mind. *I'm not going anywhere without you! I'm not leaving you!*

What if those were the last words she ever spoke to him?

He should've tried harder to find her earlier. Or maybe he shouldn't have sent her and Hei Xing the message through the trees—if he hadn't, she wouldn't have come to the palace and fallen into Fahai's clutches.

He had never felt so scared, so helpless. Even when he was shackled and caged in the wagon on the journey to Wuyue . . . at least he had, in some way, brought that fate upon himself. Qing had done nothing wrong except to heed Zhen's foolish call for help.

"Zhen?" Xian's voice broke into his thoughts.

He turned as Xian entered the room. The other boy had changed into an apricot-yellow robe—a different shade from the golden yellow he usually wore. Apricot yellow had to be the designated color of the crown prince.

Xian took Zhen's hand; the signet ring gleamed on his thumb as he interlocked his fingers with Zhen's. "How are you holding up?"

"I'm terrified," Zhen whispered. "I can't imagine what Qing's going through right now."

Xian gave his hand a comforting squeeze. "She's a snake spirit too, isn't she? Which is why Fahai thinks she also has powers that can be extracted?"

Zhen shook his head. "She became a snake spirit only because I healed her using the power of the pearl. She didn't actually consume the pearl, so Fahai won't be able to draw out any of the pearl's essence from her."

"In that case, Fahai must be using her to lure us there." Xian's tone was grim.

Zhen's eyes flashed up to Xian's. "I don't care if Fahai is setting a trap—there's no way I'm abandoning Qing. Even if it costs my life, I'm going to save her."

"I know," Xian replied. "That's why I want you to have this."

He pressed the jade amulet on its chain into Zhen's palm.

Zhen blinked. "But your mother gave this to you."

"Fahai wants the pearl, which makes you his prime target," Xian replied. "This has protected me so far, and now I want it to protect you."

Xian looped the chain around Zhen's neck and fastened the clasp.

"I will tear down every stone of the pagoda if that's what it takes to bring Qing back safely." Xian's eyes were filled with the fortitude that made Zhen understand why Xian's father had chosen him to be the future king. "And I will stay by your side"—he leaned in and pressed a quick kiss to Zhen's lips—"as you did for me."

Hoofbeats echoed in counterpoint to the rumbling thunder as Xian led the palace guard down the road along the lake to Leifeng Pagoda; Zhen rode on his right, Feng on his left. Streaks of lightning veined the impenetrable clouds, like silver fire lighting the belly of a massive gray dragon. The skies unleashed a downpour as they approached the southern shore, and they were all drenched by the time they slowed to a halt in front of the pagoda's flame-scorched base.

As they dismounted, Zhen shielded his eyes and gazed up at the series of wide eaves and brackets like armor and scales on the pagoda's eight-sided body.

Xian strode to the front entrance, and Zhen and Feng followed. The archway was etched with lotus flowers and flying lions, and on a pillar next to the door hung a banner with a string of characters written in black ink.

"He's here." Xian read the message on the banner. "He wants

Zhen and me only to go up to the top of the tower. He's watching us—if anyone else tries to enter the pagoda, he'll throw Qing from the top."

Zhen felt his blood draining from his face. "We cannot underestimate a man who thinks he has nothing left to lose."

Feng frowned. "That doesn't mean the two of you should just walk right into his trap."

"He has the upper hand for now," Xian told Feng. He drew his sword. "Do not breach the pagoda until I give the command."

Zhen took out his white fan, and he and Xian entered the pagoda. Its outer walls were constructed with brick, which had protected the wooden interior structures from being ravaged by fire. Built around the massive central pillar that supported the roof was a spiral stone staircase leading to the upper floors.

Xian ascended the curving steps first, and Zhen stayed close behind. As they drew nearer to the top, they heard Qing's voice, although the sound of rain lashing against the exterior of the pagoda almost drowned it out. She was talking to someone, but Zhen couldn't hear the other person's voice.

Zhen and Xian exchanged looks; on Xian's signal, they burst through the doorway.

Unlike the other floors, which were sectioned into rooms, the highest level was an undivided space. The wind that gusted through the arches of the four balconies at each compass point was cuttingly cold, but that wasn't what made Zhen's hair stand on end.

The thick metal steeple stood on a raised platform in the center; one end was anchored to the floor and the other rose right through the hexagonal roof, ending in the spire. Qing, dressed in a plain rú qún, was bound to the steeple with rope. A hooded figure stood by her side.

Qing's eyes widened when she saw Zhen and Xian.

"It's him!" she yelled. "Watch out—"

The hooded figure turned.

Zhen stopped in his tracks.

"Hei Xing?" he blurted out. "How—how did you get out of the palace prison?"

"Where's Fahai?" Xian demanded. "Have you been working with him all this time?"

Hei Xing let out a raspy laugh. "I suppose you could say that."

He pulled his hood lower, obscuring his face for a moment, and when he pushed the hood back again, Fahai's face stared back at them.

Fahai and Hei Xing—they were one and the same.

"Hei Xing existed first," the man continued. "But Fahai was the person he was forced to become after he was betrayed."

Zhen's heart thudded. Escaping from the palace prison would've been easy for a powerful spirit creature like Hei Xing, and with his hundreds of years of cultivation, using illusion to alter his appearance would hardly be a difficult feat. And he had managed to deflect any suspicion by coming to the palace to tell them about Qing's capture when he was the one who had taken her captive.

"Prince Xian, it seems you and I have something in common." Fahai's mouth twisted as his gaze cut toward Zhen. "We were both deceived by the same malicious, backstabbing snake."

The vehemence in Fahai's eyes sent a shiver up Zhen's spine.

"What did I ever do to you, Hei Xing?" he asked. "Why do you hate me so much?"

"You still don't know?" Fahai's face contorted with rage. "I saved your life when you were caught in that trap, you worthless creature. And in return, when you found the pearl—the pearl you *knew* I was searching for to finish my thousand years of cultivation and ascend to the heavens—you took it for yourself! I should've let you die in that trap!"

"I just wanted to be a spirit creature like you," Zhen whispered. "I looked up to you as a mentor, and I was enchanted by all your adventures. I wished for us to be the same—"

"We are *not* the same!" Fahai roared. "Did you think that once upon a time, I was merely an ordinary reptile like you? No! I was a chief sentry in the celestial realm—but I incurred the wrath of the gods, and I was banished to the earth, where I had to accumulate a thousand years of cultivation before I could return to my place. I was forbidden to set foot on the sacred Kunlun Mountains, gateway to the heavens, which meant I could not seek a spirit pearl of my own. Alone on my sojourn in this wretched world, I took the form of a tortoise, wisest and oldest of all creatures."

Before Zhen could say anything, Xian spoke.

"You're wrong, Fahai." Xian stepped forward, eyes glinting. "You and I have nothing in common. *You* betrayed *us*. My father and I trusted you, and you deceived us for years! All this time, what you were doing in your laboratory in the basement of this pagoda was never for my mother's healing, was it?"

"I delved into forbidden magic tomes and learned that, through a long, arduous process involving dark sorcery, a cultivation pool could be turned contrary to its natural purpose," Fahai replied. "And I discovered that one existed in the underground chamber of Leifeng Pagoda. I became a human, assumed the identity of genteel scholar Fahai, and insinuated myself into your father's court as a trusted adviser. When I offered to secretly seek a cure for your mother, he was more than willing to give me full access to the pagoda, where I had the time and privacy to prepare the cultivation pool."

"Did you even go and consult the oracle on Mount Emei or was that another one of your lies?" Xian demanded.

"I did," Fahai said. "The cultivation pool was finally ready, and I asked the oracle where I could find the treacherous white snake that had taken the spirit pearl. The oracle's reply was that the white snake was in Changle—and not I but the prince of Wuyue would be the one to find the cursed creature. I told your father that the oracle had directed us to Changle to find the cure, knowing full well you would insist on being sent there. I needed the connection you forged with the white snake seven years ago to lead me straight to him. And everything happened just as the oracle predicted."

Xian's eyes narrowed. "No wonder you were so eager to leave Changle earlier than the rest of us. You needed time to plan the ambush as Hei Xing."

Realization dawned on Zhen. "But your ambush wasn't meant to rescue me."

"Of course not," Fahai retorted. "If everyone believed you'd escaped on the way back to Wuyue, the last place they'd search for you would be Leifeng Pagoda. I would have enough time to extract the remaining power of the pearl without anyone knowing. But you, Xian, found a way to ruin my plans."

Fahai hadn't expected Xian to cuff himself to Zhen to stop him from getting away. Now Zhen understood why Fahai—as Hei Xing—had been genuinely taken aback when Zhen refused to let him cut off Xian's hand. They had both unknowingly thwarted Fahai's attempt to capture Zhen and secretly bring him back to the pagoda.

"After the fire in the underground chamber, I had my doubts about your alleged death," Fahai continued. "I strongly suspected that the two of you had somehow escaped and fled— which was confirmed when I received the message through the trees that you and Zhen were now working together." He glowered at Xian. "I thought that learning his true nature as a cursed white snake responsible for prolonging your mother's illness would make you hate him more, not send you running straight into his arms."

Xian moved in front of Zhen, blocking him from Fahai. He raised his hand with the signet ring. "I will never let you lay a finger on him again."

Fahai's expression flickered at the sight of the signet ring.

"Congratulations, *Crown* Prince," he replied, his tone heavy with scorn. "Your father chose well. Allow me to give you the elevated position you deserve."

With a sweep of Fahai's hand, a length of rope lying on the floor flew up like a snake. One end coiled into a noose and looped around Xian's neck; before Zhen could react, the rope hoisted Xian into the air.

"Xian!" Zhen snapped open his white paper fan and threw it upward. It flew in a graceful arc, neatly sliced the rope connected to Xian's neck, and returned to Zhen's hand.

But to Zhen's horror, Xian remained suspended in midair, as if an invisible hand around his throat were still choking him.

Fahai let out a bark of laughter. "Not a very nice feeling to be tricked, is it?"

A brilliant flash of lightning struck, almost immediately followed by a crack of thunder. Zhen spun toward the steeple to which Qing was bound.

"That was extremely close," Fahai said, a gleam in his eye. "The next one might hit the steeple. People believe that a lightning strike to the spire of a pagoda can destroy demons . . . or, in this case, a snake spirit. Who will you choose, Zhen? The prince who has given you his heart or your sister who refused to leave your side?"

Xian struggled, unable to speak. His legs kicked in vain, and both hands scrabbled at the unseen noose around his neck. Another bolt of lightning cracked like a celestial whip, lighting up the sky as brightly as midday, and a deafening boom of thunder shook the pagoda to its foundations.

Zhen's stomach clenched. Fahai was forcing him to make an impossible choice: Save Xian or save Qing. There was no way he could rescue them both; he was no match for Fahai's seven hundred years of cultivation.

Zhen swallowed hard and made his choice.

"Take me instead," he told Fahai. "You said the pearl's power cannot be forcibly seized, which was why you had to use the cultivation pool—you knew I would never surrender it to you voluntarily." He took a deep breath. "Let both Xian and Qing go. Once they're safely out of here, I will willingly give you whatever remains of the pearl's power within me. You told me there should be at least three hundred years' worth of cultivation left. You will finally have accumulated a thousand years of cultivation, and you can go back to the heavens where you belong."

"No, Zhen!" Qing shouted. "Don't give it to him!"

Fahai arched an eyebrow.

"After all these years, you still have the ability to surprise me." He let out a sardonic laugh. "Master Sun was right: If you wait by the river long enough, the bodies of your enemies will float by."

Zhen's heart was pounding. The next bolt of lightning could kill Qing, and Xian was already suffocating. He could only hope that Fahai's greed would win out over his spite. "Do we have an agreement?"

With a flick of Fahai's wrist, the bonds tying Qing to the steeple fell away. Another wave, and the invisible grip around Xian's neck abruptly loosened. Xian collapsed to the floor, wheezing and gulping for breath.

Zhen rushed to his side. "Are you all right?"

"Zhen!" Qing skidded to a halt next to them. "What's going to happen to you when you give him the pearl's power?"

Zhen's silence was the resounding answer.

Xian raised his head, his breathing still ragged. "Zhen, don't do this. Please."

Qing caught Zhen's hand. "There *has* to be another way—"

Fahai interrupted. "I kept my end of the bargain. Now it's time for you to keep yours. Send them away if you don't want them to witness what happens next."

Zhen took Qing's hand and put it in Xian's.

"Take care of her for me," he told Xian. "Whatever happens, don't turn back."

Neither Xian nor Qing moved. Zhen mustered all his resolve and pushed them away.

"Get out of here," he said. "Both of you. Go!"

The helplessness in Xian's eyes was heartrending.

"I love you," he whispered.

Zhen's breath caught in his throat. He wanted nothing more than to throw his arms around the other boy, hold him one last time, and tell him he loved him too. But he couldn't. It would break him. It would break them both.

As Xian pulled a sobbing Qing toward the doorway, Zhen turned back to Fahai. He clenched his hands so tightly by his sides that his fingernails dug crescents into his palms. As if he were desperately holding on to something that, perhaps, was never his to have. Not in this life.

"The equilibrium always finds itself, Little White One." Fahai held up his left hand, kindling a swirling orb of black light. "It's time to take back what's mine."

Zhen could sense the dangerous, volatile aura of the orb. It would consume his spirit powers and bestow them on Fahai, and Zhen would die. Fahai drew back his palm, and Zhen shut his eyes as the rotating black orb hurtled toward his heart—

Something exploded inside his chest, and the sheer force lifted him off his feet. He expected to float upward, finally weightless, separated from the part of him that was earthbound, but instead, he found himself flying backward—

His back slammed into a hard surface, and he crashed downward and hit the floor. His eyes sprang open, and he gazed up at the wooden beams and interlocking brackets that supported the pagoda's roof. Was he dead? Or still in his human body?

He raised his head. Across from him, Fahai stood ramrod straight, as if he had been petrified by some terrible, immense force. His eyes were wide and uncomprehending, and his left hand was still extended, his fingers curled like talons around the empty hollow of his palm.

Zhen looked down at his own chest—the amulet that Xian had given him glowed with blinding brilliance, like heavenly jade fire.

Fahai let out a guttural croak, clutching his throat as he staggered backward. His face began to protrude in a grotesque, rectangular shape. His eyes grew beady, narrow set, and his nose melted into its cavity, changing into two flat nostrils—

"Zhen!" Xian reappeared at his side. "Are you all right?"

Zhen couldn't contain his horror as he stared at Fahai. "What's happening to him?"

Fahai opened his mouth and let out a horrible, bloodcurdling shriek as his teeth vanished and his jaw became beak-like. His neck elongated, stretching like rubber. His skin turned brown and wrinkled, and his back began to hunch, swelling with a concave hump . . . like a shell.

Before Zhen or Xian could react, Fahai spun around and stumbled toward the balcony that overlooked the lake. As he vaulted over the balustrade, his transformation continued in midair: His arms and legs became thick stumps, his fingers and toes sprang into claws—

Then he fell, disappearing from view. Seconds later, a loud splash rose from the lake, and a flock of ducks took flight with a screech of panic.

Zhen rushed to the balcony. Below, the water had closed over Fahai, swallowing him into its depths. The rise and fall of ripples spreading across the surface was all that remained. The palace guards clustered by the edge of the lake, seeming confused.

"Zhen!"

Qing rushed forward and let out a small, choked noise as she hugged him so hard that Zhen was sure his bones would break.

Zhen held her tightly. "Are you all right? Did he hurt you?"

"I'm fine." She sniffed. "How did you ward off Fahai's curse?"

Zhen looked down at the amulet that hung against his chest. The jade had cracked in half. "It must have broken when it repelled the spell."

Understanding crossed Xian's face. "My mother once told me that if a piece of jade worn for many years suddenly breaks, it means the jade has shielded its wearer from a terrible evil."

Zhen was sure this wouldn't be the last they saw of Fahai. But he could worry later. For now, all of them were safe. That was all that mattered. All he could ask for.

Xian reached out and pulled Zhen into a fervent embrace. "For a moment I thought you . . . you were gone."

Zhen buried his face in Xian's neck and breathed in his familiar scent. Something in his chest seemed to unbolt, releasing like a dragon-claw lock that could be opened only by one key in the world.

"I'm not going anywhere," he whispered back.

When the three of them walked out of the pagoda, Feng rushed up to Xian, looking anxious and relieved. Then he turned to Qing and, unexpectedly, hugged her.

Qing blushed bright red. Xian and Zhen exchanged grins.

They rode back to the palace. This was Xian's first time returning from victory as the crown prince, but when they arrived at the outer court, instead of a hero's welcome, they were met with distressed faces.

One of the physicians came up to Xian and fell to his knees.

"Your Highness," he wept. "Your mother . . . she has died."

Chapter 37
ZHEN

Zhen's head snapped toward Xian. Seeing the disbelief and devastation that splintered across the other boy's face was a hundred times worse than being repeatedly plunged into the cultivation pool.

Then Xian seemed to compose himself. Without a word, he strode toward the inner court.

Zhen started to follow, but Feng caught his arm.

"Let him be. He needs to see her alone." Feng turned to the physician who had delivered the news. "What happened?"

"About an hour ago, she became deeply disturbed," the physician replied. "She kept asking for Prince Xian, saying that she needed to see him. Her handmaids tried to calm her down, but she became more and more hysterical before losing consciousness. We did our best to save her . . . but we couldn't."

A prickle rose across Zhen's skin. An hour ago—they were in Leifeng Pagoda, and it was about the time Fahai had struck Zhen to kill him and take the pearl's power. The jade amulet had repelled the attack, causing it to rebound onto Fahai. Xian's mother must have sensed the evil that had broken her protection charm; she thought something terrible had happened to her son, and in her fragile state, the panic and agitation had overwhelmed her.

Zhen sank to his knees in despair. Xian could've insisted that Zhen heal his mother before they went to Leifeng Pagoda to rescue Qing. But he hadn't.

Even if it costs my life, I'm going to save her, Zhen had said.

I know, Xian had replied. *And I will stay by your side.*

Later that afternoon, Zhen walked along the streets of Xifu with Qing. It reminded him of the times they'd spent together in Changle while they were on their meal breaks—lounging under the shade of scholar trees, trading gossip she'd heard from the kitchen and news he'd picked up from the stable. That had been less than two weeks ago, but it felt like a distant memory.

News of the death of the king's favorite consort—the mother of the newly appointed crown prince—had spread beyond the palace, and the atmosphere in the town was somber. Merchants selling their wares of charcoal, tea, oil, and wine spoke in hushed tones. Children were stopped from running around and playing flutes in the streets. A woman chided her husband for being drunk at such an early hour.

Zhen looked at Qing. "Where were you when you heard the message I sent through the trees?"

"I was already on my way to Wuyue to find you," Qing replied. "Hei Xing—well, the person I thought was Hei Xing—asked to meet me at a secluded spot outside the palace. When I showed up, Fahai was waiting. He overpowered me and brought me to the pagoda." She sounded morose. "I'm sorry I let him use you against me."

"He deceived all of us," Zhen said. "He expected me to bring him the pearl as payment of my debt to him for saving my life. He must have been incensed when he found out I swallowed it instead, but he hid his fury well." He sighed. "None of this would've happened if I had just given him the pearl in the first place. Little did I know I would set off a terrible chain of events that would hurt so many."

"You're the one who told me that everything happens for a reason," Qing pointed out. "Without the pearl, you and Xian wouldn't have met."

Zhen shook his head. "I would rather he had never met me and had his mother by his side, in good health. He would have been happy . . . and that's enough."

Zhen would've been an ordinary snake living in the West Lake, oblivious to the fact that just beyond the palace walls lived a prince who, in another time and place, would've been the love of his life.

He had taken what did not belong to him—including Xian's love. Xian was never meant to be his. He had stolen Xian's heart, and Xian had paid the price.

The equilibrium always finds itself.

Zhen halted in front of the stone steps leading to a small temple. During his time as a human, he had avoided visiting temples for the same reason he had chosen not to return to the West Lake. Being in a place of worship made him feel more unworthy.

The temple's outer wall was painted red; its pillars were black. There were three doors. Above the doors on the right and left, a pair of wooden boards in the shape of an unfurled scroll were each carved with two different sets of characters that Zhen couldn't read: 寶蓋 and 慈航.

"I'd like to go inside for a while," he told Qing.

"Sure," Qing said. "I'll come with you."

"Actually, I would prefer to go alone," Zhen replied. "I have something I need to ask. Can you wait for me out here? I won't be too long."

He hadn't paid close attention to which of the three doors people used to enter and exit the temple. There was no one to follow, so to be safe, he walked through the middle doorway, which was the broadest.

An elderly monk inside stared at him in astonishment, and Zhen assumed he'd made the wrong choice.

The monk came up to him and bowed his shaved head. He was dressed in a cross-collared saffron robe embroidered with the yin-yang symbol.

"It is not every day that we are honored to welcome a spirit," he said with reverence. "How may I be of service to you, my lord?"

Zhen wondered how the monk knew he was a spirit creature in human form.

"I have an important decision to make," he replied. "I hope to ask the gods for advice."

The monk held out two crescent-shaped blocks painted red. "Perhaps the jiǎo bēi will reveal their answer."

Zhen took the curved bamboo blocks. He had seen people tossing them into the air and watching where they fell—it seemed that the way the blocks landed on the floor was the answer to whatever they had asked about.

Zhen closed his eyes and spoke the question in his mind.

Can I still save Xian's mother's life?

He threw the blocks into the air.

When he opened his eyes, one crescent was facing up, and the other was facing down.

He looked to the monk for the interpretation.

"Shèng jiǎo," said the monk. If he was puzzled that a spirit didn't know how to read divination, he didn't show it. "The gods are in accord with what you have asked."

Zhen's chest constricted. Fate was cruel. Just when he thought he and Xian had finally overcome the odds, the hope that they could have a future together dissipated like incense between his outstretched fingers.

When Zhen walked out of the temple, Qing was eating a juicy watermelon slice. She handed him a bamboo skewer of candied hawthorn berries. "Try this, it's delicious."

Zhen took a bite of the dark pink fruit coated in syrup, which gave the tart hawthorn berries a saccharine glaze.

Qing wiped the back of her hand over her mouth. "So, did you get the answer you were searching for?"

An ache went through Zhen, but he pushed it down. "I did."

Chapter 38
ZHEN

That night, Zhen stepped into Xian's bedchamber carrying a tray with a bowl of congee prepared by the palace kitchen. Feng had reported that Xian had refused to eat all day; he had retreated to his chamber after returning from the coffin home, leaving strict word that no one except Zhen had permission to enter.

The room was unlit except for a single oil lamp, and the windows were all shut. A hunched figure in an apricot-yellow robe was sitting on the floor by the side of the platform bed, knees drawn to his chest. It broke Zhen's heart to see the other boy this way. He wanted nothing more than to cross the room and embrace Xian, but he didn't dare.

Xian spoke in the darkness. "The monks just finished performing tonight's rituals at the coffin home." His voice was thick, scratchy. "The rites will continue in the morning."

Zhen carefully set the tray on a table. "I brought you something to eat."

Xian raised his head. His eyes were puffy and bloodshot. "Why didn't you come earlier?"

Zhen blinked. "Feng said you needed time to be alone. And . . . I didn't think you'd want to see me."

"Why wouldn't I want to see you?"

Zhen bit the inside of his cheek. He walked to Xian and dropped to his knees next to him. They were a couple of feet apart, but it felt like a chasm lay between them.

Zhen slipped his hand into his sleeve pocket, took out the chain with the broken amulet, and held it out to Xian.

"I'm so sorry," he whispered.

He was reminded of the first time he had said these words to Xian, when his nose had bled after Xian showed him the case filled with instruments for catching snakes and he'd realized that Xian was the boy he had taken the spirit pearl from.

Then, he had hoped that Xian would never find out what he was apologizing for.

Now he had nothing more to hide. He wasn't just the cause of Xian's mother's unnecessary suffering in the past seven years—he was also the reason she had died in distress, thinking her son was in grave danger.

A long moment passed before Xian reached out and took the amulet from Zhen's palm.

"Nothing you say will ease the pain and sorrow of losing my mother," he said. A sharp pang went through Zhen's chest, but then Xian continued speaking. "Can you just hold me instead?"

The raw emotion that rose in Zhen's throat was almost too much to hold back. He put his arms around Xian, gently, like he was a bird with broken wings. Xian was the one who pulled him forward and hugged him tightly. He buried his face in Zhen's neck, and his shoulders shook with silent sobs.

"She asked for me. But I wasn't there by her side . . . at the end." Xian's voice was muffled. "I am an unworthy son."

"No, you aren't." Zhen held Xian close, hoping he sounded as fervent as he felt. "Blame me if you must. Just don't torment yourself. I can't bear to see you this way."

Xian pulled back. He looked at Zhen with red-rimmed eyes. "My only regret is that she never had the chance to meet you."

Zhen felt as if his heart had been cleaved in half, the same way the jade amulet had split in two. He took Xian's hand, helped him to his feet, guided him to the bed, and laid him down on it. He stretched out beside Xian and stroked away the stray strands of hair that clung to the dampness on Xian's cheeks.

"Tell me everything about her," he said.

Xian dozed off midway through telling Zhen that when he was little, his mother told him that eating tāng yuán—glutinous rice balls cooked in soup—during the winter solstice would make him turn one year older. Later that evening, he sneaked into the kitchen and gorged on so many tāng yuán that he threw up. When his mother asked why he'd done such a foolish thing, he told her that he wanted to grow tall faster and have a beard like his father's.

Now Zhen gazed at Xian in his arms. The other boy's brows were pinched, the edges of his mouth downturned in grief. The last time they'd shared a bed was in the bamboo hut in the middle of the forest, their bodies entwined. That had been the perfect night, as if only the two of them existed, lost in each other and in their own world, with nothing and no one to pull them apart.

Zhen had once watched a street opera in a town he'd wandered through. He sat alone in the last row, captivated by the story of the afterlife that unfolded on the makeshift stage. A person's soul journeyed to the underworld, passed through the ten courts of hell, and finally met with Meng Po, the goddess of forgetfulness. She gave each soul a bowl of mí hún tāng, the broth of oblivion. Drinking it made them forget all their memories—the bad as well as the good—so they could truly leave their past lives behind before being reborn.

At the end, the main performer had stage-whispered conspiratorially that some lovers managed to avoid drinking Meng Po's broth of oblivion. They were reborn with memories of their beloveds and found their way back to each other in their next life.

Was that possible for him? Did snake spirits go through reincarnation as humans did? Or would he lose his memories of everything in this life?

Would he forget Xian?

He spent the rest of the night gazing at Xian's sleeping face, memorizing every angle, every imperfection. It felt like they had shared an entire lifetime in the span of a few weeks—it was more than Zhen could ask, and yet it wasn't enough. Not nearly enough.

Do you believe in destiny? Zhen had asked.

I believe destiny is an excuse people give not to fight for what they really want in life, Xian had replied.

Will you fight for what you want?

Always.

At the break of dawn, Zhen carefully extricated his arm from under Xian and lowered his head onto the pillow without waking him. Xian didn't stir; his fingers reflexively curled around the piece of broken jade, as if he were clinging to a last memory of the mother he had just lost.

"Zhī jǐ." Zhen leaned down and pressed a kiss to Xian's forehead. "My soulmate."

Back in the hut in the mountains, Xian had thought Zhen was asleep when he whispered that term of endearment, but Zhen had heard it. He had carried those two words in his heart. Would carry them always.

When Zhen exited the bedchamber, Feng was waiting outside. He acknowledged Zhen with a curt dip of his chin, and together they walked out through the gates of the royal manor.

As they stepped onto the terrace, Feng spoke. "How is he?"

"Asleep," Zhen replied. "He's exhausted."

Feng's expression was sober. "He doesn't know what you're going to do?"

Zhen shook his head. "You mustn't tell Qing either." He paused. "I have one more favor to ask of you."

Chapter 39
XIAN

Xian jolted awake.

Silence echoed around his bedchamber. Outside the window, the sky had lightened. His head felt like it had been stuffed with cotton, and his lips were parched, his cheeks sticky with dried tears. His heart pounded, and his bones seemed heavy with a sense of foreboding.

He stretched out a hand—the space next to him was empty. Zhen was gone.

Something was clenched in Xian's other palm. He unfurled his fingers. It was the broken jade amulet on its chain.

He jumped out of bed, still dressed in his apricot-yellow robe from the day before, and burst out of his chamber, startling the guards.

"Where's Zhen?" he demanded. "When did he leave?"

"At dawn, Your Highness," one of the guards replied. "Royal Bodyguard Feng escorted him out of the residence."

"Where did they go?"

"I do not know, Your Highness. They did not say."

Xian frowned. Where could the two of them possibly have gone together?

A terrible thought came into his mind.

No. It couldn't be.

Instinctively, he broke into a run, ignoring the gawks he drew as he raced barefoot across the palace terraces. His chest felt like an overwound spring, tightly twisted with dread.

Even at that early hour, a small crowd had gathered in the courtyard outside the coffin home. Qing was yelling Zhen's name at the top of her voice, pounding her fists on the closed front doors of the coffin home as Feng tried to calm her. Guards hung back, unsure what to do.

Xian skidded to a halt. "He's inside?"

Qing grabbed Xian's arm. "Oh, good, you're here—he'll listen to you. Talk some sense into him!"

"Zhen?" Xian rattled on the locked doors. He turned to the guards. "Break the doors down. Now."

Feng spoke. "Zhen barricaded himself and sealed the doors and windows with his powers. There's no use trying to force our way in."

Xian rounded on him. "You—you *knew* he was going to do this? And you didn't tell me?"

Feng's expression faltered. "Xian, I—"

"Don't make things difficult for him," came Zhen's voice from inside. "It was my choice. He respected that."

Xian spun around as Zhen's face appeared on the other side of a latticed window next to the door. He and Qing rushed over.

"I don't want either of you blaming Feng," Zhen continued. "He's the only person I know who has both your best interests at heart yet can be objective enough to see why this needs to be done."

"Don't do what I think you're going to do," Qing pleaded. "I swore I would never leave you. Don't you dare make me break my promise again—I won't forgive you this time!"

Zhen managed a chuckle.

"Silly little snake," he told her. "I'm the one who broke my promise. I said I would always protect you. I'm sorry I won't be able to do that anymore."

"What's the matter with you?" Qing cried. "I told you, you can't save everyone—"

"And I told you I have to try," Zhen replied. "Listen to me, Qing, this is important. I want you to continue the journey to Mount Emei while the healing milfoil is blossoming. Remember to pick the ones in bud. They're more effective than those in full bloom." He gave her a wan smile. "They say the clouds near the peak of the mountain take the shape of snake spirits that have gone ahead of us. Wave at the sky if you see me."

Qing broke down sobbing. Xian's heart clenched. Zhen gestured to Feng, who came over and put a comforting arm around her. He led her away, giving Xian a moment alone with Zhen.

"Zhen, please." Xian gripped the window lattice with his fingers. "You don't have to do this."

Zhen shook his head. "Watching your pain and not being able to take it from you . . . the feeling is worse than death. I don't want you to grow to hate me."

"Hate you?" Xian stared at him, aghast. "I told you that I don't blame you for what happened—"

"But you still blame yourself." Zhen's tone was quiet. "For helping me rescue Qing instead of insisting that I heal your mother first. For not being around to say goodbye to her. For letting Fahai torture me in that underground chamber. For losing the pearl in the first place. For everything, and for far too long. I can see the guilt tearing you apart. It needs to stop, Xian."

"Don't make me choose between your life and my mother's," Xian whispered. "What if it doesn't work? What if I lose both of you?"

Zhen's eyes glistened. "I would give up anything to stay with you. To spend the rest of my life by your side. I'm grateful for these past seven years of borrowed time . . . most of all because it led me to you. But I have to give back what was never mine to begin with."

"Were you just going to leave without saying goodbye?" Xian tried to muster anger, but he couldn't. He knew why Zhen had slipped out of his room without a word. He hadn't wanted their parting to come to this.

"Yesterday, back in the pagoda, when you said you loved me . . . I didn't say it back." A pensive look flitted across Zhen's face. "I didn't want to make saying goodbye harder for both of us than it had to be. That's why I left without waking you. Now I know the reason snake spirits cultivated alone on Mount Emei for a thousand years—so they could leave their mortal lives behind without any sorrow." He paused. "But you showed me how to be brave. And I would regret forever if I didn't take this last chance to say it: I love you, Xian."

Xian pressed his forehead against the lattice separating them. "There has to be something else we can do." He felt sick with denial, with desperation. "We can still find a way to save you . . ."

Zhen smiled. "You already have."

A smooth gray pebble lay on the window frame between them. Zhen took the pebble and closed his fingers around it—when he opened his hand again, in the pebble's place was a white jade charm.

"You once told me that white jade is a symbol of love." Zhen's fingers brushed Xian's as he slipped the charm through the latticework. "Take this as a token of my promise: In my next life, I'll do everything I can to find my way back to you."

Xian stared at the transmuted charm in the shape of an S—a snake. Before he could respond, Zhen moved away from the window and pulled down the shade, blocking the interior from view.

"Zhen, stop! Come back!" Xian slammed his palms on the window frame—but he knew it was useless. Back on that bridge, as Xian had dangled over a thousand feet of nothingness, Qing had shouted for Zhen to escape with them. But the other boy had refused to go. Once Zhen's mind was made up to do what he believed was right, there was no changing it. Not even for the ones he loved.

Xian spun toward the guards. "Find somebody who can break the magical charm on these doors!"

Before the guards could carry out Xian's order, an intense, luminous light flashed through the latticed windows, and a sharp gust of wind sent everyone stumbling a few steps back. Then the barricaded doors let out a loud click. They had unlocked on their own, which could mean only one thing—

Xian pushed the doors open and rushed inside.

Zhen was slumped on the floor in front of Xian's mother's open casket. Xian raced toward him. Zhen's eyes were closed, and his skin was unnaturally cold and dry, like a snake's, as if all the warmth and life had been abruptly drained from his body.

"Zhen?" Xian whispered. "Can you hear me?"

"Zhen!" Qing was the next to reach him. She grabbed Zhen's shoulders and shook him violently. "Zhen, wake up!"

Zhen's head lolled to one side, and a thin line of blood trickled from the corner of his mouth. Before Xian could try to revive him, Qing pushed him aside.

"I can use my powers to save him like he saved me!" She pressed her palms to Zhen's chest and squeezed her eyes shut, tears leaking from them as she concentrated hard.

A weak cough made Xian's head snap up. He leaped to his feet in time to see his mother's eyelids flutter open.

"Niang Qin?" He exhaled in disbelief.

His mother's unfocused eyes darted around in confusion

before settling on his face. "Xian'er?"

He put his arms around her and helped her into a sitting position.

She looked horrified when she realized she was in a casket. "What happened? How did I—"

Qing's shrill, frustrated cry interrupted her.

"What am I doing wrong?" Qing threw herself over Zhen's body, pummeling his chest so hard that Xian was sure she would crack a few ribs. "Why won't you wake up, damn you!"

Feng came forward and caught her wrists. She snarled and struggled against him before finally dissolving into loud, uncontrollable wails.

"Son?" Xian's mother put her hand on his. "Who is this boy?"

Xian knelt and gathered Zhen's lifeless form in his arms, hugging him tightly against his chest as tears streamed down his face.

"His name was Zhen," he choked out.

Chapter 40
XIAN

Zhen's funeral was held on the West Lake at the break of dawn the next day. Burials were far more common than cremations, but the lake was where Zhen once lived as a snake, where he had become a snake spirit. Where he and Xian had met for the first time. It seemed fitting for him to be laid to rest on its waters.

The air was clear and crystalline, the sky rain-washed from a thunderstorm the night before. Xian had ordered that the funeral be private, attended by only the few who knew Zhen. A wide perimeter around the lake had been cordoned off, with palace guards keeping onlookers at a respectful distance.

Back in the coffin home, before they'd closed the birch casket, Xian had put Zhen's folded white fan in his left hand, pointing downward. Then he'd placed his mother's cracked jade amulet in Zhen's right palm. The amulet had protected Zhen in life;

although it was broken, Xian hoped it would continue to do so for the next phase of his journey . . . wherever that might be.

Xian stood by the water's edge as the bier was set afloat. A banner on a pole attached to the bier caught in the wind. It read: *Zhen, Beloved Consort of Crown Prince Xian.*

Xian swallowed past the lump in his throat and stared straight ahead. When the bier neared Ruangong Islet—the smallest of the three islands in the middle of the lake where Zhen, as a snake, had rescued Xian from drowning—Xian nodded at a waiting archer. The archer fired a lit arrow, which found its mark and set the casket ablaze.

Behind him stood Qing and Feng. The three of them remained quiet as smoke from the burning bier billowed, casting a gray pall that reflected on the lake like clouds of underwater algae blooms. Flames consumed the casket and the bier, finally extinguishing when the burned-out wood sank beneath the surface. The banner with Zhen's name detached from the pole and settled on the lake, facing the dawn sky.

Qing spoke.

"He once told me that the stronger the emotion, the stronger our spirit powers." She looked at Xian, her face wet with tears. "What made him able to resurrect your mother . . . was his love for you."

But it had also killed him. Xian would have to carry that knowledge for the rest of his life.

"Are you going to continue the journey to Mount Emei, like he wanted you to?" he asked Qing.

She nodded. "The healing milfoil blooms only in the summer, so I have to get going. Or I'll have to wait another year."

"You can leave immediately, if you want," Xian told her. "Feng will make the arrangements. He'll also personally escort you there and back."

Qing couldn't hide her surprise. "But he's your bodyguard."

"And you're Zhen's sister." Xian turned to Feng. "You made a promise to him. Go with her and keep her safe. Appoint another bodyguard in your stead until you return."

Feng hesitated, unspoken concern in his eyes.

Xian gave him a nod. He would be fine. He had to be. He was the crown prince now.

A prince did not cry. A prince did not show weakness. A prince should not feel heartbroken.

After Feng and Qing left, Xian stood alone by the lake. Everything was tranquil again. Peaceful. White reed catkins swayed in the breeze. Lotuses floated on the water, waving their pink flowers high on stalks. The scorched tower of Leifeng Pagoda stood on the opposite shore, a forlorn, burned-out candle held upright by a base of blackened wax.

Is Zhen the one who will save my mother's life? he had asked at the temple.

Zhen had done that . . . at the cost of his own.

For all the guilt Xian had carried, Zhen had borne even more—which had led him to that final heartbreaking choice.

If Xian had known what the other boy was planning, would he have stopped Zhen? Would he have chosen the loss of a boy he had loved for less than a season to save the mother he had loved his entire life?

Xian slipped his hand into his sleeve and took out the snake-shaped charm that Zhen had transmuted. The last thing Zhen had given him. All he had left of him.

A choked sound escaped Xian's throat. His lower lip trembled, and he bit down so hard that he tasted blood. His fingers closed around the charm. The pressure built behind his eyes, and he tried to force it back, to hold himself together—but he couldn't any longer.

Something fissured inside him, a crack splitting wide open. Tears burst free, flooding out of him. He crumpled to his knees by the water's edge, sobs breaking in heaving, fractured gasps. He felt as if his lungs had been punctured and would never hold air the same way, and he wasn't sure he could learn how to breathe again.

When his tears finally subsided, he opened his palm.

Instead of a white jade charm, all that remained was a gray pebble.

Epilogue
One hundred days later

Xian stood in the middle of the Broken Bridge and lifted his face to the morning sun.

Fall had arrived—maples turned flaming orange while pines and cypresses were still evergreen. Lotuses had wilted, their fallen petals and withered stalks floating in a sea of brown leaves. Wooden fishing boats were moored by the side of the lake, their hulls reflected on the still waters. Soon the winter frost would descend on the West Lake, turning it white, bleak, desolate . . . the way Zhen had left Xian's heart exactly a hundred days ago.

On the parapet wall of the bridge was a tray with a purple clay teapot and two undecorated porcelain cups. The teapot had lost some of its heat in the intervening time, but the tea he poured into each cup was still warm. Xian had steeped it himself just before setting out.

A hundred days after someone's death, close family and

friends would gather to remember the person and celebrate their passage into a new life. Qing was still in Mount Emei with Feng, so Xian decided to mark the day at the place he and Zhen had first met seven years ago.

"Lóng jǐng tea," he said. "We were supposed to enjoy a cup together, remember? I brewed some today for us to share."

He brought one cup to his lips and drank. The bitterness he felt had nothing to do with the tea's flavor.

"I miss you, Zhen," he said quietly, gazing across the mirror waters of the lake. "I can't drink a cup of tea without thinking of you. I refuse to go hunting again. I haven't touched a wéi qí board in three months. Nothing is the same without you."

He took the other cup and poured the tea into the water from right to left, as was the custom when people drank in honor of their dead loved ones.

A hundred days. He had felt Zhen's absence in every single one.

Xian leaned down and picked up a small cage by his feet. Inside was a brown water snake he had rescued from a mongoose by the lake the previous day. The snake stared at him with beady eyes, its forked tongue flicking out.

"You need to be more careful," Xian told the snake, opening the cage and letting it slither toward freedom. "Watch your back. Stay close to your friends. And don't trust tortoises."

"Good advice," came a familiar voice behind him.

Xian whirled around. His eyes went wide. Was he actually dreaming, still lying asleep in bed instead of standing on the Broken Bridge?

"Zhen?" he whispered.

Zhen walked toward him. He looked transcendent in a flowing white robe embroidered with metallic silver threads. The top half of his hair was twisted in a knot held by a white jade hairpin, while the rest cascaded elegantly down his shoulders.

Xian stared at him, still rooted to the spot. His hand trembled as he reached out to touch Zhen's face. He expected Zhen to vanish like a mirage the moment he extended his hand, as had happened countless times in his dreams. But his fingers brushed Zhen's cheekbone, and Zhen didn't disappear. "Is . . . is it really you?"

A curl lifted the edges of Zhen's mouth. "I promised I wouldn't lie to you again."

Xian inhaled, sharp with disbelief. "But . . . how?"

Zhen's expression turned contemplative.

"Remember the meaning of the small dot of the opposite color in each half of the yin-yang circle?" he replied. "Because I gave up whatever strength remained in the pearl to bring your mother back, I was allowed to choose: Return as a snake spirit and stay on Mount Emei in seclusion for a thousand years, after which I would gain immortality and ascend to the heavens. Or come back as a human, without any powers, and be fully mortal for the rest of my life."

"You . . . you gave up eternity to come back to me?" Xian breathed.

Zhen smiled. "It wasn't even a choice."

Xian embraced him tightly. He was still afraid to believe this was real. But Zhen was solid against his chest, and his heartbeat thrummed in counterpoint to his own.

"I told you I would give up anything to stay with you," Zhen said in his ear. "To spend the rest of my life by your side."

Xian took Zhen's face in both hands and kissed him. Kissed him like there was no tomorrow, and even if there wasn't, it wouldn't matter—they had found each other, and he could ask for nothing more than to spend his last day on earth with his soulmate.

Zhen pulled back, concern in his eyes. "How's your mother? Is she well? Has she fully recovered?"

Xian nodded.

"The physicians say her qi needs time to circulate after stagnating for many years, but she's been taking longer walks and getting stronger every day. My father has given us leave to spend the winter in the eastern palace in Yuezhou." He leaned in until their foreheads touched. "I've told her all about you. I can't wait for her to finally meet you."

Xian had never imagined he would get the chance to introduce his mother to the person who had given her a new lease on life.

Zhen looked around. "Where's Qing? Is she still in the palace?"

"Feng sent word that he and Qing arrived at Mount Emei in time to harvest the summer milfoil," Xian replied. "Now that autumn is here, they'll probably start their journey back soon."

Zhen shook his head, marveling. "I can't believe Qing actually listened to me."

"That might have something to do with you not being around for her to argue with."

Zhen took Xian's hand. "Thanks for allowing Feng to accompany her. My mind is more at ease knowing there's someone by her side. Not that she needs protection—I think he'll be spending most of his time getting her out of trouble."

"Feng told me he promised you that he'd take care of her." Xian grinned. "I have a feeling he wants to do that for the rest of his life."

Zhen chuckled.

"I'm glad I came back in time for the wedding." His eyes clouded with emotion as he touched the gray pebble that hung on a chain around Xian's neck. "You're still wearing this. It's not befitting of a crown prince."

"I thought I'd never see you again." Xian reached out and tucked a strand of hair behind Zhen's ear. "But I just couldn't let you go."

Zhen sobered. "I'm sorry I left you alone. It won't happen again."

Xian wrapped his arms around him. "You going to keep your word this time?"

Zhen smiled. He pulled Xian closer until their lips touched. "I promise."

Standing on the Broken Bridge, they had finally come full circle. This was where their paths had first crossed—and seven years later, this was where the rest of their lives would begin.

Acknowledgments

Heartfelt thanks to Alexandra Cooper, executive editor at Quill Tree Books, for believing in this story of my heart. My literary agent, Jessica Regel, owner of Helm Literary, who is the best advocate an author could ask for. Jenny Meyer, my foreign rights agent, for bringing this novel to multiple territories worldwide.

My international editors: Emma Jones and Charlie Castelletti at Macmillan Children's Books (United Kingdom); Leonel Teti at Ediciones Urano (Spain); Rodrigo Manhita at Penguin Random House (Portugal); Thaíse Costa Macêdo at VR Editora (Brazil); Valeria Muti at Mondadori Libri (Italy); Julia Jung at Edel (Germany). As an author based outside the United States, translated editions bring me exceptional joy.

I'm grateful for all the support I've received at HarperCollins Publishers: in particular, from Rosemary Brosnan, vice president and publisher at Quill Tree Books; Allison Weintraub, associate editor; Joel Tippie, associate art director; Michael D'Angelo, marketing; Patty Rosati, Mimi Rankin, and team, school and library marketing; Abby Dommert, publicity; Tracy Roe, copyeditor; Christine Ma, proofreader; Heather Tamarkin, production editorial; Tim Smith, managing editorial; Sean Cavanagh and Vanessa Nuttry, production; Kerry Moynagh and team, sales.

Special thanks to Kuri Huang, who created the cover artwork of my dreams. Sarah Rees Brennan, Vanessa Len, Ehigbor Okosun, and Sarah Underwood, authors I admire, who read this novel in advance and shared their wonderful blurbs.

Much love to my family and friends: my parents, for their unwavering love and support. My beloved corgi pups, Clover and Spade—without their interruptions, I would have completed my edits a lot faster, but our days would be filled with far less laughter and chaos.

My husband, Fred, who has been there for this story from its inception—reading early drafts, brainstorming plot ideas, and sharing his vast knowledge of xianxia tropes. You are the best partner ever. This book is ours.